VINCENT'S RESOLUTION

BOOK 1: CHILDREN OF THE DEAD FALL

SUSAN TROMBLEY

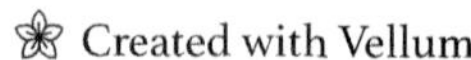

1

Gabby

"So, there's this guy who comes into the station every day...."

Oh no, here it comes. She's going to try to set me up on another blind date. My former roommate never gave up on matchmaking. Even moving out of our shared apartment into an apartment of my own hadn't saved me from her efforts.

"Val, I don't need a date for the New Year's Eve party. I'm going with Charles."

"Noooo!" Her tone left me in no doubt as to her opinion about my plans. "Gabby, *bad* girl!"

I hung my head out of habit. Val was a benevolent bully. She "managed" people for their own good. In my case, she was usually right, keeping me away from the *less* benevolent bullies. Still, I was on my own now, and I'd matured enough to make my own judgements and decisions about my life. I was twenty-six, for goodness' sake. I could date whomever I wanted.

"He's using you, Gabs! How many times does he have to hurt you before you stop letting him back into your life?"

"It's different this time," I said, struggling to put conviction in my voice. "He has a good job now, and he's more focused on a stable future. He's even left the band."

Which hopefully meant he wouldn't be surrounded by wanna-be groupies who were all too eager to sleep with a potential future rock star. It didn't help that he had a voice that was sexy as hell and a lean, toned body to match, but his determination to enjoy the benefits of playing gigs at local bars had ruined our relationship in the past. The last time I'd left him, he'd sworn that he would prove to me he could change.

"You said that last time." Val's disappointment in me came through loud and clear. "How many times does he have to con you before you wake up, Gabby? You could do *so* much better than him! You know he constantly tears you down so that you'll think he's the best man you can get. That's why you keep taking him back."

"I love him," I insisted, thinking about my panic and heartache every time I had to leave him because of his infidelity, drug-abuse, and the fact that he couldn't seem to hold down a full-time job so that I always had to support us.

Val had even threatened to kick me out of our apartment because Charles had mooched off me for so long by crashing there. She definitely wasn't one of his fans.

The fact that she despised him made her words about him carry less weight with me. Sure, I had my doubts about taking him back. He'd hurt me far too many times for me to trust his "change" completely, and he had been pretty mean to me about my weight and my body in the past.

Yet, when I'd bumped into him in the grocery store and he'd raved over my slimmed-down body and told me how beautiful I looked, I'd blossomed from the attention. He'd been so contrite about how he'd treated me in the past, and he'd sworn that he'd started his New Year's resolution to be a better man early. That meant giving up the sex, and the drugs, and apparently, even the rock and roll.

Now, he wanted me back, and he wanted to be a better man to earn my forgiveness. How could I turn that down, when he was the only man I'd ever loved? Besides, I wasn't getting any younger, as my mother kept reminding me, and it was time to start thinking about my future. I didn't want to manage an apartment complex forever.

I wanted to be a full-time wife and mom. I wanted five kids at least, and I wanted to shuttle them back and forth to all their extracurricular activities and be part of the PTA and do all the "mommy" kind of stuff that my own mother hadn't had the time for when I was growing up. I didn't want to have an "only child" because I knew how hard that was on the child, especially for an introvert. I wanted to be home full time for my children, because I knew what it was like to grow up in daycare and then afterschool programs while my mom worked my whole life. Being shy like I was made those places miserable for me.

"This guy, this regular who comes into the station daily, is such a sweetheart, Gabs! I mean, he's got that edginess you seem to love in a man, like he's got an aura of danger around him, but he's not a total poser douchebag like Charles. He's a gentleman and always holds the door for people and is unfailingly polite. And he's hot, even though I find his style a bit... strange. But you'd love it! I know your type."

"I don't have a 'type,' V."

I hadn't chosen to date Charles because he was "edgy," which apparently meant into drugs and alcohol, and unprotected sex with lots of random girls who threw themselves at the lead singers of pretty much any band that played at those venues he frequented.

I'd chosen him because he'd seemed sweet and outgoing, and filled with charm and charisma, and he burned with a creative fire that came out of him in his music. How could I not be taken in by that when I'd met him at twenty-one—a shy, overweight introvert whose only real relationships were with the characters in my favorite books? Yes, like many of the other girls he'd slept with, I'd met him at one of his gigs. I suppose, in a way, that made me just like the others, but with me, he was different. With me, it was more than just sex—is what I told myself.

Charles could have chosen to be with any number of girls that night we'd first met, but he'd chosen to take the fat, shy girl home with him, and then he'd taken my virginity.

Then he'd taken advantage of me. Used me. Cheated on me. Lied to me.

I sighed heavily, my shoulders slumping as I felt more exhausted than anticipatory about seeing Charles again. The misery he'd caused me just wore me out. I wanted more than that for my future, and I had a bad feeling Charles could never deliver it.

"V, every time you set me up, the dates are brutally awkward! The guys you meet at the gas station are always so... strange."

"Gabs, *you're* strange, okay? That's why I keep setting you up with those guys. You like all that paranormal stuff, so when I see some dude who is obviously into the same, I immediately think of you. I want you to find a man who appreciates you for the weird goofball you are. Not some jerkoff who is only using you to pay his bills while he fucks other women behind your back."

I looked down at my grim reaper-printed pajamas, plucking at the light gray fabric right beside a bloodied scythe. I'd made them myself from Halloween print fabric.

There was no bad time to wear Halloween print fabric, as far as I was concerned.

So maybe I was a bit strange. Maybe the fact that I used

Halloween decorations as regular décor, and binged paranormal documentaries and movies, and read anything I could get my hands on about ghosts, ghouls, aliens, vampires, and cryptids was a little weird.

"I'm not saying that in a bad way, Gabby," Val added in a softer tone. "It's just that you have interests that are different from most people. Chucky never appreciated that about you, and he never bothered to even try to share those interests. Hell, he never bothered to remain faithful, so why would he make an effort with any other part of your relationship?"

I cut off a giggle at her nickname for Charles. He hated that name with a passion, which meant that Valerie used it all the time, especially when she was around him.

"I have normal interests too." My defensive tone sounded weak, even to me.

I could cook, and bake, and knew all kinds of hacks on housecleaning that I'd learned from social media. My apartment was spotless, even if it did look a bit like a gothic themed house. I would be an excellent wife—once my future husband got his act fully together so we could start our family.

"I notice you keep avoiding the real issue with the Chuckster," Val said wryly.

"I get it, okay!" I shook my head as if she could see it, sighing heavily in surrender. "He's a lowdown, dirty cheater. He'll probably always be a cheater. I'm an idiot to think he'll ever change."

"Stop being agreeable *now*, Gabs. You need to stand up for yourself. Even with me."

"No, no. You're right. Charles hasn't been a good boyfriend, and I keep taking him back." I hung my head again. "Because I'm a total loser myself."

"See!" Val crowed as if she'd won a victory. "That's what I'm saying! He's got you so down on yourself that you think he's doing you some kind of favor by being with you. That's how he manipulates you!"

Val was only partially right. I'd been down on myself before I'd even met Charles. I wish I'd known Val in school, because maybe she could have protected me from the bullies that had made my life miserable and had told me in singsong chants that I was so fat and ugly that I could never get a boyfriend, and that I shouldn't even bother with a dog because it would run in front of a car to get away from me.

Kids are bastards. Funny that I wanted so many of them, but I figured I could raise mine to have empathy and maybe do my part to make the world a better place.

Or at least a more tolerable one.

"Gabs, you've changed your own life to be a stronger, more confident person. Don't take that jerk back and let him bring you down again. Let me set you up with Vincent. I swear, this time, you'll really click with him. He's super handsome, but I can tell he has some body issues too. He'll be more understanding of your self-consciousness about your body."

Valerie knew me too well. This "Vincent" now had my interest, and my empathy. Perhaps, like me, he'd spent a good portion of his childhood mocked and degraded by others because of his weight. Maybe he really could understand me, in a way that Charles never could.

I might be a gym rat now after I decided to try to deal with stress and anxiety without using medications. Endorphins from working out had such a profound positive effect on my mood that I had embraced physical activity when previously I'd always avoided it. Unfortunately, my weight loss had left me with loose skin, and I still had the roadmap of stretchmarks that had plagued me since childhood. No matter how toned I got, I couldn't change those aspects of my appearance.

I liked the thought of being with a man who was a little on the fluffier side, maybe with some squeezable love handles.

Someone who wouldn't take one look at my body and curl his lip in disgust because it wasn't perfect like all the women on social media.

"Maybe you can just give me his number and I can text him?" I wavered, even though every blind date Val had set me up for had been uncomfortable or downright terrible.

"No, because you'll chicken out and go for the familiar, and that familiar is, sadly, Chucky. Ditch the loser for New Year's Eve and go to the party with Vincent. Trust me, Gabs. I know what's best for you, and this guy is it! He's the *one*."

"God, V, you sound like you're trying to be my mother!"

Valerie snorted. "Sometimes I swear you still need one, girl."

We both fell silent for an awkward moment as I thought about the fact that I rarely talked to my real mother. She'd made it clear that I had never lived up to her expectations and that she'd wasted her youth working to support me only for me to disappoint her.

"Does this Vincent even *want* to go on a date with a total stranger?" I asked, getting back to the matter at hand.

"Of course," Val said eagerly, sensing that I was weakening, "I told him all about you, and he's looking forward to meeting you."

I groaned and rolled my eyes heavenwards. I could only imagine the kinds of things Val might think were relevant to say about me to this stranger. The other guys she'd set me up with had made some bizarre comments that told me Val got far too enthusiastic when promoting me to them.

"Val, did you tell him I'd already said yes without even discussing it with me first?"

"I knew I could talk you into it, and I did. I can already tell."

As irritating as it was that she'd already set up the date on my behalf, she knew me too well. Everyone who got close to me knew how to manipulate me. That was the problem. I'd gained more confidence in my skin, but I still struggled with social situations. I still tended to be railroaded by stronger-willed people.

I didn't like to admit that I was a passive person who tried to be agreeable to avoid conflict. People looked down on that kind of submissiveness, just like modern society looked down on my desire to be a wife and mom over having a career that didn't appeal to me. People used me and manipulated me and justified it to themselves by saying I deserved it for being so weak.

Even Valerie urged me to be a "stronger" person. Even she only saw me as someone she could respect when I pushed back against her will or anyone else's. Yet, she wanted me to agree to her plan to set me up with some weirdo she'd met at the gas station.

If I did, she wouldn't respect me because I'd caved to her. If I didn't, she'd assume I'd chosen Charles out of weakness, and she still wouldn't respect me.

"*Alright* already! I'll go on a date with him. But if he turns out to be an axe-murderer, I am *so* haunting you! And it will be a bad haunting, too. I'm gonna throw stuff around at your house and fling open doors and then slam them, and my apparition will be flipping you off whenever you see it reflected in your bathroom mirror as my ghost stands behind you freezing your ass."

I didn't cave. Not really. I just thought about the lesser of two evils. Sure, Charles had quit the band and now had a stable day job working in "sales," he said. Sure, he said he'd never stopped loving me and he wanted to give me the life I'd always dreamed about.

But seriously, I could smell his bullshit, and when I really got to thinking about it, I realized that something had changed inside me after I'd walked out on him the last time because of his infidelity.

I didn't want to go through that again. I didn't want to suffer the constant mistrust and fear of losing him to some other woman. When I thought about my upcoming date with Charles, I felt exhausted instead of anticipatory.

I'd try another blind date set up by Valerie, but this would be the last one! I knew it would likely be a disaster, and that the guy would be a real oddball, and not in the way I would hope for, but it wasn't like I had better plans for New Year's Eve, and I sure as hell didn't want to go to Valerie and Ben's party at our old apartment alone.

Again.

For the New Year, I was going to adopt a new attitude, and I might as well begin working on my resolutions early.

Gabby's New Year's Resolution #1: *take more risks and ditch the things in my life that aren't working out instead of clinging to them because they're familiar.*

2

Gabby

My body-skimming dress looked fabulous. The undergarment beneath it that belonged in a medieval torture dungeon kept all the loose skin contained and shaped my body into an hourglass.

Even though I finally had the silhouette I'd always thought I was supposed to have, I still didn't feel confident in the dress, or exposing this much of my body's contours to the world. I'd hidden myself behind baggy, poorly fitted clothing for so long that I felt almost naked in a dress like this. The golden sequins that covered it only drew more attention to me. Drawing attention was something I had tried very hard to avoid for most of my life.

This was all part of my New Year's resolution, I kept reminding myself. I was going to be a whole new Gabby for the upcoming year and ditch the old Gabby. I was going to finally have the perfect life to go with my perfect hourglass shape, just like all the beautiful women on social media.

Yes, I knew that most of thos… al lives were pr… fake. I knew that women online use… rs and photoshop fit themselves into the very narrowly de… d band of a beauty standard. What else were women suppos… o do when their value in society was judged by their beauty … her than their accomplishments?

Still, I wanted to have the beautiful magazine … ver home and attentive husband and crowd of kiddos, and fro… what I knew—from what I'd seen on every media available to me—a woman had to be pretty to get those things.

I studied my made-up face critically in the mirror, wondering if I had outlined my full lips too much, or if the brows I'd carefully covered with makeup and then redrawn were the perfect shape. The makeup made my face look like all the other women on social media, drawing attention to my naturally bee-stung lips, large gray eyes, and long, lush lashes. The heavy contouring sharpened my rounded cheeks and chin and narrowed my wide brow. It also allowed me to create the illusion of a straight, narrow nose, rather than my wider, crooked nose.

I looked nothing like myself. I could take a selfie and post it on my social media, and I would—*finally*—fit in with all the other pretty girls. Honestly, I would probably look like twinsies with most of the other pretty women.

For some reason, my success at applying this makeup after a week of following tutorials and buying the right makeup and failing over and over again, left me strangely hollow and unnerved by my drastically altered appearance.

In my pictures, I looked glamorous. In person, the makeup looked too heavy and felt like it weighed a ton on my face.

Still, I had a party to go to, and people would be taking lots of pictures. I wanted to look good in all of them.

Even if my date was a disaster in every way. At least he wouldn't be Charles.

They had to be contacts, of course, but still, th breathtaking, just like the rest of his gorgeous face.

He had very long, straight black hair that fell past the middle of his back, and some of it was pulled back from his face, leaving only a few shiny strands framing his handsome features.

He had pointed ears. Not naturally, obviously. How could they be?

It had to be some kind of plastic surgery he'd had done, and the body modification had not stopped with his eyes and ears. When he smiled at my shocked stare, fangs glinted in the reflected streetlights.

Please be Vincent! my inner sex goddess begged.

Aloud, I said, "Hi," my voice again taking on that falsely high pitch of nervousness. Then I fell awkwardly silent, still unable to stop staring at the gorgeous man's face.

I had a sense of his body being huge and bulky, though it was concealed behind a rather on-the-nose gothic vampiresque, ankle-length jacket.

I was digging the aesthetic, to be honest. It was right up my alley, which made me hope this really was Vincent, because who else would be as unusually dressed as this at Val's apartment complex on New Year's Eve? Halloween, maybe, but New Year's Eve wasn't the typical vibe for this man's look. Unless it was his everyday appearance.

His slight smile faded. "If you are well, then I must bid you good evening. I have a party to attend."

His speech was so formal and polite, his accent making me think Count Dracula for sure—only a much sexier version.

"Me too!" I squeaked in an overexcited tone.

If I was drooling and panting after him, I couldn't be more obvious. I realized that I was standing there stupidly and wracked my brain to recall the sexy, flirty actions that pretty women did to attract a man.

As he made to turn away, I flipped my hair with a giggle that made me inwardly cringe. Then I shifted my undergarment-bound body into a sexier pose, looking up at him through my lashes.

His upper lip curled slightly, revealing more of his fangs as I fluttered my lashes. I giggled again and he visibly shuddered.

Then an eyelash broke free from its painted prison and made its way right into my eye. Suddenly my blinking wasn't intentional as tears blurred my vision and I thought, "oh shit! Ow!"

I reflexively rubbed at my eye, feeling the false lashes peel away from my real ones as I no doubt smeared eye makeup all over one side of my face.

"Dammit!" I shrieked in pain and frustration, forgetting for a moment that I wasn't alone in my bathroom dealing with these lashes causing me problems for the hundredth time. "You little fake-hair goblin vomit! You demon spawn from the frozen outer reaches of Hell!"

Mr. Drop dead, Undead Gorgeous backed slowly away, eyeing me with an expression that wasn't exactly flattering. In fact, he looked repulsed as I lowered my makeup-coated fist and blinked up at him, a terrible realization that I'd said those curses towards my lashes aloud pushing my sinking stomach lower towards my glamorous pumps.

"Hey, Vincent!" I heard Val's voice saying in an overly loud and cheerful tone that told me she'd started drinking early. "I'm so glad you could make it!"

My heart sank as the gorgeous man glanced back at me, then turned towards Val, who headed towards us out of the shadows of the apartment buildings.

Then she caught sight of me.

"Who...?"

Her eyes narrowed on me, then they widened, and she blinked rapidly in surprise as her mouth dropped open.

"*Gabby*? Is that *you*?" Her gaze shifted to my car, clearly recognizing it, then back to me.

Vincent glanced from Val to me, then lifted a large, long-fingered hand to run it over his hair. "Something just came up," he said in his panty-wetting voice, "and I'm afraid I'm going to have to cancel this evening." He shot me an apologetic look that still didn't hide the way his finely shaped lips pulled back from his unnatural teeth in disgust. "Perhaps we can do this some other time."

3

Vincent

I suppose I shouldn't have been too surprised, though I was disappointed by the revelation that this woman was the one I'd come to this party to meet.

The way Valerie had described her friend made me believe I would meet a sweet, kind, *genuine* female who would appreciate me for who I was on the inside and not be obsessed with my outward appearance—or her own.

Ever since gray-father had sent me to this world so that I could begin my quest for my mate, I'd encountered one disappointment after another in trying to meet the right woman. The women in this world threw themselves at me because they loved how tall I was and how my face looked, and they assumed that I hid a muscular physique under my heavy clothing.

They were mostly correct. It was a muscular physique, though I had primarily genetics to thank for that. I did spend some time daily working out, but only because I enjoyed the physical activity.

My genetics had given me something else that human females wouldn't find nearly as attractive as the muscles that rippled over my body. I also concealed my claudas—the six venomous claws that extended from my exposed spinal ridge and were usually wrapped around my waist to tuck neatly against my abdomen.

I could get away with showing my fangs and leaving my eyes their true color. Very few humans even questioned the appearance of my ears. But I think the claudas—and my slit and stem—would give any human pause, or perhaps send them screaming for the door.

That was why I wanted a woman to fall in love with me first, before she saw my body and learned the truth about my nature. I was only half human. The other half was something far too alien for most of the humans of this dimension to understand.

If gray-father hadn't suggested this particular dimension as the place to search for my mate, I would not have come here. It seemed too risky, but he knew the most about such things, and I trusted his judgement. He would never put me in danger if it could be avoided.

But he couldn't stop me from experiencing heartache. As I spent month after month on this world, seeking the right female—the one who could love me as I am—I began to lose hope.

Valerie had said her friend Gabby would love my aesthetic—my fangs, my eyes, my ears. She mentioned casually that her friend was very much into aliens and monsters. She'd described a soft, curvy female with sparkling gray eyes and a broad, genuine smile.

"Genuine" had been the word Val had used, but all I saw before me was another painted doll concealing her true features beneath a mask of makeup that made her look so much like the other females I'd seen in this world that it was difficult to tell her apart from them. Her body appeared so tightly bound by her clothing that it was difficult to tell if there was any softness beneath the armor of her dress.

I did find her scent pleasant, faint as it was under the reek of makeup products and cloying perfume, almost overpowered by those other odors.

The most disappointing part about this female was her behavior. Like all the other women who threw themselves at me because they liked the way I looked, she was already doing the "flirting" thing that human females did.

It was true that a Fayi female would literally throw herself at a Fayi male, clambering onto him to sink her fangs deep into his flesh for his blood, but human females hadn't shown much more restraint than that in making their lust for me clear.

I supposed I should be grateful they didn't want my blood —not that I wouldn't gladly share it with my mate—though they seemed to crave my stem as much as any Fayi female based on the shockingly intimate things they said to me. The difference was that these females had no idea what they would be getting themselves into if I actually gave them what they wanted.

Amidst my crushing disappointment at the appearance and behavior of my blind date, Val insisted that I cancel my other plans and stay at her party with Gabby. My date was looking at me with an expression that I couldn't entirely read on her over-painted face, but the way her eyes glistened as if she was about to cry made me feel uncomfortable.

In truth, it made me feel like a "complete bastard", as my mother would say—usually to blood-father. He did have his moments. I was a lot like him in so many ways, but I didn't like being insensitive to women. My mother had cured me of that kind of boorish behavior at a very young age. Not that blood-father *liked* being insensitive. His was more a result of his Fayi culture. He was learning, but it was a lifelong process.

I had the advantage of growing up with a human mother who had taught me a lot about how to embrace my human half —and how to treat the human females I met.

I wouldn't have made her proud in this moment, because it definitely looked like Gabby was about to cry as she turned away from me, moving stiffly in her gaudy dress. It cinched her waist so small that I wondered how she could bear it, and it didn't seem like she was breathing easily.

I didn't really have an excuse at the ready to abandon this date. My spur of the moment declaration was inelegant and far too obvious, so I acceded to Valerie's insistence that I remain at the party, pulling out my phone to pretend that I was texting someone regarding the something that had "just come up."

Gabby wasn't cheered by this, though. She clearly didn't lack intelligence, even if her ear-grating giggle and practiced hair flip had made me think otherwise.

She knew I wasn't impressed with her, and my careless attempt to get out of the date had stung her pride. Human females had very fragile pride, in my experience. They didn't like getting rejected, least of all when they were obviously putting themselves out there for my attention. I had already learned that the hard way, and had been called many new-to-me insults, some of which were remarkably inventive.

She tried to make an excuse to leave the party, mumbling something about her mother having the stomach flu and needing her to pick up some soda and crackers, but Valerie waved away her pathetic lie as quickly as she'd waved away mine.

Even if Valerie hadn't already been claimed by a male, I would have found her bossy behavior far too close to my own mother's to be attractive to me. She grabbed Gabby's arm and hauled her along, waving for me to follow as if I, too, was her personal servant.

I had experience with strong-willed females—and with disobeying their commands. I had always been the most defiant of my siblings, the one who most chafed at being ordered about by my mother. Blood-father found my defiance amusing. Wing-father cautioned me to temper it lest it cause unnecessary pain. Gray-father merely told me that I would learn—what lesson, he wouldn't specify.

I had yet to learn anything that made me jump to a female's command. I only followed Valerie because of that look of dejection in Gabby's eyes, and my own guilt for having caused it.

I could give the woman a chance. It wasn't fair to completely dismiss her outright, simply because she looked and acted like so many of the others that had thrown themselves at me for shallow reasons without any real interest in who I was as a person.

Gabby cast a glance over her shoulder at me as I sauntered in their wake. Her heavy eye makeup was smeared all over one side of her face and her eyes looked uneven, since the false lashes on one of them had come off.

I had no idea why she wore such things. Her real lashes looked thick, long, and full all on their own, but even if they hadn't been, her eyes were so beautiful that she didn't need any additional framing to draw attention to them.

The humans of this world had such strange ideas about beauty. I missed the Dead Fall more and more as each day passed in this "civilized" place.

As I followed the two women, Valerie chattering away with a clear slur to her voice that told me she was already intoxicated, I caught another teasing hint of Gabby's scent beneath the heavy layer of chemical odors that covered it.

That, I did like. Very much. I wondered what she would

look like out of that tight dress and tottering heels and thick makeup that changed the very shape of her face.

I also wondered whether she'd remain attracted to me if she saw what I looked like out of my clothes. Would she look at my mating tattoos in admiration or see the slit they covered and freak out when my stem extended from it?

Music from Valerie's party reached my sensitive ears well before we came upon her packed apartment. Fortunately for her, I suspected, other apartments in the area were equally as packed and clearly bent on celebrating the New Year, so she wasn't getting complaints from her neighbors that would shut such celebrations down early.

The authorities in this world and the way they shut down harmless things never ceased to surprise and disappoint me. Only our leader, the Minotaur Asterius, had such authority in New Omni, and he rarely exercised it unless a disruption posed a very real danger to the life and safety of the citizens. Then, he was utterly ruthless in meting out punishment, but it worked to keep New Omni remarkably peaceful, given the often-violent nature of its citizens.

A loud party would never be shut down simply because of the noise of it.

The vibration of music warred with the loud voices of the revelers as Valerie opened the door and towed the hapless Gabby inside, passing beneath a curtain of plastic glittery fringe hanging from the frame of the door. I followed quickly as they disappeared behind the curtain, strangely reluctant to have Gabby out of my sight for long.

I felt oddly responsible for her welfare now. After all, I'd hurt her feelings. Made her feel rejected. I had to make up for that insensitivity.

The fact that I'd never felt that responsibility towards the other human women I'd rejected did nothing to stop me from charging through the curtain, my gaze seeking out my wayward date. She moved quickly now, her head down, her shoulders slumped as she dodged the revelers around her. I could sense that she was fleeing, and I resisted the urge to give chase.

She couldn't escape the party forever. She would have to face me again, and this time, I would give her a chance before judging her and finding her wanting.

4

Gabby

I felt like a complete and total loser. I hadn't been this humiliated since high school, when I'd overheard my crush telling his friend what a weirdo I was after I'd nervously handed him a Valentine's card I'd made myself with all kinds of glittery hearts—and maybe a few skulls because I was good at doodling them.

I wished I could be more normal. That was what all the makeup and the hair and the dress and the heels that were seriously destroying my feet were for. Vincent was supposed to take one look at me and fall madly in love. Or at least show some interest.

I looked the part now! I fit in! Why didn't he like me? Was I truly that unlovable? Did I give off loser vibes even through all the makeup?

He'd looked at me like I was an unpleasant insect that had just landed on his fancy jacket. He'd looked like he wanted to squash me with his expensive black calf-length boot, just to get rid of me.

And then I'd gone and made things worse by cursing at my false lashes like a lunatic!

He was so obvious about his desire to be anywhere but near me that I'd felt his excuse strike me as if it had physical force behind it. I wanted to curse Valerie for being so insistent that he stay when we both could have escaped that horribly awkward and uncomfortable encounter quickly. Then I could go home, cut myself free of this undergarment, and chow down on the leftover Halloween candy that I'd been slowly savoring for the last two months.

Val's master bathroom was thankfully empty, though I'd had to walk past a couple making out on her bed. If Valerie wasn't already drunk—and Ben even more so—I would have sought her out and told her so she could kick them out of her private space. I sure as heck wouldn't do it. That would require courage I was currently lacking.

I fled into the bathroom like a dog with my tail between my legs. Yes, my belly was yellow and that shamed me, but damned if I didn't plan on hiding in this bathroom for the next four hours before the New Year or until Vincent vacated the building.

My reflection in the mirror only made me feel worse about myself. My little eyelash incident had left me with a makeup fail of disaster proportions. This makeup was supposed to be waterproof! Why did a little watery eye and a rub of my fist make me look like I'd gone a few rounds with a champion boxer?

Sure, the other half of my face looked glamorous, all ready for social media, but I certainly wasn't in the mood for pictures now.

The sounds of people hooking up outside the bathroom door—completely unconcerned with my presence—only depressed me more. I tried halfheartedly to fix the damage to my social mask, but I didn't have any of the makeup on me, and like a dumbass, I'd left my clutch with my powder and brush in the passenger seat of my car, so I couldn't even deal with the shininess that had begun to show through my foundation.

Long-wear my ass! So much for blotting, baking, and setting!

I rifled through Valerie's bathroom drawers looking for her makeup bag and came across a pack of makeup remover wipes just as the couple began crying out like porn stars and the headboard of Val's bed rhythmically struck the wall.

I rolled my eyes, getting an odd, unbalanced view of my lashes. Then I sighed heavily as I slumped onto the toilet seat cover, staring down at the makeup wipes in my hand while I hummed aloud to drown out the sounds of sex going on outside the door.

Depressed and feeling hopeless, realizing my terrible first impression would definitely stick with Vincent the hot vampire wannabe, I tugged a makeup wipe out of the pack.

By the time I'd wiped all the mess off my face, revealing my pink cheeks and rosy nose and chin, the couple in the other room had vacated. It was sad how fast that encounter had ended.

Did no one take the time for foreplay or after cuddles anymore?

I wanted a man who would tease my body until I was begging him to take me before sex and then hold me close and tenderly caress me after sex. I wanted our lovemaking to be epic, hours-long, mind-blowing.

I had never had that. Charles screwed like the guy out there who had just banged some woman he likely had no relationship with on Valerie's comforter.

Valerie was gonna be pissed tomorrow when she found out about them doing it on her bed. Right now, she was piss drunk.

If I wasn't so miserable in my own skin at the moment, I would spend some time worrying about her alcohol consumption and how it had been increasing steadily since she'd started dating Ben. He was a nice guy who treated her well, even when he was wasted, but he got wasted a little too often, and Val seemed to be trying to keep up.

I'd already broached the suggestion that maybe they both had a problem and should cut back on the drinking. Val had dismissed my words very firmly, in a tone that said she wouldn't tolerate me bringing it up again. Not wanting to upset her or make her unhappy with me, I kept my concerns to myself after that, even though I felt uneasy every time I saw her imbibing.

I felt sorry for the woman who had just left the bedroom on the heels of the man who'd likely disappointed her. Was that all women could hope for now? A quick bang and then off to the party to look for the next physical connection?

Would Vincent have been any better?

That last question didn't matter, since I had no intention of ever seeing him again. By now, I'd been hiding in the bathroom long enough that he had to have made his apologies and escaped Val's grasp. Either that, or he'd found some other woman who was prettier than me, no doubt thinner than me, and probably a whole lot cooler than me.

A guy like that could pull any woman he wanted, even with his eccentricities. Hell, some women would dig them as much as I did. I couldn't help wondering what the points of his fangs would feel like skating dangerously over my naked skin, teasing my throbbing pulse. Would he bite?

Why did I want to know so badly, when it was obviously pointless—unlike his teeth?

My body started to ache, but not with arousal. Sitting in any position, much less slumped on a toilet seat, was cutting off my blood flow. My feet already throbbed from the egregiously high heels I was wearing. I had not trained my tootsies to endure such torture, and I had been feeling the strain from their unnatural position from the moment I had wrestled them on.

No pain, no gain, right?

Cautiously, I unlocked the bathroom door, listening for the sounds of others in the room beyond. When I heard nothing, I crept out and headed towards Val's closet. She wouldn't mind if I borrowed a few items of her clothing. Now that I'd lost significant weight, Val was a size larger than me, and I could fit in something of hers that would be far more comfortable than this shapewear and spangly dress.

To my delight, I found one of my own pair of jammies folded on her shelf. She must have found it after I moved out and forgot to return it to me. I wasn't surprised by her memory lapse. I had accidentally taken off with a couple items of clothes from her that had gotten mixed in with mine on laundry day and I'd neglected to return them out of forgetfulness.

My jammies looked so appealing in that moment that I couldn't resist snatching them up. They were yards too big, so I grabbed a tie off one of Val's pajama bottoms to cinch the pants around my waist, then retreated to the safety of the master bathroom.

Once locked inside, I began the herculean task of freeing myself from my fancy dress after kicking off the heels with a whoop of triumph.

As I unbound my body, my skin sagging again around my belly and thighs and arms, I sighed in intense relief.

Hell yes! There was no feeling as good as being able to breathe freely again after what couldn't have been more than an hour or so in a straitjacket of a dress.

My flannel jammies with their rotting green zombies wearing purple party hats pattern felt so soft and comfortable as the material skated over my reddened skin, smoothing over the marks left in my flesh from the undergarment and dress.

I swam in my old clothing, looking like I'd dressed in

flannel sheets because of all the extra material. The waist of the pants bunched up in thick clumps as I tied it off. I could have traded in the comfortable and familiar jammies for something a little smaller from Val's wardrobe, but I loved these. I'd missed them.

Now that I had them back, I could sew a new set from the material, and I decided as I hugged it to my body that I most definitely would. Somehow, after my humiliation of the evening, I already felt better just being comfortable in my own skin, in clothes that didn't aim to squish me into a different shape than I was.

I could only imagine what the gorgeous Vincent would think of me now, my face plain and scrubbed clean of makeup, my body drowning in faded and worn flannel fabric, my hair pulled up with one of Val's old scrunchies into a messy bun that had strands sticking out everywhere.

I looked ready for a solo horror movie binge night. All I was missing was my alien slippers.

Val had bunnies on her slippers. Fat, pink bunnies. It wasn't the most imaginative pair to go with my black, green, and purple flannel Halloween-themed jammies, but I would take it, since they fit me.

I don't know at what point I decided I would sneak the hell out of the apartment, past all the hopefully drunk by now revelers, and the less than vigilant intoxicated Val, but by the time I slipped my aching feet into those super soft slippers, I knew I was gonna bail.

Vincent had to be gone by now. Or he was tongue deep in some beautiful woman's mouth—or elsewhere on her body.

At any rate, he likely wouldn't notice a jammie-clad woman with a round, shiny face and messy hair ghosting through the packed apartment. I looked so different from the woman he'd come here to meet—and had promptly rejected—that he couldn't possibly recognize me even if he noticed me.

I honestly didn't want to ring in the New Year in a bathroom, and God forbid any other couples break Val's rules and breach her master bedroom to make use of her bed again. I'd heard enough of that tonight, especially with the knowledge that I wouldn't be getting any, at least not any time soon.

I wondered what tonight would have been like if I had come here with Charles. I was sure he would have appreciated my new look. That flashy, glam style was just the kind of thing he'd always go for—in other women. And he'd *always* gone for it, even when he was dating me.

Charles had cheated on me all the time because women loved the whole rock-guy thing. I could only imagine how much Vincent would cheat on me if I was his woman, given how much hotter he was than Charles. I didn't think I'd ever met a man who wouldn't cheat on his partner if he had the chance at a woman who was more beautiful and exciting. I wasn't even certain men *could* be faithful unless they lacked the opportunity to be otherwise.

That only meant that I had to avoid gorgeous men who were obviously way out of my league. Even if I could make myself up to look like a social media model.

I didn't look like that when I wiped all the makeup off, and bare-faced Gabby was the Gabby they were going to wake up to in the morning.

I wanted a man who looked at my bare face and loved what he saw, flaws and all. Did such men even exist in this universe?

Sadly, I was jaded enough to doubt it. The beauty standard existed for a reason. Clearly, it was what most men wanted to see, since the women who fit it—either naturally or artificially—were the ones who got the most attention.

Vincent wasn't for me, despite Val's certainty that we would get along perfectly. He'd taken one look at me and dismissed me, then got just a taste of my social awkwardness and had literally tried to flee our date.

That was all I needed to convince me this was a mistake. I would have had more fun with cheating Charles than meeting this stranger who curled his upper lip and bared his fangs with disgust when he saw me.

Fangs though! Damn, why was that so hot?

I shoved that question aside as I crept out of my bathroom sanctuary, then slowly opened the bedroom door and peered out to check that the coast was clear.

Bodies writhed in a swaying dance to the top hits of the year, none of which I felt particularly fond. The crowd in the midsized two-bedroom apartment was significant since Val was the extrovert to my introvert and invited many strangers into her life with a carefree abandon I couldn't comprehend. It took years sometimes for me to consider a person more than an acquaintance, and in that time, they practically had to donate a kidney to me for me to believe they actually liked me enough to consider them my friend.

Unless they were pushy, like Val, and adopted me as their friend whether I liked it or not. I *did* like it though. I wouldn't have friends at all if it wasn't for Val's overbearing at times personality.

I saw no sign of Vincent, and he was difficult to miss, given his height and sheer hotness. Most of the revelers I didn't recognize, and by this time, they all appeared to be drunk. It was the perfect time to escape.

Several dancers trod on my—well, Val's—bunny faces, leaving behind shoe smudges on the bubblegum pink material that I would have to clean off later.

Honestly, I would just replace the slippers. I felt sentimental about this particular pair now. Their cheerful appearance had brightened my miserable evening almost as much as my own beloved jammies.

I made it all the way to my car without being spotted by Val or anyone who knew me, and just like I'd hoped, all the other partiers had ignored me. I was almost home-free, ready to escape, my hand on the door handle, when a deep, sexy voice spoke behind me.

"I believe that vehicle belongs to my date. I would hate to think you are attempting to abscond with it."

5

Gabby

My heart sinking into my feet, I sighed fatalistically. At this point, what difference did it make if Vincent saw me at my worst? He'd already decided he wanted nothing to do with me.

I spun around and faced the man, my breath catching anew at how ridiculously hot he was. Seriously, it just wasn't fair for a man to be that gorgeous! If I got my ears done like his and wore fangs and contacts, people would treat me like I was a nut. I was surprised Vincent didn't have a modeling contract.

Maybe he did. Val hadn't filled me in on what he did for a living. In fact, I wasn't certain she'd even bothered to ask. Everyone was a potential friend for Val, regardless of their profession.

"Abscond?" I said with a laugh, even though I wasn't feeling particularly amused as I realized that he was even hotter than I'd recalled from earlier. "I didn't know people actually used that word."

His golden eyes narrowed as he inhaled deeply. "You are not a thief then. You *are* my date." His gaze trailed from my bun down to my bunny slippers.

I shrugged my shoulders in my oversized jammie top. "Yeah. I'm Gabby. I figured since you clearly didn't want anything to do with me, there wasn't much point in sticking around."

His gaze shot back up to my face, meeting mine as I lifted my chin, feeling hurt and angry enough to inject a little courage into my spine.

"I will admit, I did not want anything to do with the woman I met earlier. But *you*...."

He inhaled again, his beautiful eyes seeming to sparkle in the light reflected off puddles of water left from melted snow. "You are *far* more interesting like this."

This took me aback enough that I gaped at him, blinking in surprise. Then I looked down at myself, trying to figure out what kind of magical Cinderella-style transformation I'd suddenly gone through that had caught this man's interest.

I was still clad in jammies, my body still swimming in them. I lifted a hand to touch my messy bun, and yes, strands were still sticking out everywhere.

"I apologize for my earlier behavior," Vincent said, not waiting for me to respond as I processed his words. "It was rude, and I was raised better than that. My mother would not have been pleased that I hurt your feelings with my insensitivity."

I crossed my arms defensively over my chest, embarrassed that he'd picked up on that. "Don't flatter yourself, buddy. I was only doing Valerie a favor by agreeing to a blind date with you."

He chuckled, baring those sexy as hell fangs that had to be dental installations that must have cost a pretty penny. "I suspect you *were* doing her a favor. She mentioned something about your...," he cocked his head as he regarded me curiously, "*loser* ex-boyfriend, I believe were the words she used."

He glanced around in an exaggerated fashion that made me bristle, then returned his gaze to my face, a smirk on his lips that managed to be both mocking and sexy at the same time. Curse him!

"Should I flatter myself that you chose to meet me over bringing him?" He stepped closer to me, reminding me how tall he really was.

He had to be well over six feet. Maybe even approaching seven. The guy was a giant!

My eyes shifted to take in his jacket-covered body.

A bulky giant!

His jacket curved outwards from his chest down to his hips, which told me he was probably concealing a beer belly or even a full barrel under that fabric. It made him seem more relatable to me. He was still hot as hell, but that "flaw" made him a little more human.

And maybe more squeezable and plushier. I had no problem with a little plushiness.

It was my turn to cock my head, eyeing him with a deliberately appraising look. "Maybe you flatter yourself too much. Perhaps you should try a little humility."

He laughed instead of responding as if he was offended. "You are likely correct. Perhaps I have 'grown too big for my britches' as my mother would say."

"You seem to respect your mother, or at least her words." I wondered what it felt like to have a mother I could respect, and maybe one who could respect me.

He nodded briefly. "I have a deep and abiding love and respect for my mother and all my fathers."

My mouth gaped open again, and I probably looked like a fish struggling for air. "*All* your fathers?"

Okay, I knew about polyamory. I wasn't a complete innocent. Still, I'd never actually met anyone who was connected to that lifestyle in any way. I hoped Vincent wasn't the kind of guy who expected to have an open relationship with multiple partners, but then wondered why it mattered. He hadn't been interested in me before, and now he seemed more curious than anything, probably because I looked so drastically different from earlier tonight. Worrying about relationship matters was really jumping the gun.

"I have multiple fathers," he said, eyeing me with his enigmatic contact-lenses gaze. "But when I find my mate, I have no intention of sharing her with anyone."

"Well, good luck on your search," I said, turning towards my car again.

Clearly, he didn't think I was "her," this future "mate" of his. I'd felt a bit of an eyeroll coming on at that term but had managed to restrain myself.

At least the guy seemed to hold his mother in high regard, though he wasn't putting out "mama's boy" vibes. Something about his demeanor made me think he disobeyed his mama as often as he obeyed her, if not more so. Since he was a grown man, that was probably a healthy thing to do. Our mamas didn't always know best. Mine had proved that time and again. Sometimes, a little disobedience was necessary.

"Perhaps my search is over," he said in a thoughtful tone that caused me to pause and glance over my shoulder at him.

The intent way he watched me made a blush rise in my cheeks, no doubt only increasing the frustrating redness of my face.

Val was the drunk at this point, but I always looked like I'd been hitting the bottle a little too hard when I didn't wear makeup to even out my skin tone. Most of the time, I didn't even drink alcohol. It didn't seem fair, but I supposed no one had promised me life would be fair.

I turned my face back towards the car window, seeing my reflection in the tinted glass, but unable to tell if my color was higher than normal. "If that's the case, you'd better get back into that party and claim her then, because it was getting pretty wild in there, especially in Val's bedroom."

He made a little growling sound that had my spine tingling in both fear and excitement.

Did the dude just growl? Like a werewolf? It seemed like he was having a paranormal being identity crisis.

Why the hell was his growl almost as hot as his fangs?

"What happened in Val's bedroom? Is that why you have disrobed and changed into these different items of clothing? Were you entertaining another man while I waited for you to emerge, foolishly believing you were in the bathing room?"

Okay, he was not sounding very happy and cocky right now, and, honestly, red flags were shooting up like New Year's fireworks at that possessive tone.

Literally just met the guy, and he'd shown next to no interest in me until now.

I spun around to face him, crossing my arms over my chest and lifting my chin. "What I do in a bedroom or bathroom is none of your business, *stranger*." I emphasized that last word. "After all, you made it clear in no uncertain terms that you weren't interested."

He took another step closer, and I wondered if I should step backwards until I pressed against the driver's side of my car, or step up to him with defiance against his obvious attempt to invade my space and intimidate me.

Oh, I knew guys like this. Sure, they usually weren't nearly as hot—nor as huge—but I'd dealt with them before.

And kinda backed away, to be honest. But then again, I wasn't cornered like I was right now. Instead of making a choice this time, I ended up paralyzed by indecision.

"I suppose you are right, Gabby," he said, practically purring my name in his deep, gorgeous voice, "I have no claim on you. Our first meeting has not gone well, and I am to blame for that." He inhaled audibly as he towered over me. "But you were not with any other man tonight. I can tell that now. Why did you change your clothing?"

"*Again*," I stressed, wondering how the hell he could tell that I hadn't been enjoying myself with another guy in Val's bedroom, "that's really none of your business."

"I don't want to be a stranger to you, Gabby. I would like to start over on this date."

I peered up at him, my neck craning a bit just so I could meet his eyes. "Look, Vincent, you're... *interesting*," my gaze returned to his bulky body, imposing and now so close that I could reach out and touch the swell of his belly, "but I'm not sure I can handle 'interesting' at this point in my life. I'm really looking more for safe and stable."

He leaned down until his face came close to mine, his warm breath sighing over me. It smelled like he'd eaten some chocolates, likely snagged from Val's candy bowl, and I wondered if I could taste the lingering sweetness of them if I let him kiss me.

"Safe and stable sounds boring," he murmured. "I assure you, my kind of interesting is what you'd prefer."

"You know nothing about me," I muttered, resisting the urge to lift on my toes to kiss those sexy lips.

"Valerie told me a great deal about you." His gaze roved over my face. "She convinced me that you were perfect for me. When I saw you earlier, I wondered how she could be so wrong. But seeing you now...."

I lowered my gaze from his intense features, hoping that not seeing how beautiful he was would help me resist him, because he was putting out some serious attractive vibes, red flags and all.

"Seeing me now? In oversized jammies, with no makeup, and my hair a mess?" I lifted a foot and wiggled it around, causing the bunny ears to flop around. "Hell, I'm even wearing slippers!" I lifted my eyes to meet his again, holding my arms out at my sides. "What the heck would make you interested in me now, when you weren't before while I was looking my best?"

He straightened, moving the temptation of his lips away from me. "You weren't looking *your* best then. You didn't look like the woman Valerie described. You looked like an unnatural doll—stiff, cold, painted. Now," his golden eyes gleamed as they shifted from my face to trail down my body, "you look soft, warm, and real."

He lowered his gaze to my feet and chuckled in a way that made my core tighten. "I like your clothing now much more than before. It makes you look fun." He met my eyes again. "Cute."

His grin flashed plenty of fang. "*Interesting.*"

6

Gabby

"I'm not really in a partying mood right now," I said, sucking in a deep breath filled with the heady scent of him.

He looked good, smelled amazing, and put out some seriously fascinating vibes. He was damned near irresistible to me, and I wondered what the harm would be in just a little taste of attention from the sexiest man I'd ever met.

He glanced towards the apartment buildings, where Val's party no doubt raged on, everyone growing more intoxicated as the clock ticked towards the New Year. "I would prefer to spend time with you rather than all of Valerie's revelers."

"Well, we could always ring in the New Year in a more private setting." I shrugged one shoulder casually, as if I wasn't just suggesting a hookup with a near stranger.

Okay, it would be living dangerously, I'll admit. I'd impulsively slept with Charles the first night I'd met him and had paid for it with years of being in a miserable relationship. Still, even Charles hadn't been as interesting as Vincent was, and I really wanted a little excitement in my life.

Gabby's New Year's Resolution #2: *Be bold and chase my destiny instead of waiting for it to come to me.*

I'd just made that one up on the spot, because it wasn't like Vincent was my destiny or anything, but damned if I didn't feel drawn to him in a way I'd never experienced before.

"I like the idea of a more private setting." His slow grin exposed those sexy, fake fangs. "Your place, or mine?"

It would probably be safer to go to his place in my own car so he wouldn't know where I lived in case things went sideways. Of course, if he had a sex dungeon or something, it would be easier for him to lock me away in it if I delivered myself to his door.

At the same time, suggesting we split the difference and just rent a hotel for the night seemed a little seedy.

I could text Val. Let her know I left the party with Vincent and ask her to call the cops if I didn't text her again tomorrow. Then head over to Vincent's house and hopefully have the best sex of my life, or at least a lot of heavy petting with a man who smelled like heaven. I wasn't even certain what scent he was wearing or if it was just his soap, but the more I stood there breathing him in, the more I wanted to get closer to him to lick him and see if he tasted as delicious as he smelled.

I was sure he would be terrible for my man-diet. Very high in heartbreak potential. As long as I didn't catch any feelings tonight, I couldn't come up with a reason why I shouldn't have some fun, though.

"I think your place would be good," I said, unable to affect a flirtatious tone as I suddenly felt awkward again at the thought of being alone and naked with this gorgeous guy.

What if he grew disgusted again when he saw me naked, saw the loose skin? Would his lip curl in that repulsed expression a second time, cutting me deep? Could I handle another rejection like that in the same night?

He lifted a hand to brush aside some strands of hair that had slipped free of my hasty bun. Then he lowered his head and kissed me, his lips demanding as they caressed mine.

Well, decision made then.

I moaned as his tongue slipped past my lips, tasting as sweet as chocolate and twice as rich. Oh, he was a good kisser, I'd give him that. Hell, at this point, I'd give him anything, which I supposed was the point of that seductive kiss. Maybe he'd sensed my doubt and had moved to chase it from my mind.

He kissed me into submission too easily, until I was leaning towards him as he lifted his head and pulled away.

He hadn't taken me into his arms, and I realized that he'd kept a hand on my shoulder to keep me from moving close enough to him to brush my body against his.

Val had said he had body issues too. Perhaps he didn't want me to feel his plushy belly and be turned off by it. Maybe he was worried about *me* seeing *him* naked. I wondered if that would make him more tolerant and forgiving of my imperfect body.

Then I recalled the men who'd been full-figured themselves but had mocked my body and said they only wanted to date "hot" women who looked like the flawless women on social media.

"We should go, before I forget myself and take you right here against your own vehicle," he said in a gruff tone, as if he struggled to speak after our kiss, despite holding me off from getting too close to his body.

My core clenched at the desire in his voice and the clear implication that he wanted me badly. Maybe as badly as I wanted him. Honestly, I couldn't have predicted the night would go like this after our disastrous first meeting, but I wasn't about to ruin a good thing.

Nothing like ringing in the New Year with a hot guy balls-deep inside me. Especially *this* hot guy! This kooky, vampire-wannabe whose aesthetic was right up my alley and really floated my yacht—because my libido had well surpassed a mere boat after just one kiss from him.

"I'll follow you to your place," I said in a breathless voice, licking my kiss-swollen lips.

His gaze shifted to my vehicle, and for the life of me, I couldn't see the ring of a contact lens around his fascinating irises. They really made those things undetectable now! His unnatural eyes looked as real as his unnatural teeth and his unnatural ears, which, even upon a closer inspection, had no visible scarring from the plastic surgery.

I honestly wasn't certain what kind of scarring there might be for a procedure that shaped the ears into points. Makeup maybe? Prosthetics?

"There are intoxicated drivers on the road." He regarded my vehicle with doubt. "I would prefer to have you ride with me rather than in this... vehicle."

"Hey!" I turned to regard my little Honda affectionately. "Phoebe is perfectly serviceable!"

"Phoebe?" He quirked his black eyebrows, a crooked smile tilting his beautiful lips.

I shrugged. "I always liked the name and never had kids or a pet to give it to, so I named my car that."

"Phoebe." He nodded slowly. "It is an interesting name."

"I liked it a *lot* better than Gabriella."

"Gabriella is a beautiful name," his gaze returned to me, his smile turning sultry, "for a beautiful woman."

I wanted to ask him if those contacts were impairing his vision but knew better. I would keep my insecurities to myself from now on. No reason to give a man ammunition for those moments when he really wanted to go for the jugular during an argument. Charles had certainly used my own body issues against me on numerous occasions.

Gabby's New Year's resolution #3: *Don't voice my body issues to hot guys who seem to be into me.*

"Come, Gabriella," Vincent purred, taking my hand in his, his palm warm against my chilly fingers.

Jammies weren't exactly winterwear, even flannel PJs.

"I will drive you to my home. I can bring you back here tomorrow." He shot an amused look at my car. "I'm sure Phoebe will patiently await your return."

"Wait!" I said, recalling my clutch, even as I allowed him to convince me to let him take me to his place. "I have to get my purse."

It had my phone in it, and I needed to make sure to text Val. I knew I was being reckless, not to mention potentially setting myself up for an embarrassing encounter and the awkwardness of having to contact a cab for my walk of shame in the morning—or ride of shame, I guess. Still, I didn't really feel like driving to his house, potentially getting lost.

Or more likely, chickening out and turning around to head home.

Then I would miss out on whatever delights Vincent promised, and based on his kiss alone, I suspected he had all kinds of delights to offer.

He waited as I unlocked my door and grabbed my clutch, then he took my arm and guided me to his vehicle, which he'd parked a fair distance away from mine in the crowded parking lot. I liked the old-fashioned gesture, even though it would be considered more on the domineering side nowadays. It felt more like he was keeping me from slipping on the patches of ice or stumbling into the puddles of melted snow rather than controlling my movements.

When we reached his car, I gasped, then released a low whistle. "Wow! Your car is gorgeous! What do you call her?"

He chuckled in his sexy way, the sound causing a delicious fluttering low in my belly. "Chevelle SS," he said with a half laugh. "It doesn't sound as lovely as Phoebe, I suppose."

I studied the red muscle car with black stripes on the hood in admiration. "Oh, she's lovely enough that she doesn't need a pretty name. Although Chevelle isn't so bad a name after all. I might name my second daughter Chevelle."

"It has a nice ring to it," he admitted, then steered me to the passenger door and unlocked it. "How many daughters are you planning for?"

I glanced at him quickly, wondering if he was already freaking out, worried I'd trap him by getting pregnant. "I'm on birth control, and I have a couple condoms in my clutch." I held up the gold bag. "So, you don't need to concern yourself about that."

He frowned slightly, his finely shaped brows pulling together. "It wasn't concern that made me curious. I'm interested in finding out more about you, Gabby."

I stepped into the vee made by the open door, passing close to his big body, brushing against his belly. It felt hard, rather than as soft and plushy as I'd expected, so maybe he had a body shaping garment on, too.

"Well," I turned and tilted my chin to look up at him standing close enough to me that a stray biting breeze blew several strands of his silky hair against my cheek, "if you're that curious, I'm actually hoping to have at least five children. I want my kids to have lots of siblings to play with, so even the introverts among them won't be lonely."

He grinned, baring those sexy fangs. "Having many siblings isn't always a joy for a child. Mine could be... *difficult* at times." He shrugged one shoulder. "Though I suppose the same would be true of myself."

Intrigued, I paused before lowering myself into his car. "How many siblings do you have?"

"I am one of ten offspring, for the moment, though my mother claims she is done 'breeding little monsters' as she puts it."

"Ten!" I blinked in surprise, unable to fathom what it would be like to grow up in a family that large, surrounded by so many people who were blood-related to me and might have stuck up for me when the kids at school got really ambitious in their bullying. "You're so lucky!"

He barked a laugh. "I take it you've never had siblings if you think that." His grin remained broad as he studied me. "Although I do love all my brothers and sisters, some of them didn't make it easy. Alex, Ria, and I are triplets, and yet we struggled to get along the most. Alex and I fought throughout most of our childhood, and Ria would egg us on. My brother is a 'kiss ass' I believe it's called. I found that irritating growing up, since he would always try to get me in trouble to score points with our mother."

My curiosity only increased at this revelation about my unusual date. "You're a triplet? How cool is that!"

He rested his palm on the shiny roof of his car, patient, despite his intention to get me back to his place for some bedroom adventure. "I suppose you might think so. There were moments when we were closer than ever, but it is really my brother Eren who is my closest sibling—though he was close with all of us. He's the eldest and has always been... *special.* Empathetic, even when he was a child."

I could tell by his tone that he was fond of his family, even if his siblings drove him nuts. There was affection in his voice even when he mentioned Alex and Ria, and I really wished I could meet them.

I didn't assume a casual affair with him would earn me that opportunity, but the thought of being embraced by a family so large was appealing. Charles's family barely spoke to him, since they were sick of dealing with him and his constant pleas to borrow money that he could then blow on drugs and women.

"I would love to meet your family someday," I blurted without thinking, quickly regretting it as it sounded presumptuous.

We were just going to his house to have sex, I had to keep reminding myself. I couldn't assume a future with this guy. Honestly, even with my New Year's resolutions in mind, I still couldn't believe that he wasn't out of my league.

I could have sex with a guy who was out of my league, but I couldn't keep him. At least, that had been my experience with Charles.

"I would love to introduce you to them." His golden eyes glittered with some emotion I couldn't interpret. His gaze shifted from my face to lower, where the fabric of my oversized PJ top bunched as I crossed my arms, subconsciously reacting to the chill in the air. "But for tonight, I'd like to have you all to myself."

He gestured with one hand towards the spotless black interior of the car. "You look cold. I have kept you out here too long. Get in and I'll get the heater going."

He had a point, though I still wanted to ask him lots of questions. I supposed I could do so while he was driving us to his house. After all, chattering away about other things would help me deal with my nervousness about getting naked with Vincent. I could distract myself from worrying about what he would think when he saw my body.

At the same time, I *really* wanted to get naked with Vincent, and take a peek at his huge body. Then the licking could commence. I'd gladly go first, but I was hoping he'd want to join in.

7

Vincent

I glanced over at Gabby after settling into the driver's seat, wondering as I usually did why I hadn't gone for the spacious SUV rather than the more compact muscle car. Still, I loved the Chevelle so much that I wished gray-father would approve me bringing it back to the Dead Fall. After all, we'd been building roads in New Omni for years now, and my Chevelle wouldn't have been the only vehicle using them at this point. It would just be the fastest vehicle using them, as the max speed of the conveyances in New Omni were kept to a safe limit to accommodate the amount of pedestrian traffic on those same streets.

I would ask him, though I was certain he'd reject my request. He had strict rules about taking objects from their home dimensions. The Chevelle likely wouldn't qualify, as its absence could cause changes in this dimension that would disrupt its flux. Gray-father liked to minimize our impact on parallel dimensions to only what couldn't be avoided to achieve our objectives, whatever they might be.

The car I could leave behind. Gabby, on the other hand, I might just have to steal away from this dimension, though mother insisted we only bring willing travelers into the Fall. The Artificial Intelligence, NEX, that managed the Nexus dimensional portal to our dimension would snatch anyone up from any dimension anchored to the Nexus if gray-father told it to. It lacked morals or ethics or anything else that hindered the rest of us. I supposed I wouldn't exist if it hadn't been so unconcerned with the feelings of the people it abducted from their home dimensions.

Honestly, I thought as I started the car up, pleased with the roar of the 454 coming to life, gray-father would probably let me take Gabby without asking first, if my mother wouldn't flip her top from him doing so. She was the voice of his conscience, and from what I'd heard about their past, he hadn't been much different from NEX when they'd met.

Love had changed him. I wondered if it would change me as well, and if so, would I be proud of the male I'd become for my mate?

I noted that Gabby shivered a little in her oversized clothing that looked almost as soft as her pink cheeks and little, round chin. I quickly turned on the heater, then shifted into reverse to back out of the parking space.

It turned out that Valerie had been right. Gabby, as she truly looked, definitely appealed to me in a way that her heavily painted and lacquered appearance had not. I hoped this was the Gabby she intended to be on a daily basis. The way Valerie had described her best friend had made me think she was like this, and that earlier tonight had been the anomaly.

"What year is this Chevelle?" she asked with a little quiver in her voice that I hoped came from the chill rather than from nerves at being alone with me.

"Nineteen Seventy-one," I said, still impressed by the mint condition of a car that was fifty years old by this dimension's time.

In the Fall, most of the objects we found were decayed, though gray-father could now take resources from other dimensions. He put the same limits on how much we took and how often we took it to avoid interfering too much outside our own dimension. We often still made do with what we could salvage or scavenge from the Fall.

New Omni's advancement and the quality of life that her citizens could have there was a testament to how much we could accomplish with what we found in the Fall.

"Wow, she's a beauty, especially for her age!"

I glanced over at Gabby, comfortable enough now with the operation of the motor vehicle to take my eyes from the road briefly, though they didn't stray from my path for too long.

"Her beauty pales in comparison to yours, Gabby."

My date's cheeks flushed with blood that I could hear rushing through her veins. My mouth watered to taste it, but that would definitely not happen tonight. I would have to satisfy myself with the taste of other parts of her, and I already hungered for more after just one kiss.

"You flatter me," she said, and I heard the doubt in her tone. "Although," I felt her gaze settle on me as I focused again on the road, "she *is* a car with a nice big trunk, so maybe a comparison could be made between us."

I chuckled. "You don't believe me? About how beautiful you are?"

Gabby shrugged. "I'm just a little surprised that you didn't think I was beautiful earlier, when I was really trying."

I frowned, mentally kicking myself again for behaving the way I had. I should have made a greater effort to be polite and hide my distaste for her earlier appearance, but I had dealt with so many women like that hitting on me that I'd grown frustrated. Valerie's descriptions of Gabby had raised my hope and sense of anticipation for the kind of mate I was looking for.

"I prefer your natural look." I smiled as I shot her another glance, noting that she seemed to be warming up, no longer shivering as she held her hands out to the heater vents. "You don't need all that paint to be beautiful."

She smirked, her lusciously full lips tilting crookedly. "Maybe I enjoy wearing makeup."

There were plenty of females in the New Omni who did, as well as many males. It would be wrong of me to insist she keep her face bare simply because that was how I preferred it.

It would be wrong to *insist*. No one could fault me for *suggesting*.

"I would ask then, why you prefer it? If you simply enjoy painting your features as an art form, then I can appreciate your skill. Your face with makeup on looked nothing like it does now. However, if you cover your face because you don't like the way it already looks, and you think it would be more beautiful if it looked like so many of the other faces I've seen in this world," I sent her a smoldering look that had all my hunger for her in it, "then you are doing yourself a grave disservice."

She seemed to mull this over for a minute, rubbing her hands together in her lap to encourage circulation to them. I regretted keeping her out in the cold so long. I'd sensed that she might be skittish about allowing me to drive her to my home so I had taken it slowly rather than rushing her to my car with the eagerness I felt to get her alone.

I also sensed she was as hungry for me as I was for her, which was no doubt the deciding factor of her coming along. I hoped she found more to be intrigued about me than only my physical appearance, because when she saw the rest of my body, she might be a lot more skittish if she wasn't already invested in who I was as a person.

"You have any family?" I asked in an attempt to break the

awkward silence that fell between us. My homesickness for my own family inspired the question.

While living in this "civilized" world had initially interested me as I sought out lodging and transportation and encountered so many humans in different shapes and sizes and shades, I missed New Omni. I even missed the Fall, despite how wild and dangerous it remained, even as New Omni expanded outwards with the ancilla forest. Gray-father might control the Nexus now, but the creatures within the Fall had created their own complex eco-system among the ruins and junkpiles, as well as an entire second civilization beneath the ground, below the ancilla's root system, and our scouting and salvage parties often ran across unexpected and uncharted dangers. Even our flesh worm spies couldn't see everything.

Gabby's reply brought me back to the present, reminding me that we still had a long way to go before I was certain she would be the mate I brought back to my dimension.

As much as I wanted her to be, as her scent not only filled my car, but also seemed to intoxicate my senses. I salivated with the desire to taste her everywhere.

"I don't have any family who cares about me, so if you're planning to axe-murder me or lock me away in a sex dungeon, you won't need to worry about a search party knocking on your door." She tried for a joking tone, but I sensed genuine nervousness behind it.

The mention of a sex-dungeon made my stem eager to extend, but I pushed down the urge, keeping it behind my tattooed slit with an act of will, even as my claudas shifted beneath their binding. Fortunately, she didn't appear to notice the movement of my clothing, staring instead out the window as I drove us to my small home in a middle-class neighborhood. Nothing too flashy, gray-father had warned as he'd given me enough currency to make my way in this dimension without being forced to seek employment that could draw unnecessary attention to my differences.

"I have no intention of harming you, Gabby," I said with as much reassurance in my tone as I could, "I realize my appearance can be *alarming* for some people, and they assume things about me that aren't accurate, but I'm harmless to you."

Harmless because I would never hurt her, or any innocent female. Not one of my fathers would condone that, even if I was of that nature. That would have been beaten out of me at a young age, I was certain, had I shown any proclivities like that. Fortunately, I'd never felt the urge to hurt a female, and that could be more because of my Fayi blood than my human blood. The males of my blood-father's species might be domineering, but they didn't hurt females unless given no choice, and it was a rare instance where they weren't able to overpower them to keep them from being forced to make such a choice.

She smiled, but it was a small and uncertain expression. "You don't look harmless, to be honest, but I do like the fangs."

I grinned, baring those fangs. Hopefully, she would discover they were quite real and very functional at some point, but for now, I'd let her believe they were fake, as all the other humans I'd met had assumed. It was useful that humans in this world had come up with many ways of modifying their appearance to look more like the creatures from their myths and legends. That made it much easier for me to fit in, even though I stood out.

"Note that I said harmless *to you*, Gabby. If you ever need me to defend you...."

She released a soft laugh, the tension in her body escaping with her breath. "I sure coulda used you back when I was in junior high and high school!"

Her tension might be gone, but her words and tone made my body tense up. My claudas shifted again, and I quickly lowered my elbows onto my stomach to block the view of that movement and willed them back into place. Someone had hurt Gabby badly enough to convince her that she had to look completely unlike herself simply to be accepted by others. Perhaps it was a kind of camouflage she used to fit in with her fellow humans so that she wouldn't be targeted.

Anger burned through my blood, causing drops of paralyzing venom to leak from my claudas' claw tips. I wanted to make those who had hurt her pay, but I doubted gray-father would appreciate that. It might draw too much unwanted attention to me.

I knew my mother had been cruelly treated by her fellow humans while in these "schools" the humans of worlds like this attended. I'd been outraged by some of the stories she'd told, though she'd been able to tell them with more amusement than Gabby had in her tone right now.

I didn't know what to say to her that wouldn't make the direction of my thoughts obvious, or the fact that I wanted to be the one to protect her from ever being hurt by another again. Though I felt an intense connection to her that only seemed to grow the longer I spent in her company, I couldn't expect her to feel the same so quickly. In this region of her world, dating was a strange thing. Humans might have sex with each other very early in their dating ritual, often on the first date, yet would take sometimes many years to commit to each other.

For most of the residents of the Fall, they knew very quickly if they were meant to be together. They didn't need to perform a complex and often pointless—in my opinion—dance around the topic of commitment.

Another long silence fell between us, though her heartbeat sounded stable rather than rapid with nervousness. Maybe I had reassured her that she wasn't risking her life by coming with me.

Then she broke the silence by gasping and opening her

little purse. She pulled out her phone and unlocked the screen. "I almost forgot to tell Valerie where I'm going!"

As she rapidly pressed the letters on her phone to send a text, I smiled knowingly. "Perhaps your family has failed you, but your friend seems very protective of you."

She glanced at me after pushing send, then nodded. "Val is a good friend, even if she can be a bit overbearing at times."

I huffed in amusement. "She reminds me a lot of my mother. Always managing people, but also possessing a huge heart and boundless compassion."

"That describes her perfectly!" Gabby's smile faded as she bit her sexy lower lip. She glanced down at the phone in her lap. "I'm worried about her though. She's been drinking a lot more lately than she used to."

I'd also noticed Valerie's intoxication, but only at her party. I had not sensed that she consumed alcohol while on her job at the gas station where I'd become a regular. I had assumed she was merely partying as humans did on such occasions as the turning of a New Year. Since I could not make a real comment on that, I remained silent, allowing Gabby time to continue speaking if she wished.

My silence seemed to give her permission, and she took it eagerly, spilling out her growing concerns for her best friend, as well as sharing some of their past and how Valerie had taken Gabby under her wing.

I learned as much about my date as her friend. Valerie might be the extrovert with the big heart, but Gabby also possessed one too, though she was often too shy to reveal her concerns for others because she felt she might impose on them. I suspected she didn't want to have any uncomfortable conversations with Valerie over her drinking, despite her obvious concern about that.

Gabby's sudden candor about a subject that had nothing to do with our current date might have had something to do with the fact that I'd turned onto my road, and we were rapidly approaching my house. I could sense her heartbeat increasing, and she was worrying her lower lip more as she cast glances my way.

She was nervous about what the rest of this night would bring. I wanted to reassure her, but I also felt nervous, though I hid it better. Alex would have mocked me for showing any type of uncertainty or nervousness, and Ria was so fearless and feisty that I wasn't even certain she'd ever felt nervous.

I liked Gabby—a lot. I wanted her to like me a lot in return.

Enough that my claudas wouldn't send her screaming into the night. Enough that she would welcome my stem inside her.

Enough that she would leave everything she ever knew behind and return with me to my own dimension.

8

Gabby

When Vincent turned off the car and the powerful purr of the engine fell silent, I feared that my gulp would be audible to his pointed ears.

This was it! I had let a strange man drive me to his house, and if I followed him through the front door of his middleclass tract home, I could be risking my life, or maybe just my heart. I wasn't certain which would be worse.

Would he turn out to be just like Charles? Charming and complimentary at first, then a real bastard once he had me hooked?

While I sat there debating whether this was a good idea, or a really, *really* bad one, Vincent opened his heavy door and maneuvered his tall, bulky frame out of the vehicle. Before I had a chance to decide whether I would chicken out and a make a break for it, he'd made his way to my side of the car and opened my door.

He offered a hand to help me out, and I took it with my own

hand slightly trembling and feeling a bit too clammy to not embarrass me. Still, the warmth of his palm and fingers was heavenly as his hand closed around mine and he gently tugged me out of the vehicle.

This was the point of no return, because he didn't release my hand. Maybe he sensed I could make a break for it. Or maybe he really did like touching me—even my cold, clammy mitt.

The ears on my bunny slippers flopped with each step I took in his wake, past the lawn that looked like every other lawn on the block, to the door that was painted the exact same color as every other door.

When he reached the door, it unlocked on its own, prompting a low whistle from me.

"Fancy! You have one of those new home security systems, eh?"

He grinned down at me. "I like technology, even the more primitive tech."

"*Primitive*?" I laughed. "That's cutting-edge technology. Did it use facial recognition to unlock your door?"

He nodded, his devastatingly handsome, toothy grin growing broader. "It is primitive compared to the things my father has in his lab, but I did enjoy toying with it and modifying it."

"Who the heck is your father? Nikola Tesla reincarnated?"

He merely chuckled at that question, then swept his free arm towards the entry door of his house as it swung open on its own.

Since he didn't move to step forward, I took it that he wanted me to go in first. As nervous as I felt, I complied, because I also felt a lot of anticipation. This evening could wind up being a disaster—or I'd have the best time of my life.

It looked like his entire house had ceramic tile flooring, and I saw plenty of signs of his tech-obsession when I entered. He had a fully tricked out gaming rig in his living room with a basic couch that showed a lack of interest in any décor that lacked circuitry.

He also had the fancy refrigerator that had a touch screen on the front, and a door that would change from opaque to translucent so you could look inside it without opening it.

He led me into the kitchen, which was open to the dining room.

"Would you like something to drink?" he asked, tapping the refrigerator door so it turned transparent as I paused on the other side of the wide kitchen island that had a bland beige granite countertop.

A variety of different juices as well as water bottles filled the interior. Beneath the liquid selection sat a couple of containers whose contents I couldn't determine because they were opaque, but they were likely leftovers.

"I'll have whatever you're having," I said, feeling overwhelmed in my nervousness by the choices.

He opened the refrigerator, plucking out a pomegranate juice that he passed to me, then another bottle that lacked a label, but had suspiciously dark red fluid in it.

He caught me staring at it and smirked. "I figured you'd prefer pomegranate to my usual beverage."

I raised my eyebrows. "Are you... are you seriously drinking *blood*?"

"Would it be a problem if I was?" he asked in his ridiculously hot voice as he uncapped the bottle.

"I mean...," I shrugged, "I dunno." I had anticipated this possibility when Valerie had told me about Vincent, but I still hadn't come to a conclusion about how it made me feel—other than nervous. "Where exactly do you source it from? Is it animal, or...?"

I lifted both hands to cover my neck reflexively, shooting a quick glance at the front door that fortunately wasn't that far away.

He laughed aloud, then caught my wrist and pulled my hand towards him. My resistance against his grip didn't stop him from dripping a few drops of the garnet red liquid onto my palm. Then he released me and straightened on his side of the kitchen island.

"Taste it," he said with a sharp smile as his fangs gleamed in the overhead can lights above the kitchen island.

I didn't particularly want to taste blood, but it was only a few drops.

Well, I had known from first seeing him that he was into the whole "vampire" thing, and I'd been digging it up until this point. I supposed it was hypocritical of me to have an issue with it now, when it came down to the actual defining trait of a vampire. I cautiously lifted my palm and licked one of the drops, praying it came from some other animal rather than a human one.

It tasted sweet and syrupy.

I lifted my head, smacking my lips, and narrowed my eyes at him. "Hey! This isn't blood!"

"Disappointed?" He grinned crookedly.

I licked the remaining syrup off my hand as I shook my head. "You really had me going! Is this a trick you play on all your guests?"

He shrugged as he took a swig from the bottle of what tasted a lot like cherry syrup, fortified with vitamins, I suspected, since I caught the hint of a minerally aftertaste to the sweet flavor.

"I rarely have guests," he answered after he swallowed, licking the cherry syrup residue off his lips.

I propped my hands on my hips. "I can't imagine why," I said sardonically, my smile wry as I eyed the bottle of cherry juice he held.

He set the bottle down on his granite kitchen countertop. Then rested his forearms on it and leaned towards me, moving his mouth a lot closer to mine as his smile faded into a more intent look.

"Valerie tells me your home is decorated like a haunted house—all year around."

I nodded slowly. "That's true. I like my skulls and skeletons, and witches, and werewolves—"

"And *vampires*," he said with a wink.

"What made you decide to get the fangs?" I asked impulsively, though I'd promised myself I wouldn't be nosy about his choice of lifestyle.

He straightened, then came around the kitchen island to stand on my side of it, next to the three stools that fronted it. He lifted a hand to my bun, then unwound it so my hair fell in full waves around my face.

"There was no choice about the fangs." His voice rumbled as he lowered his head.

He nuzzled my mussed hair, inhaling deeply. Then he kissed along my cheek until I lifted my head to meet his lips.

I tasted the cherry syrup sweetness on his lips and then his tongue as it slipped inside my mouth. I moaned in pleasure, savoring the flavor of him as I sucked it the way I wanted to suck another part of him.

His answering moan shot heat directly to my core as his arm wrapped around my waist and pulled me closer to his bulky body. I felt the hardness of his belly, but I was too caught up in the deliciousness of his hungry kiss to contemplate whether he'd take off the shapewear beneath his overcoat.

Then his hands shifted to the buttons on my flannel top. He deftly unhooked them, freeing my breasts, which, to my embarrassment, sagged from my weight loss, just like the excess skin beneath them.

I tried to pull away to cover them and maybe convince him to take us into a room where it would be pitch dark.

He didn't release me, his hands trailing down my collarbone to capture first one breast, then the other. His thumbs teased my nipples into hard peaks. He didn't make a single sound of disgust or disappointment at how much they sagged.

His lack of judgement still seemed too good to be true when he broke the kiss and dropped to his knees in front of me.

I tried to pull the sides of my flannel top closed as he got a good look at my sagging flesh, but he caught my wrists and held them still. Then he leaned forward and captured one of my nipples in his mouth, suckling it so skillfully that I nearly came just from that stimulation. He only freed my hands once he'd captured my breast, knowing I couldn't close my top now.

I buried my fingers in his thick, silky hair, pulling his head closer to my body as he teased my nipple with his lips and tongue.

Then he freed it to focus on the other, leaving it tight, hard, and eager for more attention as the cool air kissed flesh damp from his mouth. His fingers returned to tease it when I whimpered in protest, causing me to sigh with pleasure.

My knees threatened to buckle under the onslaught of his lips and tongue and fingers. I leaned my butt against the bar stool to brace myself, awash in the pleasure he was giving me.

Then he untied the cord that held up my PJ bottoms and I felt another wave of panic, fearing he wouldn't be so turned on if he could see my thighs sagging.

He released my nipple with his mouth and trailed kisses down my belly, nipping at the extra skin as if it didn't bother him in the least and it was just another part of my body that he desired.

Then the cord was loose, and the flannel bottoms slipped down my legs, exposing my lower body to him. Underneath them, I wore only the sexy thong that I'd originally had under my New Year's party dress. The shapewear had left marks on my skin, and Vincent kissed along those marks as his hands stroked over my lower body, his fingers straying closer and closer to that scrap of gold fabric.

I gasped and my knees parted when his fingers slipped beneath it to feel the slickness of my entrance. He growled in pleasure against my belly, then licked his way lower, over rippled, stretch-marked flesh with the same ardor as a lover might show a woman with the perfect body.

He caught the crotch of the thong and tugged it downwards, exposing my mound to him, inch by inch, his tongue licking a trail down to my landing strip of pubic hair. He nuzzled the springy curls there, inhaling deeply again.

Then he planted a kiss right on my clit. The fingers of one of his hands parted my folds so he could suck it between his lips. His other hand yanked my thong down to my ankles.

I cried out with the pleasure of him suckling my clit the way he had my nipples. Then I writhed my hips as he began to stroke his long, thick tongue over the hypersensitive flesh.

Once he'd disposed of the thong, his fingers returned to my entrance, then delved inside me as he licked me towards my peak.

I came quickly, my inner muscles convulsing around his fingers as they thrust inside me. He made a low rumble that was almost like the purr of his muscle car with his satisfaction.

I tried to pull away, but he wasn't finished with me yet. With one hand, he pushed my thighs further open, then withdrew his fingers from my opening to replace them with his tongue.

I gasped and moaned as his tongue licked inside me with the fervor of a starving man at a five-course meal. He rubbed my clit with his fingers until I came again, his tongue stroking my inner muscles as they convulsed around it. I had no idea how he got it so deep inside me, but it felt amazing as it teased my g-spot.

I could definitely forgive Vincent his eccentricities, even if he was a blood drinker, if he promised to do this to me every day!

As I trembled from my second orgasm, leaning heavily against the kitchen island, my naked buttocks braced on the stool, he withdrew his tongue from me and planted a kiss on my throbbing clit, then he sat back on his haunches, looking up at my face with a satisfied smirk.

"I didn't even bite," he said, his tongue licking his lips. "Though I was definitely tempted."

I sagged against the kitchen bar, struggling to catch my breath as he slowly rose to his feet, his height imposing when he stood this close to me, but I was done with feeling nervous in his presence.

He really knew how to break the ice.

His hands stroked over my thighs, and he seemed so unfazed by the skin that I'd spent so much time agonizing over. It was surreal to have this drop-dead gorgeous giant of a man caressing my flawed body as if he couldn't resist touching it. It was like I'd conjured him out of my hottest dreams into reality.

Then I had a sudden panicked fear that I *was* dreaming, and that I would soon wake up to the invasive alarm clock and end up being miserable when I found myself alone in a cold bed.

"Can you pinch me?" I said quickly.

He cocked his head, his dark brows pulling together with confusion. "You'd prefer I pinch you rather than bite you?"

I shook my head with a nervous laugh. "I just want proof that all of this is really happening, and I'm not just enjoying the best dream of my life!"

He lifted his hands to cup my face, his golden gaze intent as it met mine. "Am I your dream man then, Gabby?"

"Oh, you are *way* hotter than my dream man, Vincent!" I

reached to stroke his chest, but he stepped away from me, just out of my reach, leaving me confused and feeling rejected.

Embarrassed, I pulled the sides of my flannel top closed, the excess fabric covering my bare crotch as I settled more fully on the stool. “I guess I’m not your dream woman.” I lowered my head as I laughed shortly with embarrassment. “I’m not surprised.”

He caught my chin and lifted it, forcing me to meet his eyes. “I think you’re the woman I’ve been waiting my whole life to meet, Gabby.” His gaze trailed from my face down to my concealed lap. “You are beautiful, and you taste more delicious than I’d hoped you would. You *are* my dream woman.”

I made to shake my head, but his grip on my chin wouldn’t allow me to.

“No, I won’t hear any negative comments you would say about yourself. I realize now why you tried to hide your beauty behind a false façade. You do not fit the mold of what your people claim is beautiful.”

He gestured with his free hand to his own body. “Neither do I, Gabby. I assure you, my body is much farther from the human ideal than yours.” He leaned closer to me. “But I don’t give a damn about human ideals, because I am not entirely human.”

9

Gabby

With that statement, he released my chin. "Would you like something to eat?" He gave me a cocky smile. "Now that *I've* feasted."

I was still a little self-conscious, but his words, bizarre as they might seem to some people, actually made me feel much better about myself. I suspected he meant that bulge beneath his jacket, which wouldn't be the human "ideal" for a man, but if he wanted to pretend he wasn't human, then I would get in on the game.

Why not? If it made him feel better about himself, allowed him to feel acceptance for himself as he was, then I could appreciate that. I'd been uncomfortable in my own skin for most of my life. I'd struggled to fit into the mold my mother insisted I fit into so that the other kids at school would stop picking on me and maybe be my friends.

"Were you ever bullied in school, Vincent?" I asked impulsively as he strode to his living room and grabbed a blanket from the back of his couch.

He brought it to me, then took my hand to urge me to stand and step out of my slippers and the thong and pajama bottoms that he'd left wrapped around my ankles. When I made to protest, he kissed me to silence me.

Those poor innocent bunnies had witnessed some naughty things recently. I hope they'd had their ears covering their eyes the whole time.

"I want easy access for later," he whispered into my ear before stepping back and releasing my hand.

I shivered in anticipation at the promise in those words as I unfolded the blanket and wrapped it around my waist, feeling his hungry gaze on my bared lower body until I successfully covered it up.

"You didn't answer my question," I said, feeling bolder in his presence with each complimentary word or gesture he showed me.

Okay, so I bloomed under praise, since I received it so rarely. I could admit it. Charles had used that weakness in me to his advantage, doling out praise in tiny doses to get me to do what he wanted, and I'd repeatedly fallen for it—hook, line, and sinker. That self-awareness didn't make me proud, but I was certain a therapist could make something out of it.

Probably a car payment.

He returned to the fridge, this time opening the door to expose the contents to me. Then he glanced back at me over his shoulder as he regarded the meager selection of food. "Where I come from, we didn't attend a *school* like your people do." He grinned toothily. "But I have siblings, remember? I understand bullying perfectly."

I propped my elbows on the counter, leaning forward with interest. "Where *do* you come from?" He spoke perfect English, but with an unfamiliar accent that I couldn't place.

He slowly closed the refrigerator door and turned to regard me fully. "A place very far away." He jerked his chin towards the fridge. "Perhaps we should order out. I don't keep much food around."

I could tell a dodge when I heard one, but I wanted to know more about him, and I wasn't feeling hungry for *food* at the moment either. "I'd rather talk about you than eat right now."

His nostrils flared as his gaze trailed from my face downwards. A slow smile tilted his lips as he raised his eyes to meet mine again. "Are you certain all you want to do is talk?" His gaze turned smoldering. "Because I definitely want to do more."

I smiled seductively, feeling like a regular sex-kitten in the aftermath of two incredible orgasms the likes of which I'd only received from dream men in the past. Gotta love that oxytocin! It made me want to marry Vincent at this point. I didn't give a damn what his body looked like under that jacket, as long as he kept using his mouth on me the way he did.

"If that's so, why did you pull away from me?" I walked my fingers across the kitchen bar in a teasing way, looking up at him through my lashes.

With a pound of makeup on and my body bound into a shapewear garment, I hadn't felt this sexy. In fact, I didn't think I'd ever felt this sexy in my life. Something about Vincent made me feel damned good in my skin, flaws and all. It was probably his apparent hunger for me, and the fact that he made no effort to hide that he desired me.

The only sticking point was that he'd pulled away from me when I'd gone to touch him in return. I was *so* ready to lick him like a lollipop and make him come in a shuddering orgasm the way I had.

His expression grew closed off and he looked away from me, his hand dropping reflexively to cover his stomach. "I don't think you're ready to see my body yet. I want you to get to know me better before I show it to you." He returned his gaze to me. "So you understand that I'm not a monster."

I slowly shook my head, feeling an intense burst of compassion for him and his insecurities. Didn't I know them all too well myself?

I dropped my gaze to his belly. "I don't mind a little extra padding at all! Trust me, I like a little softness to hold onto in the bedroom."

My words seemed to have the opposite effect than I was going for as he looked away again, his brows pulling together in a concerned frown. "What if I'm not nearly as soft as you think, Gabby? Would you still like me in the bedroom?"

I wondered now exactly what he was getting at, and his words really began to work their way into my brain, knocking aside preconceived notions about reality.

What if he was telling the truth, all plain and out in the open? In fact, what if he truly wasn't human, and he was hiding in plain sight because he knew that no one would assume his appearance was anything other than artificially created?

I straightened in my seat, regarding him with new eyes, noting the impossible golden gaze, the pointed ears with no sign of surgery scars or movie makeup effects, the fangs that looked so real and natural in his mouth, as if they belonged there.

"When you said you weren't entirely human, what exactly did you mean by that?"

I'd naively and hastily assumed he meant that in his *mind* he wasn't entirely human, thinking that he'd taken on a mindset that allowed him to separate himself from a world of people who had a narrowly defined standard of what was normal and acceptable. As an oddball myself, I could totally understand why he'd taken that extra step mentally.

But what if it wasn't all in his head?

"I am only half-human," he said after a long moment, his

eyes fixed on my face as if he wanted to see my reaction. "My mother is fully human, but my father... is not human at all."

I pondered this, my face probably showing my lack of reaction, because I genuinely wasn't sure what to think at this point. My eyes shifted to study the bulge of his stomach with a new perspective.

"Are you really some sort of vampire?" I asked, feeling a sense of excitement, rather than the fear most people would probably experience at the thought.

He shrugged one broad shoulder. "Some sort, I suppose."

I leaned forward excitedly. "Are you serious? You're not just pranking me, or messing around with me, or really getting into character, are you?"

Please, please don't let him disappoint me by saying it was all a game he was playing! The thought that there might really be something beyond the reality we knew, the reality we were allowed to accept without being called delusional or crazy, was almost as good as discovering that the man of my dreams was real. I didn't think I could handle my disappointment if I found out otherwise.

He braced his hands on his side of the kitchen island, regarding me with a curious expression. "You sound more excited about the prospect of me being a vampire than scared or worried."

I nodded quickly. "I am, Vincent! You have no idea how much I want it to be true. I've spent my whole life believing in things that everyone told me didn't exist. I would love to have some validation of all those beliefs."

He seemed to ponder my words, his eyes studying my face intently. "You aren't like any of the other women I've met here."

I shrugged. "Trust me, I know I'm strange. I've been told that my whole life."

"Where I'm from, *strange* is the norm." He grinned. "I assure you, I am much closer to human than most of my acquaintances."

I leaned forward on my elbows, practically bouncing on my stool with excitement, unable to look away from his face and the unusual appearance of it. "Where *are* you from? You keep teasing me by mentioning all these details, but you never come right out and say it."

He sighed and straightened. "That's because I can't discuss it with you yet. There are things I must know about you before we have such a conversation."

I jumped off my stool and rushed to grab my clutch purse. He watched me with raised eyebrows as I opened it and pulled out my driver's license. I returned to the kitchen island and slapped it on the counter then pushed it towards him.

"Here's all my personal information. They even put my blood type on there." I eyed his fangs thoughtfully. "Does it hurt when you bite people?"

He smiled crookedly at me. "Are you asking me to bite you? So soon in our relationship?"

I shrugged, blushing with embarrassment at his teasing. Was I too eager? Did he think I was a freak? I suppose most people would. Who asked someone to bite them on a first date?

"We can... uh, we can wait," I rubbed my neck reflexively. "I guess." I tried not to sound too disappointed, though I did feel oddly let down that he didn't jump at the chance.

He chuckled as he pulled my driver's license close, then picked it up and examined it. "This wasn't exactly what I meant when I said I needed to know more about you."

"Well, I can answer any question you have. I don't have a resume on me or anything, but I can describe my work experience and—"

His bark of laughter cut me off as he set down my driver's license. "Gabby, you silly woman! I don't care about your work history." His wide smile faded as he regarded me affectionately. "You are as adorable as those slippers you wore here."

I flushed again with embarrassment, realizing how ridiculous I'd sounded in my eagerness to get more confessions out of him.

And maybe get a peek under his jacket at what inhuman bits he was hiding. Inquiring minds definitely needed to know. Forget that "wanted" shit! I had a *need* inside me—well, I needed whatever he was packing to be inside me.

His nostrils flared as he inhaled and his gaze shifted to my neck, where my pulse pounded as my heartrate increased with my arousal. "You're making it difficult for me to concentrate on our conversation."

"C-can you tell I'm...?" I covered my mouth, cutting off my admission. "Is it like... like a sense of smell or...."

"I can smell your desire, and hear your heartbeat," he said in a guttural growl.

Then he licked his lips, and I realized that his tongue was longer than I'd ever seen for a human tongue. He'd been careful to conceal the length of it from me before, but he wasn't hiding it now.

He really wasn't human! A sane woman would be running for the door right now, but all I wanted to do was beg him to open that coat already.

"What would you like to know about me? Ask me anything! Hey, I got an idea. We can play twenty questions."

"There's no hurry. We have all night." He gestured to his couch. "This date hasn't gone quite the way I'd anticipated, but I'm happy we made it to this point. I wouldn't want to rush things before either of us are ready."

"I am *so* ready, Vincent!"

I couldn't help it. I knew I sounded like a lunatic, but I was beyond curious and into the realm of frantic to see something completely and unequivocally inhuman that I couldn't pass off as plastic surgery or body modifications. Somehow, given his hesitation to show me what was under his coat, I knew what he had would fit the bill.

Either that, or it was a beer belly, and he didn't want this game to end and for me to realize that he was just playing around.

10

Vincent

Gabby wasn't afraid of the idea that I wasn't human. If anything, she was almost too eager for proof of my claims. It was just as Valerie had said about her. Gabby craved the strange, the weird, the unusual. She was perfect for me.

The only problem was that I was now experiencing stage fright about exposing my body to her. Hers was so beautiful and she tasted delicious. My mouth watered at the thought of tasting her again, of delving my tongue inside her as she came, her nectar sweet and heady to me, like a drug that I could easily grow addicted to.

I'd been unable to resist tasting her so soon after getting her into my home, and I knew that I was rushing things. Putting the "cart before the horse" as my mother would say, quoting her own long-lost father. I'd heard that phrase many times while growing up. Along with my defiance came a whole lot of impatience that had driven my mother crazy.

I guess I still struggled with that impatience, even now.

I was supposed to get to know Gabby as a person before I dived into her tongue first. At least I resisted the powerful urge to bite her and drink from the blood that rushed through veins so close to her fragrant and luscious heat.

Now that I knew Gabby was the kind of woman I was looking for, I didn't want to mess things up by throwing open my coat and scaring the shit out of her. She was still thinking I was the kind of vampire the people of her world dreamed up. I didn't know how to tell her I was likely closer to a tick than an undead creature of the night.

My claudas twitched beneath my coat, even bound as they were by the tight garment I kept over them. They were eager for her to see them, but that was because my stem wanted to extend so badly that my slit ached from the desire to set it free. Once she was comfortable with my body, I hoped she would welcome my stem.

Dare I hope that would happen so soon? On our first date?

It seemed like too much, too soon. I'd spent months in this world hiding the truth about myself, knowing that I would be in danger if I was revealed for the inhuman creature I was to the authorities that ruled this world. Now, I had already told Gabby the truth, but she hadn't actually seen the irrefutable evidence.

What if I was wrong about her? What if she wasn't the right woman, even though she tasted like perfection and her body made my stem almost too eager to contain?

A mating wasn't all about the physical appearance. Gabby and I had a rocky first meeting, and I'd almost screwed things up by reacting too hastily. I didn't want to make the same mistake again. My impulsivity was getting me into trouble.

I'd been warned about that in the past. Dammed if I'd listened.

This was too important though, because if Gabby turned out to be the wrong woman and freaked out and ran screaming from my home to call her government officials or the police authorities, then I would have to relocate again, go deeper into hiding, maybe even be forced to use the camouflage gray-father had provided.

I'd eschewed that technology because I wanted my future mate to see me for what I was from the very beginning. I realized that she would still be misled by thinking some of my features were modified, but at least she would appreciate my true aesthetic rather than a more humanized version of my appearance.

"Vincent?" Gabby said with a worried expression since I had remained silent for too long after she swore she was ready to see the true me.

"Perhaps we should order some food," I insisted as a delaying tactic.

I could eat and gain sustenance from food, thanks to my human side, but I could also subsist entirely on blood—or in my case, a sweet, flavored syrup I'd created with blood, since I had a fierce sweet tooth.

Her shoulders sagged forward, and her expression fell. "I... okay," she capitulated. "Sure, I, uh, I'm a little hungry."

Now I'd disappointed her, and I could tell she was doubting the truth of my claim of not being entirely human. She probably thought I was toying with her for some nefarious purpose.

Or just to be a creep.

I didn't know what to say to undo yet another hasty mistake. In my over eagerness to strip her naked and feast upon her body and bury my stem inside her, I'd rushed things inelegantly. I was showing my inexperience with dating and relationships.

"What kind of foods do you like?" I pulled open a drawer and withdrew a stack of menus.

I collected them because I liked to try the different types of foods in this region of the world, having never had access to some of them before. I enjoyed experiencing new flavors, although in truth, it was only Gabby's flavor that I really wanted to taste right now.

"I take it you eat out a lot," she said with a little laugh.

I met her eyes, unable to stop the slow, knowing smile from touching my lips. "Not as much as you think, but when I hunger for something, I'm impatient to taste it."

I heard the increase in her blood flow as a blush darkened her cheeks. My mouth watered as I caught the scent of her increased arousal. Beneath that blanket, her lower body was naked and wet for my touch. All I had to do was walk over to her and pull it away, then kneel before her and—

"Since it's New Year's Eve, a lot of those places won't be open." She pointed to the stack of menus. "We might be better off digging something up out of your pantry or freezer."

I had forgotten that businesses around here closed for holiday celebrations. I wasn't accustomed to that. In the Dead Fall, though we had several annual celebrations—the biggest being the blooming of the ancilla trees and the resultant orgies that took place during the flurry of petals—vendors stayed open throughout them, usually making maximum profits because of hungry and thirsty revelers.

Gabby stood from the stool, tucking the blanket around her like it was a robe. "Let me have a look in your fridge and pantry. I'll see what I can make from what you have here. I'm sure I can whip something up for us."

I pushed aside the stack of menus, regarding her curiously. "You can cook?"

She pushed a lock of her wavy hair behind one ear, smiling shyly. "Yeah. I've been cooking for myself since I was barely tall enough to stand at the stove. Granted, I had to teach myself how to cook, so back then it was only basic stuff like grilled cheese sandwiches, but I've been learning lots of new recipes lately. There are some good ones that I can whip up with basic ingredients most households keep around." She made her way around the bar into my kitchen area, trailing the end of the blanket behind her like a train. "Life hacks," she said with a little laugh as she moved towards the pantry door.

She paused there, looking at me with a cute expression of uncertainty on her round face. "Is it okay if I take a peek in your pantry?"

I gestured for her to go ahead, hoping I had something of use in there. I purchased groceries every couple of weeks, though I was often unsure what to buy, since I'd already secured a supplier of fresh animal blood for my nutritional needs. My desire to try new flavors had led to me buying a wide variety of odd things, most of them turning out to be disgusting and overprocessed.

I had also ambitiously selected ingredients to make my own meals but found my interest in cooking to be as undeveloped as my blood-father's. I was too impatient for the tedious task of food preparation, and I was more likely to simply resort to drinking blood instead. Hence, why most of my culinary exploration happened thanks to takeout menus.

She opened the pantry door and flicked on the light, then perused my shelves thoughtfully. I heard a little chuckle from her as she plucked out a bag of "chips" that I'd found repulsive after a few bites.

"I didn't expect to find these kinds of munchies in your pantry." She shook the bag. "You seem a little too refined for Pork 'N Doodles."

"I thought I'd give them a try." I shrugged. "They were less than pleasant."

She regarded them with an expression of disgust. "They were never my favorite. My mom had a boyfriend who loved this stuff, so for the year that he lived with us, it was always one of the few things in our pantry. I can crush it up and make a topping for a casserole, but honestly, it's not the tastiest ingredient to use."

"They're probably stale." I gestured to the bag. "I bought them some time ago."

She tossed the bag on the kitchen bar. "In that case, I'd throw them out if I were you. No sense leaving them in here to clutter up your pantry."

She returned to the shelves, propping one hand on her hip as she murmured to herself, reading off labels and making comments below her breath that she no doubt thought I couldn't hear. I found them all amusing as she questioned my tastes and wondered if it was because of my nonhuman nature that I liked all the odd items in my pantry.

I would tell her later that my nonhuman side was fine with only blood for a diet. It was my human side that craved different flavors.

For now, I enjoyed watching her ravage my pantry, clearing out all the stale chips and crackers and nearly full boxes of cereals that had initially satisfied my sweet tooth, but still tasted too processed for me to enjoy for long.

Where she was timid in other interactions, she seemed to take charge of my kitchen, snagging several ingredients out of my pantry to set them on the counter, then moving on to my refrigerator and freezer after she formed a pile of groceries for me to dispose of that were stale or past their expiration dates.

I could see she was in her element, and I stayed out of her way, enjoying watching her move around my kitchen while having to keep pausing to tuck her blanket around herself as I caught intriguing glimpses of her naked lower body each time it slipped.

She tugged open the refrigerator door, humming thoughtfully as she shifted aside the many different beverages I'd purchased to experiment with while creating my flavored blood drink. Then she examined the containers of leftovers.

She lifted the top one and popped the lid off. Then she shied away from the contents, wrinkling her nose.

"Vincent! Are you trying to rediscover penicillin?" She turned the container towards me, revealing the green fur coat the food inside had taken on.

The mold that had grown over the food was so thick I couldn't make out what it had been before.

I shrugged, feeling the heat of embarrassment at her disgust. "Sometimes, I forget about the food in there."

She shook her head as a broad grin crossed her face. Her expression looked almost affectionate as she regarded me. "I'm afraid to check those other containers."

She set the lid back on the container in her hand and put it on the counter beside the refrigerator. Then she squared her shoulders and lifted her chin. She tossed me a saucy wink then faced the fridge.

"I'm going in," she said with a mock solemn tone as if she was about to face combat.

I stifled a laugh at her teasing, intrigued by the way she began to systematically decimate my spoiled food collection.

Her expressions as she checked each container were so entertaining that it was almost worth the discomfiture of having her discover the evidence of my neglect.

"Yes!" she cried out in victory, holding up a shrink-wrapped sausage I'd purchased recently but had yet to try. "I can use this." She cast me an arch look. "I was beginning to lose hope I'd find anything edible in here."

I pointed at the storage bins below the shelves. "I recall purchasing some cheeses and produce fairly recently."

She gave me a skeptical look, a smile playing about her lips. "Dare I check your drawers, Vincent?"

I grinned, catching onto her double entendre. Having a human mother from a dimension nearly identical to this one had given me a good understanding of the language and its multiple meanings.

I leaned against the counter, regarding her with all my hunger for her in my eyes. "You might like what you find in there," I said in my most seductive tone.

I hadn't had much experience using seduction prior to coming to this world. In fact, as my brother Alex often pointed out, I was a virgin, choosing to wait for my mate rather than visit the pleasure houses in New Omni that had been set up by entrepreneurial females from many different dimensions. He insisted that our Fayi blood demanded we satisfy our sexual urges as often as possible, and he made frequent visits to those places. I was proof he was wrong, but whenever I pointed that out, he claimed that I was just a human with claudas, not a true Fayi.

Of course, he never said such things around our mother.

Now, I almost wished I had more experience with women, because I was very nervous about taking things to the next step with Gabby.

Her gaze immediately lowered to my groin, which was currently well concealed behind the flaps of my jacket. "I'm sure I will, when you get around to opening them for me." She cocked her hip, one of her naked legs peeking through the concealment of the blanket. "Or you could let me open them for myself."

When she waggled her brows as she eyed me appraisingly, I tensed with the battle to control my stem and keep it from extending.

She was very ready for me, and the scent of her desire was driving me almost as wild as her teasing tone and the hungry look in her eyes. My claudas strained against the binder, my claw tips stinging with the paralytic venom that welled from their glands. Recalling the hurdle I had to get past with showing her my body, and fearing how she would react when she finally saw what she wanted to see so badly, I decided that now wasn't the time for this conversation.

I pointed to the bins. "I'm pretty certain the cheeses are still good. I'm not sure about the produce, but this refrigerator is supposed to keep food fresher longer."

Again, her shoulders slumped, and her lustful look faded into one of disappointment as she turned back to the refrigerator. She opened the right-hand bin and perked up a little as she examined the contents.

"You have enough cheese here to make a dozen pizzas!" She pulled out several bricks of cheese to show them to me. "I can whip up a five-cheese pizza and put some sausage on top." She nodded her chin towards the kitchen bar and the ingredients she'd pulled from my pantry. "I can also make us a cheesy pasta, if you'd like."

The food sounded interesting, but what made my mouth water was Gabby herself. I only wished I wasn't experiencing this fear of exposing myself to her. In fact, the more time I spent with her and the more I enjoyed her company, the greater the fear I felt that she would run screaming from me when she saw my body.

I supposed I wanted to procrastinate, despite my overwhelming desire for her, because I didn't want this enjoyable evening to end in disaster.

I also wondered how long I could hold off when the scent of her arousal hung so heavily in the air that I could taste it.

11

Gabby

Vincent let me putter around his kitchen, going through all his groceries, without a peep of protest. He even got out a couple of garbage bags and began stuffing the expired food into them, then dumped out the stinky spoiled food from his fridge and rinsed out the containers as I prepped the pizza dough.

Once he had that task complete, he joined me at the kitchen island and watched as I went about the process of preparing our meal. When I felt his gaze shift from my hands to my body, I glanced up from my work and caught his hungry eyes.

I would have stopped mid-cheese-grating to take a break in his bedroom, but when our eyes met, he looked away quickly, returning his focus to the bowl of cheese.

It was only our first date. I shouldn't be too pushy, even though he had tongue-fucked me as soon as I walked into his house. That had felt pretty damned intimate, so it was strange that he was now acting so shy about having sex.

Then again, he seemed really nervous about showing me his body. It could be because he really did have some scary alien bits under that jacket, or it could be that he had a normal human body, and he was enjoying the role he was playing as an alien bloodsucker too much to have it end.

I liked Vincent. If he ended up being a normal human with a quirky need to play at being something else, I could accept that, even though I wouldn't deny that I would be disappointed. I just wanted him to be honest with me.

And if he truly was alien, as he said, then I wanted him to trust that I wouldn't flee from the sight of his naked body. Though, given his caution, I really had to wonder what he was hiding under there. My mind supplied all kinds of possibilities.

Tentacles topped that list, and I didn't hate that idea, even if it would be strange at first to feel them writhing against me. Then I thought maybe ginormous teeth, like maybe his stomach was actually his real mouth. I also considered the possibility that he had a hideous creature in his stomach like the mutant Kuato from Total Recall, but I pushed that idea aside, because that one would probably throw me off the most.

My imagination was too good, and it was even beginning to freak me out, until I had to hide how my hands shook as I mixed up the homemade pizza dough.

Fortunately, I convinced Vincent to check the produce drawer for fresh tomatoes, since I wanted to use them along with the homemade pizza sauce I was preparing with the canned tomato sauce and paste I'd found in his overstuffed pantry. While his back was turned, I got myself under control, calming my nerves and anxiety about what I might end up seeing when he parted his jacket and pulled up his shirt to show me his body.

If he had a normal human body, I would have to conceal my

disappointment because I didn't want to hurt his feelings. If he had a mutant sticking out of him, I would have to conceal my disgust—also because I didn't want to hurt his feelings.

Or have his mutant stomach guy psychically mindfuck me.

It occurred to me that I should check my phone to see if Val had texted me back, so after I finished mixing the dough, I cleaned off my hands and made my way to his couch to retrieve my clutch. I was very aware of my naked lower body as I moved, and even with the blanket, I felt uncomfortably exposed.

Still, I also recalled how good it had felt to have him tonguing me so hungrily, and I wanted that again, so I was hoping he meant it when he said he wanted easy access.

My bunny slippers looked forlorn and abandoned beside the kitchen barstool along with my jammie bottoms and thong, but I forgot about them when I looked up and saw Vincent watching me, two ripe tomatoes in his hands.

He regarded my clutch as I brought it to the kitchen bar.

"I'm worried about Val," I said quickly. "I just wanted to check to see if she texted me back."

My words weren't entirely false. I was concerned about her. I wanted to make sure she remained at her apartment and didn't go for a drive anywhere. Usually, she and Ben were very good about locking up their keys and those of their guests during a party, but she might have been less cautious this time.

He set the tomatoes on the cutting board, then leaned on his elbows on the kitchen bar as I pulled out my phone and checked to see if I had any notifications.

There were none. Val hadn't responded at all to my text about going over to Vincent's house.

I also noticed something else.

"It's twelve forty-five!" I said as I regarded the phone in surprise. "We missed the ball dropping!" I glanced towards the huge monitor in his living room.

We should have had the countdown on as soon as we

walked in the door, but we'd gotten distracted. Very pleasantly distracted.

I wouldn't mind being that distracted again.

"Is it so important that we see it drop?" he asked curiously. "Will the year not end for you if you don't see this event happen with your own eyes?"

I laughed, setting my phone down face-up on the kitchen island. "No, of course not!" I shook my head at him as I made my way back around the island to join him at the cutting board. "It's just that I've never missed the ball drop, or the celebration immediately afterwards."

I shifted closer to him as I looked up into his face. My gaze focused on his sexy lips.

"Usually, we share a New Year's Day kiss with someone nearby," I said with a hopeful tone.

He lowered his head and claimed my lips, kissing me so thoroughly that I forgot to worry about mutant belly people and writhing tentacle teeth. When my hands moved to encircle his waist, he pulled away, his extra-long tongue withdrawing from ravaging my mouth.

I sighed and turned back to the cutting board.

"I like that part of the celebration," he said as if he hadn't just broken up our delicious kiss. "Is there more to it? Can I kiss more of you now to celebrate?"

I chuckled as I picked up the knife. "If that happened every New Year's Day, the parties would all turn into orgies."

"And?" he asked as if the suggestion was no big deal.

I laughed aloud as I shot him a disbelieving look. "*And* that kind of thing can't be broadcast on live television. That's definitely a Pay-Per-View type of show."

He looked thoughtful as his gaze focused on his living room.

"Pretty sure that kind of thing isn't happening right now, Vincent," I said, my amusement in my tone. "You perv."

He grinned at me. "I don't need an orgy. I never did join in on them. I only want you."

I paused in mid-slice, the tomato smushing a bit under my knife. "Uh, what do you mean, you never joined in on them?" I gave him a sideways look. "How many orgies have you been to?"

He shrugged his broad shoulders. "I haven't been to them. That's what I meant. If you're caught in the petal flurry during the Ancilla Breeding Festival, you will be compelled into joining an orgy, or at least mating with someone nearby."

"Where the heck is this festival," I asked, regarding him with all kinds of sexy thoughts in my mind, "and how am I only *now* hearing about it?" I set down my knife. "And how do I book tickets?"

He laughed at my tone. "Who's the 'perv' now, Gabby?" He crossed his arms over his chest, resting them on his belly bulge. "I hope you only want to attend the festival with me and no other male. I don't want to share you with anyone."

I was only teasing him, but he sounded dead serious. "Vincent, there isn't anyone else I'd rather be in a sex-festival with at this moment than you." I let my gaze trail down his body. "In fact, I don't even need a sex-festival. I'd gladly get naked and celebrate the New Year with you right here and now."

His lids lowered over smoldering golden eyes and his long tongue snaked out to lick his gorgeous lips. I could practically feel his desire from the intensity of his expression.

Then his belly shifted in a strange way that didn't look like normal human muscle movements. As I gasped in surprise, his hands covered it and he turned his back on me.

"I'll be right back. Please, continue with your meal preparation. I'm getting hungrier as the evening goes on."

As he strode down the hallway to disappear in what I assumed to be his room, closing his door behind him, I shook my head at myself, irritated that I'd made my surprise obvious.

Way to give him a complex, Gabby!

Or *more* of one, I suppose, given that he was already hesitant to show me what hid beneath his jacket.

It wasn't human, and that meant he was telling the truth. He really wasn't a human. In that, I knew now that I wouldn't be disappointed.

Excitement filled me, along with no small amount of nervousness and even a little fear, belated though it might be. I still wanted to see proof of the existence of intelligent life that wasn't human—or entirely human—and I still found Vincent incredibly sexy. Perhaps, even more so now that I knew he wasn't human. Yet, that fully human part of myself that had a healthy survival instinct was wondering if maybe I hadn't bitten off more than I could chew.

Or maybe when he said he was hungry, he wasn't talking about food or sex. Maybe he was planning to eat me for real, and I was sitting there like a sex-starved idiot, seduced by the attractive part of the alien into getting close enough for its belly teeth to chomp me to bits, sending fountains of my blood spraying everywhere.

Curse this imagination—and my love of monster movies!

Obviously, I knew biology didn't work the way the horror movie gore suggested, but I couldn't quite put the concern out of my mind that Vincent's beautiful face might be the lure of a horrible monster ready to make a meal out of me. Like the angler fish with their enticing lure that led unsuspecting fish right into their toothy maws.

It would honestly be the perfect trap for a lonely woman—a man so handsome that he seemed computer-generated to fulfill a woman's fantasy.

Especially this woman.

Still, there was more to Vincent than his pretty face. He was amusing, thoughtful, and sweet. He said the nicest, most complimentary things to me.

And I was a sucker for nice, complimentary things. What better way to lure in a meal than to compliment it?

I looked down at the cutting board, splattered with juice from the tomato. The knife lay beside it, waiting to be taken up again. But to finish cutting the tomato slices for the pizza, or to defend myself, probably fruitlessly, against a bloodsucking alien monster?

Common sense said for me to flee, to sneak out the door while Vincent was in his room, hopefully unaware of my escape. That would be the wise thing to do, but just by coming to his home with him, alone, in his vehicle, I'd already proven that I was lacking in common sense.

I grabbed my phone and texted again. My eyes focused on Vincent's bedroom door rather than my phone. I pushed send without really looking at the text, hoping Valerie wouldn't think I was the one who was drunk, given what I'd said in the text.

Vincent isn't human. If you don't hear from me tomorrow, call the military, or FBI, or national guard, or something.

Val would either think I was just drunk off my ass, in which case she'd do nothing of the sort unless I really didn't contact her tomorrow, or she would take me seriously, in which case, I could trust her to wait for the prescribed amount of time, because she was probably the only other person I've ever met who would take something like finding out a guy is actually an alien in stride.

It would be a shame to finally convince Vincent to show me what he looked like naked, only to have the "men in black" bust into his home and take him into custody.

In fact, I was already regretting my impulsive text, and I was about to send another to Valerie to tell her it was a drunken joke, when Vincent walked out of his room.

The phone dropped from my nerveless fingers as I stared in shock at him. He had removed his jacket, and his shirt.

He had finally decided to let me see what was under it all.

12

Gabby

My first thought as the claws around his belly spread outwards was of crab legs. They were chitinous and jointed like crab legs and had sharp tips. There were six of them and they moved independently of each other, like fingers.

"Oh, wow!" was all I could manage.

"I am not a monster," Vincent said, his crab leg claws pulling close to his belly as if to protect it. "I didn't know how you would react when you saw these, so I was going to wait until we knew each other better." He lowered his golden gaze to regard his belly claws. "Then I realized that I didn't want to know you too well if you would only end up running from me the moment you saw these."

"They're actually really cool," I said quickly, making my way around the kitchen island to move closer to him. I wanted a better look at his claws.

My fear of earlier seemed hasty and unnecessary. I would definitely have to text Val and tell her it was just a drunken joke. Vincent didn't look like he was about to eat me. He looked uncertain and defensive, like he was afraid I would run screaming into the night.

My words seemed to please him, and a small smile lightened his solemn expression. His claw tips tapped on his ripped abdominals as if showing off.

His body was model perfect, just like his face. He was incredibly handsome, even with his unusual limbs.

"You're beautiful, Vincent," I said as I slowly moved closer to him, my gaze fixed on those claws.

A part of me still felt uncertain if I was walking into danger, but if Vincent truly meant harm to me, he could have hurt me many times already tonight. I pushed that primal fear of the unknown aside, allowing my *fascination* for the unknown to take its place, even as my attraction to Vincent returned in full force.

He cocked his head, regarding me with gleaming eyes. "So are you. Will you take off your shirt now?"

I crossed my arms over my chest, feeling reluctant to reveal my sagging body in full light even though he'd already seen it. "I'm already half-naked. Just like you. You have to strip the other half of your body first."

Uncertainty returned to his expression. "I'm not entirely human down there, either." His claws curled on his belly again. "I have a—well, we call it a 'stem.'"

I gestured to his belly claws. "You've showed me this much of you, and I'm not running away. I think I can handle the rest." I sucked in a breath, shaky from my growing arousal, thinking about seeing all his beautiful body naked. "In fact, I'm looking forward to it."

He glanced around the room as if he was the one looking for an escape. Then he returned his gaze to me. "I want you, Gabby. When I expose myself to you, I don't know if I can keep my stem from extending."

My brows rose as my eyes widened. "Extending?" I stepped a little closer to him, my eyes fixed on his groin, frustratingly covered by his pants. "Oh, I *have* to see this!" I pressed my hands together in front of me. "Please, please show me your stem, Vincent."

I smiled seductively at him, feeling my core tighten in anticipation. "I promise I'll make it worth your while."

Despite his obvious hesitation, an answering smile tilted his lips as he unbuttoned his pants. "If you insist. But I'll hold you to that promise."

I eagerly waited, watching fixedly as he opened the fly of his pants, exposing an elaborate tattoo that covered his groin where a penis would be on a human man. It was beautiful, and alien, just like his lack of visible genitalia.

As I made an admiring sound, he traced the outer line of the tattoo. "They're mating tattoos, used by the Fayi to differentiate fully grown males from juveniles, so the females know who they can feed from and mate with. A juvenile isn't strong enough to feed females."

His words distracted me from the sight of that tattooed groin as he pushed his pants down. I looked up in surprise to meet his watchful gaze. He was noting my every expression and reaction. I wanted them all to be positive for him, and thus far, he hadn't shown me anything that wasn't appealing to me.

"The females *feed* from the males?" I regarded his groin again. "Like, do they drink your... um... you know...."

I motioned to his groin with one hand, feeling a blush burn my cheeks.

He looked momentarily confused, then understanding dawned in his eyes as he laughed aloud. He shook his head, then tapped his naked chest. "They drink a Fayi male's blood, not our seed. Though I suppose they might gain nutritional value from that too, but it is Fayi male blood that sustains them."

I fidgeted nervously with the edge of the blanket that was tucked in around my chest. "So, how many females have you... uh, fed, since you got your mating tattoos?"

Insecurity filled me at the thought that I might have to compete with females as gorgeous in their way as Vincent. How could I possibly do that with my flawed body?

He shook his head as he dropped his pants to his ankles, then stepped out of them, one foot at a time, drawing my attention to his bare feet briefly. They had normal human toes on them, wriggling a bit under my scrutiny.

"I have never fed or mated with any female, least of all a Fayi one."

I glanced back up at his face quickly, unable to hide my shock. "You're a virgin?"

It was difficult to believe that a man as gorgeous as Vincent—and as sensual, based on the way he'd eaten me out so hungrily—would not have actually done the deed before.

His uncertain expression returned very briefly before his face shifted into an impassive mask. "I wanted to wait for the right woman to come along. Is that an issue? Do you think that I'm less appealing because I lack experience? I assure you, Gabby, I know how to use my stem. I am not ignorant of the act. I just haven't performed it before with a partner."

I blinked stupidly for a moment before the meaning of his words really registered. "You mean... do you want to give your virginity to me? Am *I* the right woman?"

We had only just met, yet I understood why he might feel this way, if he was experiencing anything like I was. My attraction to him was unsurprising, but my feeling of attachment to him did surprise me as it was even stronger than it had ever been for Charles. It seemed like it should be too early to be this into a guy, even one as hot as Vincent.

Maybe there really was something like a "fated mate" and Vincent was mine and I was his. He wasn't human, but I was.

Would I really be able to feel it, if that was the case? Because I certainly felt something strong when I was with him that I hadn't ever felt before.

"*Are* you?" he asked as if he needed me to answer that for him.

I nodded slowly, my gaze trailing down his body to return to his tattoo. "I think I might be. I really like you, Vincent. More than I've ever liked anyone."

"Just *like*?" he asked, his deep voice gone husky.

"Much more than like," I admitted, feeling vulnerable saying so this soon after meeting him.

At the beginning of the night, he'd made me feel like a total loser, yet now he was offering me something he'd never given another woman.

Then I saw the center of his tattoo part, and it was the first time I noticed that he had a slit there. I watched as a chitinous shaft extruded from it, bone-white like the claws that now spread on either side of his belly. The shaft had an imposing pointed tip and looked girthier than any human erection I'd ever seen. It extended well past eight inches, closer to ten probably, and I had the uncomfortable suspicion it could have extended further. There were several knobs on it, and as it curved upwards, bending at one of those knobs, I realized they were like ball joints. The separation of the chitin around them was so subtle that I wouldn't have noticed it until they bent.

"Wow," I said in a complete understatement.

I noticed that Vincent was breathing heavier, and realized that I was too, my heart thudding in my chest and my stomach fluttering. My thighs had grown slippery with my slick as I regarded that beast of a dick with both desire and trepidation.

Then the tip of the shaft split open in four pieces that spread out like petals around an inner tip. That fleshier inner tip had rounded petal-like flaps surrounding a hole that dripped with a bead of precum. Those flaps fluttered as I stared, pushing the liquid outwards as the chitinous tip casing pieces folded backwards to lay flat against the shaft.

I whistled softly, oddly aroused by the very alien penis when it probably should have scared me. Even as it bent at the joints on it, like it was straining towards me, I felt compelled to move closer to him, wanting to touch it.

"I can still scent your arousal," Vincent said, his nostrils flaring as he inhaled deeply. "You aren't frightened of me."

"Not in the least," I murmured, inching closer to him, still hesitant, because I sensed this was a big moment for both of us.

Maybe too big for a first date, but I felt like we had already passed the point of no return.

"Can I touch it?" I stretched a shaking hand towards it as I moved close enough to reach it.

He laughed huskily, and I could hear his desire in the sound. "I was hoping you would."

I laughed a little too, releasing some of the tension growing between us, but not all of it. When I softly touched the chitinous shaft, it bent into my fingers as if seeking more contact. I reflexively pulled my hand away.

Vincent apologized quickly, his fist closing around the base of his shaft. "I'm sorry, Gabby. I swear sometimes it has a mind of its own."

"It's cool how it can move like that."

He stroked his hand up the length of his shaft, rubbing his fingers over each joint along the way. "It's actually an extension of my spine, like my claudas. I suppose they are more like tails than claws." He moaned softly as his hand reached the bent-back chitinous shields that normally covered his tip. "There are sensory hairs along the length of my shaft that allow me to feel any touch to it, but the most sensitive part of it is the exposed tip and the flaps." His gaze shifted to my fingers. "Will you touch me there, Gabby?"

The knuckles of his hand turned white as if he was gripping his shaft hard to keep it still while he waited for my response.

Without hesitation, despite the twitch of his length as if it fought his hold, I stroked my fingers over the flaps on the tip of his shaft. They fluttered against my fingertips. The ones closest to the opening were wet with his precum.

He groaned, his head dropping back and his eyes closing. His throat worked as I continued to stroke the soft flaps.

"Cold Mother's Dark Nest, Gabby! Your touch feels so good, I don't think I can hold on much longer. Your scent has been driving me wild this entire time, and I can still taste you on my tongue. You have no idea how much I wanted the night to end with you touching my stem."

My lips parted on a slow exhale as I watched my fingers moving slowly over the fluttering flaps, small, soft, rounded petals, layered over each other like fish scales around his opening. I enjoyed the sounds of his moans and watching his big body shudder. His claws spread away from his body, bending and straightening as if they grasped for something they couldn't find. If he wanted them to, they could have touched me, but he kept them away.

I wondered what it would feel like to have them folding around my body the way they did around his waist. Would they close around me if I was pressed up against his muscular chest?

"I'd like to taste *you* on my tongue," I said impulsively.

His head straightened as he opened his eyes wide. "You want to taste me?" One of his claws stabbed into his own flesh, cutting a line deep enough that blood welled from the wound. "I figured it would take longer for you to feel comfortable enough to feed from me, but I'm eager to feel your mouth against my skin."

"Whoa!" I pulled back my hand as I stared at his blood dripping from the cut. It was red like human blood but had a milkier consistency. "Vincent, I meant I wanted to suck your dick, not drink your blood! Oh, honey, you didn't have to hurt yourself for my sake."

His laugh sounded strained as his shaft struggled against his own grip. "It doesn't hurt me to cut myself, Gabby. Trust me. But if you want to put your mouth on my stem, I definitely won't stop you. I hope someday you will also feed from my blood. It is good for you. I promise."

I struggled to come up with a response to that, because I didn't want to outright reject his desire to have me drink his blood. At the same time, I couldn't imagine doing that. It just seemed like a step too far, a bit too strange, even for me.

Instead of replying, I dropped to my knees before him, bringing my full attention to his shaft and the bizarre tip of it. His "stem" shifted in his hold as if it fought a battle to be free.

I licked my lips, wondering if he would taste like a human, or like something completely alien. Then I leaned closer and licked the fluttering flesh around his opening to find out.

13

Vincent

Gabby's tongue felt so good on my tip that I thought I would lose control and climax right then and there. It was a struggle not to shoot my seed right into her mouth, especially when she spread her lips wide and took the whole tip into it.

The feeling of my stem being engulfed by her hot, wet mouth was unlike anything I'd ever experienced before. When she began to suck on it, like a Fayi female would suck blood from a male's flesh, I saw stars in my vision and had to grip my stem harder than ever before to keep it from thrusting deeper into her hungry mouth.

"Gabby!" I cradled her head with my free hand, my claudas spread wide to keep their tips from poking her.

The venom they produced allowed me to cut myself without feeling much pain and kept the wound from healing rapidly so that it would bleed freely for my female to feed. But that same venom would not be so pleasant for her. Or perhaps it might be. I'd heard that it could cause the same euphoric sensation as the saliva from our bites, but I wasn't willing to test that on Gabby. At least not this time.

My blood *would* be enjoyable for her though. It would cause a powerful sensation for her as it absorbed into her bloodstream through her throat and stomach lining. There was a reason beyond hunger that Fayi females practically attacked the males to drink their blood. I knew from my blood-father's words that human females also felt the same exuberant sensation from consuming Fayi blood undiluted from the source.

The trick was to get Gabby to suck it as voraciously as she sucked my stem. For now, all my focus went into not spewing my seed into the back of her throat without warning.

I had heard about some females doing this but had never experienced the like. Now I understood what all the fuss was about and why males loved it so much. The difficulty was in not coming, because all I wanted to do was relax into my orgasm, but I had to hold it back.

The wet sounds of her sucking my sensitive flesh as she teased the tip with her tongue, her mouth working down onto my chitinous shaft, did not help me hold back my climax. If anything, the sheer eroticism of those sounds made things much more difficult.

In desperation as I felt the tightening in the flesh beneath my chitin casing, I gently tugged on Gabby's thick, wavy hair to pull her head away from me. "I can't take much more! I am already so close to coming."

With one last long lick over my tip, she looked up at my face with a wickedly seductive smile. "You taste delicious, Vincent."

I shuddered, unable to conceal how much her words and her voice affected me. "I'll get payback. I promise you that."

She watched me through her thick lashes as she slowly stood, running her palms along my abdominals as I forced my claudas to remain spread open and away from her vulnerable body. "I did say I would make it worth your while."

I nodded, swallowing thickly. "You did. You definitely kept your promise."

I buried my fingers in her hair, lowering my head to claim her full lips in a kiss, not trying to hide my hunger to bury my stem in her as my tongue thrust between her lips.

Gabby moaned in pleasure, her palms sliding up my chest to my neck where she laced her fingers together at my nape. She pressed her warm body against mine as I claimed her mouth. Her lower body pushed my stem against my belly, and it bent willingly, though it still strained eagerly towards her heat.

Unable to keep them from her any longer, I let my claudas close around her back, pinning her against me. One of them stabbed into the fabric of the blanket and jerked it away from her body. I lowered my hands to push aside the flaps of her top, seeking the hard peaks of her nipples.

As her naked flesh met mine, my stem jerked against her belly, needing to be inside her. I caught her around her waist with both hands and lifted her off her feet, pulling her up against me so I no longer had to bend to kiss her. Now, her wet entrance sat above my stem. My hands slid down to her thighs and tugged them apart. She obliged me by wrapping her legs around my waist.

My stem sought her heat, the hypersensitive tip probing her opening. It was slippery with her heady arousal, and the head of my stem slipped inside her on that lubricant. We both moaned at the same time as it did. Then Gabby whimpered in pleasure as my stem pushed deeper, working itself in to the first joint. The increased thickness of that knob caused her body to tighten around my shaft. I felt Gabby's tension in her grip around my nape and forced my eager stem to pause.

My kiss seemed to relax her, and her inner muscles loosened around the joint, allowing it to pass into her tight, wet heat.

By the Grove, she felt so incredible!

She welcomed the second joint in my stem with more ease, sighing softly against my mouth as I buried my stem all the way inside her. There was more length within my body that I could have extended, but there wasn't a need, as the fit was perfect, and my tip kissed the opening of her womb.

I pumped my hips, drawing my stem out a bit, then thrusting it back inside her. I knew the motions to go through, but even if I hadn't, the feelings would have been instinctual. Buried inside her, I had no desire to do anything other than thrust. She moved in a rhythm with me as if we'd done this before, many times. My claudas held her body close to mine and my hands under her thighs urged her up and down on my stem. Her legs tightened around my waist as her body moved against mine.

Again, I felt the tightening of my shaft inside my casing as the delicious friction against my tip and sensory hairs drove me to my climax. Not wanting to come without her, I shifted one hand to play with her clit, enjoying the way her body shivered in my hold. She broke away from our kiss to gasp with her pleasure, her breaths panting with each thrust. Her eyes were closed as her head fell back on her shoulders. Her fingers shifted from my nape to slip through my hair.

I felt no pain at all when she clutched locks of it in the throes of her passion. Nor did I protest when she rocked her head forward and bit my shoulder. In fact, my stem jerked inside her and the urge to come was almost overwhelming as her teeth closed on my flesh. My fingers moved faster on her clit and her hips thrust against them, her inner muscles clenching my shaft tight.

I felt her passage convulse as she shuddered in my arms, releasing my skin with her teeth to cry out with her climax in the most beautiful series of sounds I'd ever heard. Her release allowed me to seek my own and I thrust wildly into her, finally letting myself tip over the peak.

My seed shot into her, my flaps fluttering in rhythm with each spurt of it to push it towards her womb. I pumped into her until she was so filled with it that it began to seep from around my shaft. Still more came out, surprising even me. I'd never had so much spill from me while pleasuring myself. It was like it had been waiting for this moment to be released.

I was eager to give Gabby all five of her children. Perhaps I could convince her to have even more. I could picture our little ones easily. They would have her beautiful eyes and my Fayi strength.

I had finally found my mate, and I couldn't wait to take her home with me to the Fall.

14

Gabby

I felt blissful starting off the New Year with a bang, literally.

Gabby's New Year's Resolution #4: *Bang an alien when I get the chance!*

I could cross that one off my list even as I came up with it, though I hoped I got a lot more chances with Vincent.

It was amazing to feel his strange stem inside me, the knobby joints thick inside my channel, rubbing against my g-spot. The heat of his seed still warmed my womb, even as he slowly withdrew. The entire time he'd pumped inside me, he'd stood holding me up as if my weight was inconsequential. Prior to this, I would have never felt comfortable being held or carried by a man.

Vincent was no ordinary man though. I could tell he was inhumanly strong by the way he'd plucked me off my feet without any sign of effort. I could feel the power of his body as he'd thrust into me, pinning me with his fascinating dick and the claws that wrapped around his body.

As he let me slide down his body once he'd withdrawn from inside me, my hands slipped from his hair to slide down his back. My palms encountered the ridge of an exposed spine, encased in hard chitin like his claws and stem. It was yet another alien aspect of him that fascinated me, and I wanted a closer look at it, but the gush of liquid spilling from my entrance reminded me that I needed to clean up first.

It also reminded me that we hadn't used a condom. Fortunately, I was on birth control, and Vincent said he was a virgin, though I wasn't even certain I could catch the kind of STDs he might have carried. I knew I didn't have any, though Charles had cheated on me so much that I had been very lucky he hadn't passed any on to me. I'd been tested since I'd last broken up with him, and I hadn't slept with any other men, despite a handful of attempts at dating that had ended in the typical blind date disaster.

"I need to clean up," I said feeling strangely shy given what we'd just done as his seed dripped down my inner thighs.

I still felt a little shellshocked that I'd had sex with an alien being. One who might be partially human, but had very alien attributes, especially in the genitalia department. I hadn't been lying when I said he tasted delicious. What had been an unpleasant chore with Charles had become a delight with Vincent.

I looked forward to doing it again, if I could get past this current shyness.

"Let me show you the bathroom," he said, his deep voice husky, his lids low over his golden eyes as his gaze dropped to my thighs.

He took my hand and led me down the hall to his bedroom. It was as spartan in decoration as his living room, but it had a huge bed in the center of the room that drew my attention. I thought of spending the entire rest of the night there with him, wrapped in his arms.

And his claws. They'd felt strange when they'd banded against my back, pushing me closer to his naked body. Yet, it had been an exciting kind of strange. The kind I wouldn't mind feeling again.

His master bathroom was typical of most tract homes. It had the basic garden tub and walk-in shower beside it, the ubiquitous oak cabinets, and granite counter tops. It was upscale, but not exorbitant. It also didn't say much about Vincent himself. The hand towels and bath towels were a charcoal gray, as was the bath rug.

It was clean, at least. I appreciated that he managed to keep his home well-kept, even if he didn't go through his groceries often enough.

That reminded me that I still had a dinner to make, though by the time we were done here, it would be an early breakfast.

Vincent released my hand and turned on the shower. Then he turned back to me and tugged my jammie top off my shoulders, his appreciative gaze trailing over my breasts as if I had the body of a supermodel. I still couldn't believe that I was lucky enough to meet a man like him. Perhaps it was because he was alien that he didn't care about the extra skin and stretchmarks.

His body, on the other hand, was absolutely perfect, even with his alien features. In fact, they only enhanced his appeal for me. There was just something so sexy about those dangerous claws and that groin tattoo that again concealed his alien manhood.

He bent to kiss me, and I met his lips eagerly, even though his seed was making its way to my feet and would soon drip on the tile floor if I didn't hop in that shower. I moaned against his mouth as he cupped my breasts and his fingers toyed with my nipples.

His claws scraped along my bare belly, then moved to embrace my waist and tug me closer against his powerful body.

"You are so beautiful, Gabby," he said after he broke our kiss so I could catch my breath. "I don't think I can ever get enough of you."

I cut myself off before I could blurt out a demurral, recalling resolution #3. If Vincent thought my body was beautiful, then who was I to disagree with him? He certainly seemed to mean it, based on the way his stem made a reappearance, pressing the tip into my belly as it extended from his slit.

"You're sexy as hell, Vincent." I pulled away far enough to look down at his stem, and his claws relaxed around my waist, allowing me to move while not releasing me fully. "I like what you're packing down there. Very much," I said on a low moan as I recalled the feeling of having it inside me, joints and all.

His stem twitched towards my mound, bending downwards so the second joint of it rubbed along my clit. I moaned again at the pleasure that shot through me.

Vincent released me long enough to open the shower door, then he stepped inside it, capturing my hand again to tug me into it after him.

I had never taken a shower with a man before, but I made a new resolution on the spot when Vincent picked up the bar of soap, wet it, then began to soap up my body, his warm palms sliding over my slippery skin.

Gabby's New Year's Resolution #5: *Shower with a sexy man as often as possible.*

My hands roved over his body as he soaped me up, working me into a lather even more than he worked up those soap bubbles. By the time he washed between my legs and along the crack of my butt, I was already rocking my hips against his talented hands. When his slippery touch moved from between my folds to rub over my clit, I gasped in pleasure.

He lowered his head to capture one of my nipples in his mouth, suckling it as he stroked my clit. I combed my fingers through his damp hair to clutch his head, pulling him closer to me. His belly claws grasped for my body, scraping gently along my waist and sides.

When I was on the brink of an orgasm, he slipped two fingers inside me, stroking my clit in time to the thrust of them into my eager opening. I orgasmed hard, crying out as my entire body shuddered from the power of it. His claws pulled me against his body as he lifted his head, cradling me to his hard muscles as my trembling subsided and I caught my breath.

"Whew," I said once I could speak again. "You really know how to get a girl clean!" I looked up at him, enjoying the steely grip of his claws around my back. "While being dirty." I grinned, rubbing my belly against his stem, which had been pressed between us when he'd pulled me close.

"Are you ready for me again, Gabby?" His tone sounded genuinely concerned, like he didn't want to burden me with his desire.

I shifted my hips to free some space between our groins so I could encircle his stem with one hand, then I teased the exposed tip with the fingers of my other hand while smiling seductively up at him. "I am *so* ready for you again!"

When he made to lift me up in his arms, I raised one hand to stop him, then turned my back to him, bracing my palms against the tiled wall of the shower. I glanced over my shoulder at him as I pushed my hips back, exposing myself to his gaze.

"Let's try a different position," I said, my voice husky with my arousal.

I was thinking of sparing him the trouble of picking me up and holding me again, but I didn't regret my decision at all when he entered me from behind. His jointed shaft had to bend downwards to reach me, but its unique structure allowed him to do so without bending his knees in an uncomfortable half-squat given our height difference.

I had been correct about him having more length than he'd

originally shown me. He had a third joint exposed by the time he buried himself inside me until his tip brushed against my womb. At that point, he was inhumanly long, but then again, there wasn't anything human about that part of his body, and I had zero complaints about that as he slowly began to thrust into me from behind.

He curved his upper body over me, his claws closing around me until the tips of the top two teased my nipples, the dangerous points sliding over them carefully. The four lower claw tips dented my skin as he rocked me forward with each thrust.

I gasped with delight as he increased his rhythm, enjoying the sounds of pleasure he made as he chased his own orgasm. Then his fingers stroked my clit again, and the hypersensitive nub responded quickly, rocketing me up to my own peak. When my inner muscles convulsed around him, I felt his stem jerk inside me, and he washed my womb in his hot seed.

I had never been with someone who made my pleasure a priority before seeking theirs. As his cum pumped into me, he lowered his head and kissed along my shoulder. Then his lips sucked at the point where my shoulder met my neck. My head tilted to the opposite side, exposing my neck fully to him.

It was an automatic response as I submitted to him. I had forgotten about the fangs until he buried them in my throat.

15

Gabby

The initial stab of his fangs into my flesh shocked me, but by the time I recovered from that, the pain had faded, replaced by an almost euphoric pleasure as he sucked my blood from me. Something in his saliva seemed to make the wounds numb, but I felt the pull of his lips and the stroke of his tongue as he drank my blood.

His stem remained buried inside me, and he began to slowly pump it into me, even as his seed spilled out from around it. I groaned with pleasure as he returned to stroking over my clit and thrusting. Soon, he had me gasping with each thrust as he continued to suck my neck.

"Ah, Vincent!" I cried, my voice echoing in the bathroom. "Yes!"

His claws pulled me tight into his thrusts, the bottom two sliding to my hips to pin them in place as he pumped deep.

I felt a lassitude settling over me even as I orgasmed, my body sagging in his alien grip. His cum spurted into me again.

Then he released my neck with one last stroke of his inhumanly long tongue over his teeth marks. He pulled out of me and spun me around before I could recover.

As I watched him, my body shivering with the pleasure he'd given me, his claw scratched his chest, and he tugged me closer to him. One of his hands cradled my head and pushed my lips against the cut he'd made.

"Taste my blood, Gabby," he pleaded, his lips wet with my blood. "I promise you won't regret it."

Feeling better than I'd ever felt before, I licked the wound he'd made in his own flesh. His blood made my tongue and lips tingle. I took another exploratory lick, then another as more blood welled from the wound. Before I consciously thought about it, I latched onto his flesh, sucking hard at the cut, drawing in more of his blood with each hungry pull of my lips.

I felt like I'd suddenly been granted superpowers. I had this insane idea that I could fly, or at least leap tall buildings in a single bound, or something equally impossible. I felt incredible, even beyond the druglike euphoria from his bite. My entire body throbbed as his blood trickled down my throat and into my belly, warming it like a healthy shot of whiskey.

He moaned with each suck from my lips and stroke of my tongue, as if the very act of me drinking his blood gave him pleasure too. It must have, because his stem found my slippery entrance again, and he buried it back inside me as if he hadn't already spent an ocean of his seed in me.

He shuddered with pleasure, pulling me off my feet again and pinning me against him as he thrust. My lip latch on his chest broke momentarily at the abrupt motion, but he pushed my mouth back against his flesh with his hand on my head, and I obediently began to suck again, more than happy to drink more of his heady blood.

My belly filled with his alien blood, some of it escaping from my lips to drip down his chest as he chased his orgasm.

He wouldn't let me stop—not that I was overly inclined to, given my current superpower euphoria—until his stem tensed and then twitched inside me, spurting more of his seed against my womb, the fluttering of his flaps like little kisses against the opening of it.

He growled as if he was trying to keep in a howl of pleasure with his release, then kissed my hair, inhaling deeply as the shower continued to spray over us.

When he pulled out of me, a gush of his ejaculate followed. He released my head and I lifted it, licking the last drops of his blood from my lips as I looked up at him. My vision felt sharper, my hearing keener, my skin hypersensitive to changes of the air and the water temperatures. My sense of smell even seemed enhanced, and I imagined I could smell the tomato juice staining the cutting board in the kitchen, even from here in the shower in the master bedroom.

Even the mild aches and pains I'd felt in my body—little things caused by an over enthusiastic workout or sitting too long in an office chair—had completely disappeared. I felt amazing. Better than I ever had before.

His claws opened to release me as he bent to set me back on my feet. While I was still mustering the ability to speak, he picked up the soap again and lathered it up. Then he stroked his soapy hands down my belly to my mound.

He washed away the fluids from our combined orgasms that dripped from my entrance and down my thighs, then claimed my lips in a hungry kiss. I could still taste the iron of my own blood on his tongue. In fact, like all my other senses, my taste seemed enhanced.

When he finally lifted his head I gasped, shaking my own as I stared up at his face. "Am I superhuman now or something?"

He chuckled as he cradled my face between his big hands. "Temporarily, you may have gained some enhanced senses. Also, gray-father says Fayi blood has healing properties beyond anything even his people have ever encountered. It will make your immune system stronger and increase cellular regeneration and slow any signs of aging—or even halt them with regular consumption."

My mouth dropped open in shock as I regarded him, still processing his words. "Is that why you were so insistent that I drink it" I lifted a hand to rub my neck, startled to discover that the bitemarks had completely disappeared. I pulled my hand away from my neck and stared at it, seeing no signs of blood.

"I'm healed."

He nodded slowly. "Yes. I would not have hurt you, Gabby. Not if I thought the wound would last for longer than a few minutes."

I stared at the wound he'd made in his own flesh, my eyes widening as it knitted back together impossibly fast, healing right before my eyes.

Even though I still felt the vestiges of euphoria, I experienced a rush of uncertainty as I met his eyes. He was so far out of my league that he was like some god-like being I couldn't hope to hold onto. He had superhuman blood running through his veins, and I was just Gabby. What could I possibly hope to give him long-term that would keep him coming back to me instead of moving on to another woman when he got tired of me?

Right now, he seemed to be really into me. If I could believe everything he'd said, he'd given me his virginity, and that meant something to him. It meant I was important to him. But what if he'd lied? Or what if he only thought I was important, but now that he'd done this with me, he'd be looking around to try it with someone new?

Charles had fooled me. What made me think Vincent would be any different?

"Gabby?" he asked, and I thought I saw a mirror of my own uncertainty in his alien eyes. "Are you okay? I didn't hurt you too much, did I?" His gaze shifted to my healed neck. "I should have asked if I could drink from you. I'm so sorry! I got carried away."

I hastened to reassure him, clutching his hands as he lowered them from my face. "No, it's okay! I enjoyed it." I laughed at the understatement. "A *lot*!" I patted my chest, where my heartbeat was only just returning to normal. "In fact, I still feel fantastic. Like I could take on the world and win!"

He nodded knowingly. "That's one of the side effects of our blood. It causes the release of hormones in your body that give you that feeling."

I shook my head in amazement. "Imagine if you could bottle that stuff and sell it. You would be a billionaire."

His expression shuttered, and I realized that he might have mistaken my words as being serious.

"That is what humans have already done to my father's people," he said shortly, then he reached behind him and turned off the shower.

"Vincent," I said quickly as he turned to throw open the glass shower door and step out. "I was just kidding. I'm sorry. I didn't realize that had been done to your people."

He paused with his back to me, and I got my first good view of his spinal ridge. It looked a lot like a bony spine, with each pair of claws originating from different vertebrae. At the base of his spine, just above the crack of his buttocks, the bone disappeared back into his flesh. I wondered if that was the origin of his stem. I also wondered where the hard stem lay when it was inside him, and if it was within a hollow part of that spine.

"Does money matter to you, Gabby?" he asked with his back still turned to me, his shoulders tense and his body stiff.

I blinked in surprise, my gaze lifting from his very nice buttocks. "What? *No*! Why would you ask that?"

He turned to regard me without a readable expression.

"Because making money was your first thought when you learned about what my blood could do."

I gasped, shaking my head in denial. "Vincent, you've got me all wrong!" I held up both hands to reinforce my denial. "I grew up in a world focused on gaining money over any other pursuit. That's why my thoughts immediately went to that. But I was only teasing you. I realize now it was insensitive, but I *swear*, I don't give a damn about pursuing wealth. I only want to have a family and a home where we're safe and happy, and my children can grow up surrounded by people who love them."

Perhaps it was the druglike euphoria that made me so honest with him—and with myself. I'd just admitted my deepest desire to this alien who was a near stranger, when I'd never voiced it to Charles throughout the years we'd been dating.

To my relief, the tension melted from his body, and he turned around and reached for my hand to help me out of the shower. Not that I needed it. I felt like I could bound out of the shower—and maybe climb the walls while I was at it. Still, I took his hand gratefully, happy to see that he'd accepted my sincerity.

I would have to be more careful what kind of jokes I made. Clearly, Vincent's people—at least the "Fayi" side—had been through some shit.

"Did your father meet your mother because of what humans were doing to your people?"

I wondered where humans had found the Fayi, and I also wondered how they'd kept the existence of them a secret from the wider population.

Was some secret world government carrying on a war with an alien race right under our noses, while we focused on posting selfies and chasing clout?

Vincent pulled me closer to him with one hand, while he plucked a towel off the rod with the other. "The story of my parents is a complicated one. Perhaps it would be best to save it for another time."

He wrapped me in the towel, and I caught the upper edge of it with one hand to hold it around me, pressing the other to his chest where my index finger traced the now nonexistent cut he'd made in his flawless skin.

Then my eyes widened as I recalled the pizza dough. "Oh! I need to finish making our meal!" I rushed towards his bedroom, then realized that I was buck-naked under the towel and still soaking wet.

I paused in the bathroom doorway and turned to look at him as he calmly grabbed the second towel and began to dry himself off. "Do you have any clothes I can borrow?" I regarded his huge, tall body doubtfully.

My jammies would probably fit better than his clothes.

He grinned at me, his gaze trailing from my head down to my painted toes. "I think I can find something for you."

16

Vincent

I watched Gabby putter around my kitchen in the shirt I'd given her that hung on her frame like an oversized dress. She looked so adorable in it that I struggled not to snatch her into my arms every time she moved close enough to be within reach.

I felt incredible, the taste of her hot blood still lingering on my tongue, the memory of her lips sucking my blood teasing me until I had to fight my stem to keep it within my spinal core. I could hold out long enough for her to finish preparing the meal she insisted upon. After all, she was not sated by my blood the way I was by hers. My own blood would keep her from feeling exhaustion after what I'd taken from her, though it had only been a small amount in comparison to what I might pull from someone I didn't care about like I did her.

She might be hungry, or she might simply need a break, since her body was human and perhaps couldn't go for another round so soon after the last one. I wasn't certain, since I'd never done this before. All I knew was that I couldn't get enough of her, and I wanted more, even when I was spilling my seed inside her. I could have gone all night, but I was trying to be considerate of her needs.

She was the one. My mate. I knew it in my blood—both Fayi and human. She belonged to me, and I couldn't wait to take her home to introduce her to my family and friends and show her the beauty and wonder of New Omni, and the remains of the blasted wasteland of the Dead Fall that hadn't yet been claimed by the expanding ancilla grove.

Alexander might claim he was content to spend himself in a dozen females or more a night. He might speak of returning to my blood-father's home world to seek a nest to join, but I knew he craved something more. Just like I had. He would be envious of my mate, and perhaps he would finally admit that he wanted one too. He wouldn't be happy with a nest filled with vacuous Fayi females seeking his warmth only for his blood and seed, unconcerned with his interests or concerns or his emotions.

I'd known from a very early age that I wanted the kind of relationship my parents had, though I didn't think I could ever bring myself to share my female with any other male. My mother's situation had been different and had happened in a time when there were few females in the Dead Fall and sharing them among multiple males had been more common.

Though it still happened, it wasn't as frequent. Not now that NEX could bring more females of every species into our dimension, provided they were willing. Even my mother had expressed surprise at how many were not only willing, but eager to leave their dreary dimensions for a life in New Omni with a male unlike any they could have found in their own worlds.

I hoped Gabby would also be eager to leave this world, though it had its charms. I wouldn't bring up the subject just yet, or even mention that I'd come from a different dimension. I didn't want her to freak out about such a huge decision on our very first date.

We had already gone way farther than I'd dared to hope when Valerie had set up this blind date between me and her best friend. I couldn't believe how fortunate it was that I'd made that gas station my daily stop and ran into her. Although it was possible that it hadn't been fortune at all. Gray-father had given me the coordinates for this town to begin my search. It was likely that either he, or NEX, had seen something of Gabby and her life and knew that she was a strong candidate for my mate.

NEX often chose targets based on suspected compatibility. How the AI knew such things or determined them remained a mystery to me. It wasn't a topic gray-father encouraged anyone to discuss, and NEX remained isolated from the residents of New Omni. Only gray-father spoke to it where it was contained within its prison. And lately, Sherakeren, who was learning our father's work in the hopes of someday taking his place so that gray-father could "retire" as my mother put it, and spend more quality time with her.

I couldn't be happier with their choice, if that was what Gabby was. She appealed to me on many levels, though I knew it was too soon to call this rush of emotions love. All the things Valerie had told me about Gabby had made me intrigued to meet her and—barring the initial disastrous impressions we'd gotten of each other—those things were turning out to be true.

Gabby smiled warmly at me as she finished prepping our meal, sliding the pizza over to me to finish sprinkling on the cheeses that were all mixed together in one bowl, then turning to the boiling pasta.

"Someone needs to teach you how to cook," she said with an amused tone, slanting her gaze towards the pile of takeout menus. Then she returned her focus to me with a sly smile. "I'll volunteer, if you pay me in kisses."

"And other things?" I asked, not bothering to conceal the arousal in my voice as I grabbed a handful of cheese and sprinkled it on the pizza.

I didn't pay much attention to where it landed, but Gabby did, grinning broadly as she left the boiling pot on the stove and joined me at the counter.

She leaned against my side, reaching to spread out the pile of cheese I'd dropped on the pizza. "I think you'll need a lot of training." She turned her head and bit my triceps teasingly.

My claudas jerked outwards, knocking the pizza pan across the counter, sending shredded cheese flying.

Gabby only laughed at the destruction I'd caused to her meal, then bit me again, following up with little kisses along my arm.

"I'll bite you back," I said in mock-warning, baring my fangs in a crooked smile that wasn't nearly wide enough to reflect how good it felt to spend this time with her.

She looked up at me through her full lashes, fluttering them playfully as she deliberately licked her full lips. "I might like that."

"You're killing me," I groaned as I pushed my groin against the side of the kitchen bar to keep my stem from extending, because I'd lost the ability to control it at the hungry look in her eyes. "I thought you wanted to finish making this meal."

She stroked her palm over my naked chest, pressing another half dozen kisses along my arm. "I do, but you just look so tasty standing here half-naked."

I chuckled, lifting a hand to capture hers. Her touch was making it even more difficult to control my stem. "I have to admit that I usually don't bother with shirts when I'm home. It's more comfortable to be half-naked." I shrugged my shoulders, my claudas pulling close to my stomach again now that they'd done their damage. "Although my aunt makes some really comfortable shirts that accommodate our claudas."

This information was enough to distract her, and her expression shifted from hungry to curious as she pulled slightly away from me to regard me with a more direct gaze. "Is your aunt a Fayi, like your father?"

I shook my head, smiling at the thought of Aunt Alice being anything but human. "No, she's my mother's sister. She loves to sew, and she's always designing clothing to fit everyone in the—"

I cut off my reminiscence before I revealed too much. If I said "in the Fall", she would ask the obvious question of where on Earth that was, and then I would be forced to demur again, which I could tell bothered her. Or I would have to explain to her.

The second option was what I wanted. I would love to tell her about my home. I felt the weight of homesickness as a heavy burden on me, and I wondered how my cousin Friak could stay away from our home dimension so long in search of his "spark." It had been several years now since he'd left.

I wanted to tell Gabby about my family and all their eccentricities. I wanted to see her reaction when she heard the lengths some of them would go to in search of love. I wanted to describe the ancilla grove and all its stunning beauty. I wanted to talk about the mother tree, and my cousin Pavdan's relationship to it.

There was so much about my home that I missed and that I knew she would find wondrous with her love of all things strange and paranormal. I knew I could bring that fascination to her expression again, the way I had when she'd seen my claudas for the first time.

She would want to go there. I just knew it.

But not enough to feel confident that now was the time to explain. If she rejected the idea of leaving this world behind, our beautiful date would end in disaster. She might even flee from me and refuse to ever see me again.

She'd cocked her head, her gaze sharpening at my near slip, but when I turned my attention to retrieving the pizza pan, she sighed and shrugged her shoulders, giving me one last kiss on my arm before turning back to the boiling pasta.

Gabby dug a pasta shell out of the bubbling water, testing to see if it was finished, without making another comment about that topic. I desperately searched for something else to say that would break the uncomfortable silence that fell between us.

"I know you don't want to tell me where you come from," she said neutrally as she turned off the stovetop and lifted the pot by the handle, "but will you tell me about your people? The Fayi?"

I watched her move to the sink and turn on the faucet so cold water poured out. Then she used the pot lid to strain the pasta into the sink. I debated the wisdom of answering her request. If I described the Fayi, then she would have to know that they didn't exist on Earth. That would bring many questions I didn't feel it was time to answer yet.

Still, if I wanted Gabby to know me as I truly was, I had to be honest with her and tell her at least something about myself.

"The Fayi are... not at all like humans," I said lamely.

Gabby turned from the sink and glanced down at my claudas, her brows lifting and her expression telling me that was already obvious. She smirked, then chuckled at my shrug, which included my claudas spreading outwards.

"You don't say." She grinned as she poured the pasta into a glass casserole dish I hadn't even realized I had until she'd unearthed it from the back of a lower cabinet.

It was possible the previous resident had left it behind, but Gabby had dumped out the insect corpses inside it and cleaned and sanitized it before deigning it ready to use.

"I mean their culture," I added belatedly as she spread the pasta shells.

She finished that task and joined me at the counter again,

setting down a potholder, then the casserole dish on top of it. She swept the cheese that had come off the pizza into her palm, then tossed it into my trash, brushing her hands together afterwards.

As I watched her spread cheese over the pasta, she glanced up at me. "So, what makes Fayi culture so different?"

"The males, uh, provide for the females, who create the nest and bear all the spawn."

She huffed as she looked up from her work, her expression wry. "That's not all that different from some human cultures, Vincent." She shrugged one shoulder. "I mean, that's kind of the life I want, though I suppose it's not politically correct to admit it anymore."

This confused me enough that it distracted me from my concerns over how much I should share. "What do you mean, you can't admit it?"

She sighed heavily and then grasped another handful of cheese. "It's not important. I'm admitting it to you, since you probably should know that I want lots of kids, and I would rather be a homemaker than chase a high-powered career. You know, before we get too serious or anything." Her gaze lowered to my bare chest, then dropped even lower to where my groin was hidden as I kept it pressed against the side of the kitchen island.

Her focus returned to my face, and she watched me closely, waiting for my response to her words as if there was something about them that would bother me.

"I didn't realize we weren't serious yet," I said, my own gaze making a path from her head to her bare feet and taking in all the scenery along the way.

She looked down at the casserole, spreading the cheese as though the placement of every shred of it mattered. I didn't think her concentration on the food was because it did, though. "I like you, a lot. Maybe too much for a first date." She picked up a shred of cheese and broke it into crumbles. I didn't think that was part of the process of preparing the casserole. "I just don't want to fall too hard for someone who doesn't have the same ideas in mind for our future together."

She glanced up at me, her uncertainty clear in her expression. "Charles was—"

She cursed beneath her breath and shook her head hard. Then I heard her mutter something that she probably didn't think I'd pick up clearly.

"Gabby's New Year's resolution number six—never discuss my ex with the hot guy I'm dating."

"Gabby," I said, pausing until she met my eyes again, "I'm not your loser ex-boyfriend. I want to be with you. I think that's obvious at this point. I'm not looking at this," I pointed to myself, then her, "as a casual thing." My claudas spread as if to prove my point. "I wouldn't have gone this far with you, shown you this much, or even told you the truth about myself, if I didn't want a future with you."

She smiled but I still saw the uncertainty in her eyes. "Is it too soon, Vincent? I feel like it should be, but it doesn't feel to me like it is." She pushed the casserole dish aside and leaned her forearms on the counter. Her breasts shifted enticingly beneath the fabric of the shirt she was wearing as she moved, and I tried to keep my focus on her face and our conversation. "Is this normal for your people? Feeling so connected to each other so quickly?"

I shrugged. "Gray-father says some people have 'keys' in their DNA that draw them together and make them feel like they are destined for each other. In that case, the connection seems to happen quickly. I don't know if that's what happened here, though. Only gray-father could tell us that."

"Gray-father? I've heard you say that before, but I wasn't sure if I misheard your pronunciation. What do you mean by *gray*-father? Is he like, your grandfather with gray hair or something?"

I had already revealed some of my family's information, including that I had three fathers. There was no reason not to explain at least a little more. "Gray-father is one of my three fathers. He isn't my blood-kin, he's not Fayi, but he is the Dominant of our nest. At one time, he was the leader of our whole city, but he turned that responsibility over to another so he could focus on his other work."

"He's not Fayi? Is he human, like your mother and aunt?" Her expression was filled with avid curiosity, and I couldn't help myself from sharing more with her.

Especially since I wanted to share it all. I wanted to trust her with everything and believe that she would return with me to the Dead Fall without hesitation.

I wanted to believe she wouldn't reject me when she discovered what she would have to sacrifice to be with me.

I also wanted to believe that she wouldn't change her mind after returning with me and demand to go back to her own dimension, leaving me heartbroken and alone in the Dead Fall. It had happened before, and some of the males had simply walked out into the ruins and never returned after their mates left them.

"Gray-father is not human," I said cautiously, reining in my desire to spill it all, to discuss my family openly, without fear that I would reveal too much, too soon. "None of my fathers are human, like my mother and aunt. And Auntie Lauren, who isn't blood kin but is still family."

There were other human females in New Omni, and they had grown close to our family over the years, but not like Aunt Lauren, who had met my mother and aunt in the very early days of New Omni's founding. She'd practically raised us right along with my mother and aunt.

"So, your, uh, gray-father can tell us if we're fated mates or something?" She watched my face as if everything rested on my answer.

"Is that important?" I asked, knowing that we no longer needed the "keys" in order to successfully have hybrid offspring.

Not now that gray-father had access to technology he'd gotten from my Uncle Kisk many years ago.

She straightened, fussing with the cheese in the bowl again, before she grabbed a handful and sprinkled it evenly over the casserole. "I guess I just wanted an explanation that would make it all feel okay."

"What do you mean by that?" My claudas tapped their tips against my abdominals, a nervous habit I thought I'd broken by now. "You don't think this is okay?"

Her eyes widened and she dropped the remainder of the cheese and held up her hands in a demurral. "I think you and I are okay, of course." Her lids lowered over her beautiful gray eyes as she regarded my naked chest. "I meant how I feel about you. I'm afraid that I'm falling too fast, and it doesn't make sense unless it's a fated mate situation." She lowered her gaze to the casserole, poking at the cheese piles. "Or, I'm just so desperate for love and affection that I'm falling for the first man who treats me like he cares about me."

I stiffened, torn by the implied suggestion that I wasn't who she might want and by the genuine sadness in her tone. I decided to not be offended and instead ask why she felt that way. "Do you really think you wouldn't want me if you weren't desperate?"

She looked up quickly, her mouth opening in immediate denial as her gaze roved from my face down to my body. "Are you *kidding*? You're so far out of my league that we're not even in the same dimension!"

I didn't know if she'd said that because she might suspect the truth about where I was from, or it was just a coincidental choice of words, so I focused instead on the ridiculousness of her statement. "How am I out of your league?"

She huffed in disbelief and gestured with one hand towards me, then to herself. "I mean, Vincent, seriously? Look at you, then look at me!"

I couldn't stop looking at her. I didn't want to look at anything else. Certainly not the same face I'd seen in the mirror for twenty-two years. "You're beautiful, Gabby. But I don't understand why the way we look is even important if we like being around each other and want to be intimate. What difference does our looks make?"

My parents all looked so different from each other, and they still loved each other and wanted to spend their lives together. Wing-father had once believed that females who were featherless were unattractive. Then he'd fallen in love with my mother. Gray-father hadn't even been attracted to any creature. Then he'd fallen in love with my mother. And blood-father had considered humans to be the enemy and despised their very appearance. Then he'd fallen in love with my mother.

Her looks had not been what drew them to her, any more than Gabby's appearance had been my main concern. Valerie's words about Gabby had first gotten my attention as she'd told me about exactly the kind of woman I always knew I wanted. Then I met Gabby, and her scent had drawn me to her even when her appearance had repelled me. Then I'd seen her genuine appearance, free of all the unnecessary artifice, and her beauty had stolen my breath.

She lowered her head. "I guess looks have always been important to humans. At least every human I've been around." She turned the cheese bowl in a way that suggested she was fidgeting rather than preparing to do something with it. "Except for Val. She doesn't give a damn how anyone looks, as long as she thinks they're friend material."

"Do looks matter to *you*?" She hadn't shied away from my

claudas, nor my stem. My looks hadn't seemed to disgust or frighten her.

Gabby lifted her head and shook it. "No. I've always just wanted someone who would be kind to me, and not take me for granted. Be it a friend or a lover. I never cared what they might look like."

I caught her wrist, pausing her spinning of the bowl. "I will always treat you like you're precious, Gabby. I would move the world for you, if you asked me to."

She met my eyes, then returned to my side, using her free hand to stroke one of my claudas. "You already shifted my entire world on its axis. You've proven to me that I didn't spend my entire life being wrong about there being more to our world than what we could see on the surface."

I didn't know how to tell her that her world was just as mundane as the humans here believed it to be. If only I was certain she would leave this place behind for good, I would explain that I could take her to a place far more fantastical than this.

A place where even my inhuman attributes seemed ordinary.

17

Gabby

Vincent helped me finish preparing our meal and as we waited for it to cook, we sat at his kitchen island, talking as if we had known each other for years.

Unfortunately, he still didn't seem to entirely trust me, so he often cut off his words in the middle of a sentence to avoid revealing information he didn't want me to learn. This bothered me more and more as the morning went on, but I could understand why he was cautious. He was an alien hybrid in a human world. The truth of his nature could put him in serious danger.

I ended up filling in those awkward gaps in our conversation with my own stories, and Vincent turned out to be an excellent listener as I poured out my past like some word dam had broken inside me.

I told him about my mother and how I had never won her approval, no matter how hard I'd tried. She'd been a popular cheerleader and homecoming queen in high school. She'd had a bright future ahead of her. Until she'd discovered she was pregnant with me and couldn't or didn't want to identify the father. Her parents had made her keep me, and then they'd gone and died in a car accident when I was still a toddler, forcing her to put aside her own life goals to raise me.

She'd never forgiven me for that. Nor had she forgiven me for being too weird to make friends in school, and too fat to be a cheerleader, and too shy to be a homecoming queen. She'd wanted to relive her best years through me, and I'd failed her on every level.

Vincent expressed disbelief and shock when I told him how my mother had never let me forget what a disappointment I was. That gave me the opening to ask about his mother, and the way he described her and her love for her children filled me with such longing and envy that I didn't sift through his words looking for more clues about where he came from.

Instead, I focused on the clear affection and love he had for his mother and his siblings. I held off with my curiosity about his "fathers," though I really wanted to ask more about such an unusual relationship.

Not that having a single alien lover would be all that ordinary.

In fact, I supposed I was now in an unusual relationship, though I still couldn't believe how fast it had all happened, nor how much I wanted this to last forever. I could already picture us sitting at a kitchen island in a home of our own, with a half dozen kids playing around us, and the two of us talking about our day as we waited for our family meal to finish cooking.

The image filled me with more longing, but obviously I didn't mention it to Vincent. I didn't want him to think I was a crazy woman, already planning our wedding on our first date. Though, to be fair, I'd planned my wedding a hundred times over by this time. As a teenager, I'd sketch out black wedding dresses and macabre centerpieces for my future gothic-themed wedding.

Charles had laughed at my descriptions of what I'd wanted at our wedding, telling me that would be entertaining to see, but he doubted I'd be seeing it anytime soon. The fact that he'd added the "soon" to that statement had led me to believe it would happen someday with him. I'd just thought he wasn't ready. He never seemed to be ready to even consider it.

I wanted to get Vincent's opinion on a gothic theme wedding but kept my questions to myself. He would look amazing in a tuxedo designed just for him to fit the theme. If anyone would make a perfect groom for a gothic wedding, it would be Vincent.

In fact, he would make a perfect groom for me simply because he was exactly the kind of man I would create for myself if I had that power. That was another one of my concerns. I worried that Vincent might be part of an elaborate dream, and even though I could feel every pinch I gave myself when he wasn't looking, I still feared my alarm would suddenly go off, and I would discover myself alone in my bed, my heart aching after another dream that was far better than my reality.

When the timer went off, I pulled our food out of the oven and set it on the island counter as Vincent fetched paper plates left over from a local takeout restaurant, since he had only one plastic dish to eat off of. Honestly, I was surprised he had the pots and pans, but he said he'd intended to learn more about cooking, so he'd bought a set but never got around to using it.

The pizza had homemade sauce from the ingredients I'd found in his pantry, cans of tomato sauce and paste buried beneath boxes of sugary cereals. He also had an impressive collection of spices that were barely used, and I'd found more than enough to make the sauce and spice up the casserole.

Vincent expressed his appreciation vocally, then licked his lips in a way that reminded me of what his inhumanly long tongue had felt like inside me. I could definitely go for that again. As the thought of it aroused me, he breathed in, then his nostrils flared as he sucked in a deeper breath, his gaze shifting from his pizza slice to meet my eyes.

He smiled a slow, knowing grin, then licked his lips a second time as his gaze lowered to my lap, which was currently concealed by his long shirt.

"Vincent, if you keep looking at me like that," I said in a breathless voice, "I won't be able to concentrate on eating."

"I can't stop thinking about eating," he said with a seductive smile that bared his fangs. "I want to eat you all night long."

"I suppose it's technically morning," I said, even as I shivered with my arousal at his husky tone.

He had the sexiest voice I'd ever heard, and I had dated the lead singer of a rock band for years. Charles had nothing on Vincent—in any capacity.

He shrugged one broad, bare shoulder, and I enjoyed the sight of his muscles rippling beneath his pale skin. "I'm not concerned about the time, as long as I get to spend it with you."

Since I had New Year's Day off, neither was I, but his words did get me wondering. "What do you do for a living? Valerie never told me."

His expression shuttered, and I immediately regretted my question and wanted to kick myself. He must have noticed my regret in my expression, because the tension that suddenly tightened his shoulders relaxed along with his impassive features.

"I work with gray-father and my brother, Eren, on building and maintaining the technology in our city."

I wanted to ask what city he meant, picturing everything from an underground civilization below our feet to a city under domes on the dark side of the moon to some hidden ruins in the thickest parts of the Amazon jungle.

Instead of trying to take the conversation where he clearly

didn't want it to go, I focused on his job description. "So, it sounds like you really are into technical things. I imagine a job like that satisfies your interests."

He grinned, his expression relaxing fully. "Some of them." His gaze took in my rumpled appearance with appreciation that left me in no doubt as to what other interests he might have. Then his eyes returned to studying my face. "Valerie said you work for an apartment complex?"

I nodded, then shrugged. "It's not the most exciting job, but it has its moments. Some of the residents can be a little...," I regarded his belly claws, then smiled ruefully, "strange. Though I suppose their oddness would seem pretty mundane compared to your experiences."

Vincent's claws drummed along his abdominals like I might tap my fingers on a countertop. "I *have* seen some pretty unusual things," he said thoughtfully, winking at me as some of his claws spread outwards, then waved in my direction.

I laughed at his playful gesture. It was amusing to see such deadly looking limbs moving around like someone's fingers.

"I like some of the unusual things I've been seeing lately," I said with all honesty. "I like them a great deal."

His expression grew more serious as he regarded me intently. "Do you, Gabby? Do you think you'd like to be surrounded by unusual things?"

I leaned forward on my stool, pushing aside my plate with my half-eaten pizza slice. "Are you *kidding*? I love the strange and unusual! It would be a dream come true to be surrounded by wonders that I've been told my whole life don't exist!"

His smile told me that I'd said the right thing. "That makes me happy to hear it." He set his own pizza down on his plate next to the cheesy stain that was all that remained of the huge serving of casserole he'd already consumed. "I knew the appearance of my body would be a huge hurdle for the woman I wanted to be with. I feared the sight of it would chase you off, and that was why I was delaying showing it to you. You have pleasantly surprised me at every turn tonight, Gabby."

I warmed at his words, and it wasn't the heat that he normally caused in me. This time, it was centered in my chest as he looked at me like I was special.

This incredible hybrid between a human and an alien who had blood that was practically magic in its properties thought *I* was the special one.

"I'm so glad the night turned out the way it did." I touched his hand where it rested on the top of the counter. "I've had the best night of my life, and I don't want it to end."

He turned his hand to clasp my fingers in his. "Nor do I. Since it's morning, would you spend the day with me too?"

I nodded without giving it a second thought. Hell, I would spend my life with him at this point, if he asked. Though I didn't dare hope that would happen. Not on a first date.

"I can't think of anyone I'd rather spend it with, Vincent." I cocked my head after saying his name. "Hey, does everyone call you Vincent, or do you have a nickname, like Vin, or Vinnie?"

He chuckled at my question, tugging me closer to him, until I left my stool to stand next to him. He pulled me off my feet and onto his lap, arranging my legs to straddle his thighs. I rested my arms on his broad shoulders, toying with the strands of his silky hair. His claws wrapped around my back, holding me steady and close to his warm body.

"My mother and aunts call me Vinnie. Most of my siblings call me Vin, but Vincent is what people other than my family call me." He kissed me briefly, then lifted his head as I leaned into him. "If you want to give me a nickname, I'm open to suggestions." He kissed me a second time, his beautiful lips teasing on mine. "If not, you can take your pick of what to call me."

"I like all those names, but I think Vincent is my favorite. It's sexy as hell, just like you." I gazed into his unusual eyes feeling so happy to be in this position with him that I never wanted this moment to end.

"Do you always go by Gabby?" He punctuated his questioned with a kiss on my forehead, then nuzzled my hair and inhaled audibly.

I shrugged, my arms shifting on his shoulders. Then I tugged playfully on his hair, and he rewarded me with a chuckle. "'Gabriella' is the only name my mother will call me by." I ran my fingers through his hair, pulling some strands over his shoulder to smooth them between my fingers. "Maybe that's why I hate that name so much." I focused on his hair rather than looking into his eyes, uncomfortable with that confession and how it made me seem vulnerable.

He caught my chin and lifted it so I had to look at him directly. "If you never want me to use that name for you, Gabby, then I won't."

I shrugged like it didn't matter, but suddenly it did. It was just a name, and therefore should be no big deal, but I felt like it was. "Maybe if you called me Gabriella in your beautiful voice, with that tone you use with me that makes me feel special, I would learn to love hearing my name."

"Any time, *Gabriella*," he said, and it sounded as sexy and delicious as I thought it might when he purred my name in his seductive voice.

I shivered with pleasure and felt his response as his stem pushed against his pants to prod my slick opening, which was bare and accessible beneath his shirt. He reached down with one hand and unzipped his pants.

We both moaned as the tip of his stem slid into my entrance. It extended from his body, pushing deeper inside me as he claimed my lips again in a kiss filled with hunger that had nothing to do with the food we'd just eaten.

18

Gabby

Vincent kept me up all morning, and it was the best sleepless night I'd ever had. I didn't hesitate to say yes to spending the entire day together but knew that even with another taste of his blood, we couldn't spend it all in the bedroom.

And the kitchen, and the living room, and his entryway, and even the back patio where we'd gone to watch the first sunrise of the New Year.

I suggested we go see a movie, and he told me that he didn't care what we did, as long as we were together. Things like that kept me floating on a cloud well into the morning as I whipped up a breakfast for him after digging around in his fridge and freezer for ingredients.

As the time for the matinee approached, I realized that I had nothing to wear but my jammies or his shirts.

"I need to go home and change!" I said, smacking my forehead as I turned from the sink where I was washing up the pan and dishes I'd used to make our meal. "I can't go out looking like this."

I looked down at my current outfit, which was another of his shirts. I had nothing on underneath it, including underwear.

That last was because he wanted easy access and I really enjoyed when he had it. Especially since he'd rewarded me for making breakfast for us by eating me out with climactic strokes of his talented tongue.

"I need to pick up my car and then I can drive back to my place, change, and come back here before the movies."

He turned to look at me as he dried the dishes, shaking his head with a slight frown. "I don't want to be away from you that long on our first day together. How about I drive you to your place? I can take you to pick up your car later."

I didn't really want to be away from him either, so I didn't object to that, because even the short drive from Val's place to mine seemed like too long to be separated from the most exciting and incredible man I'd ever met. I was afraid if I let him out of my sight, I'd never see him again. Like he would just poof into mist and disappear forever, or it would turn out that I'd had some delusional episode where I only imagined he was real.

After finishing the dishes, he lent me an oversized jacket to bundle up in. He'd moved his car into the garage so that I wouldn't have to walk outside on the slushy ground in my purloined bunny slippers to get into it. As I climbed into the dark, clean interior, I inhaled deeply, taking in the scent of him that lingered on the seats. Then he climbed into the driver's seat, his long legs bent in a way that looked uncomfortable, even as the binding over his claws kept them pressed tight against his body.

I wondered if I was making him suffer being uncomfortable

by going out to a movie when he'd rather be at home with his shirt off.

Then he looked at me, noting my worried frown. "You okay?"

"I was just thinking that we don't have to go out anywhere if you would rather be comfortable at home."

He smiled, patting his bound claws with one hand. "Trust me. I've done this many times, and I'm used to it. It isn't as bad as you might think. I'm not bound as tightly as you were in your garment last night. I'm actually fairly comfortable like this."

I chewed my bottom lip, hoping he wasn't saying that just to ease my concerns because he wanted to spend time with me and felt like I wouldn't do so if we stayed at his house. "I just want to make sure you're enjoying yourself, Vincent."

He leaned towards me and caught my chin in his hand, lifting it so my lips were easily accessible to his. After a long, arousing kiss, he lifted his head, grinning down at me.

"I am enjoying myself immensely, Gabriella," he said in a voice husky with his arousal.

"You make my name sound so beautiful," I said on a happy sigh as he sat back in his seat and inserted the key in the ignition.

"A beautiful name for a beautiful woman." He cast a heated glance at me as he turned the key and the car rumbled to life.

"I've never felt beautiful before, but you make me believe it when you say it while you look at me the way you do."

He gave me one of those looks I was referring to, an intense, hungry look that said he would gladly take me back inside and strip me down and lick every part of my body, flaws and all.

"I'm glad you believe the truth, Gabby. You *are* special to me. Very special."

He pushed the button on the garage door opener, then stroked his hand over my thigh where the long coat had split to reveal my naked skin as we waited for the door to open.

"You're insatiable, Vince!" I rested my hand over his, then slowly guided it upwards towards the slickness between my legs. "I like that."

"Vince," he said thoughtfully, slipping two of his fingers inside me. "I like *that*. No one else calls me that."

I moaned softly as he fingered me. "Do you," I said breathlessly, laying my head back on the seat and closing my eyes, my knees falling open as my hips rocked forward. "Then it will be my name for you."

He leaned towards me, kissing my lips as they parted with another moan, his fingers moving faster inside me as his thumb rubbed my clit. He teased my lips as his fingers teased me lower, then he kissed his way to my neck.

I gasped, my eyes rolling back in my head as he buried his fangs in my throat, my orgasm crashing over me moments later as he began to suck, the euphoria of his bite filling me along with the intensity of my climax.

"We won't make it to the movie like this," I said in a shaky voice after he lifted his head and licked my blood off his lips.

"There's a later showing," he said with a satisfied smirk.

I nodded, my smile wide and no doubt goofy with the emotions rushing through me. "I don't mind if we miss it. Especially not when you do that to me."

He chuckled, the sound deep and resonating in the confined space of the car. Then he put the car into reverse and backed out of the garage. "I want to do that to you all the time. I want to touch you and taste you and feel my stem moving inside you forever."

I glanced at him in surprise at his word choice. "Forever, huh?" My stomach fluttered as he shot me a golden-eyed look filled with intensity. "I must have been one hell of a first date!"

He laughed aloud, reaching to stroke my hair away from my face affectionately. "You are amazing. Absolutely perfect and amazing!"

"You just keep thinking that, Vince. I certainly won't try to convince you otherwise." I sighed sappily as I studied his flawless profile. "I made a resolution not to do that."

"I suppose I'm supposed to make a resolution too," he said as he shifted the car into drive. "What should it be?"

I pointed at my chest, my brows lifted. "You're asking me?" I laughed. "Trust me, you don't want to take life advice from this girl." I eyed his gorgeous face and sexy body, thinking about those dangerous and yet still playful claws beneath the bulge of his jacket. "Besides, there isn't anything you should resolve to change about yourself, Vince. You're the one who's perfect."

He shook his head with a skeptical huff of laughter. "I wish that was true, but I have my flaws, though I don't think I should share them with you so soon." He caught my disbelieving look when he glanced at me again and grinned. Then his smile faded to a more serious expression. "I'll make a resolution right here and now. I'll resolve to make Gabriella the happiest woman in this world or any other."

My mouth dropped open in surprise at his words. Then I snapped it shut, lifting my hand to stroke my fingers down a strand of his hair that framed his face. "You've already done that."

His expression grew heated as he turned his head to kiss my fingers. "Then I'll resolve to *keep* Gabriella happy and let her know every day that she's special, just as she is."

Hope sprung up inside me that he was being serious and not just riding some endorphin or hormone high from drinking my blood or from having a night of incredible sex. Dare I think he wanted to make this a forever thing?

"You'll have to give me directions," he said as we stopped at the intersection leaving the housing development.

For a moment, I thought he meant about how to keep me happy, and I almost said he didn't have to do anything but be himself. Then I realized he meant directions to my apartment, and I laughed internally at myself. He'd really shaken me in the best possible way with his resolutions. They sounded even better for me than my own.

The drive to my apartment passed quickly, though it was some distance away from his house. I didn't pay much attention to the route we took, noting it only long enough to tell him what streets to turn down.

When we reached my complex, he parked in my space and climbed out of his side of the car. He reached my side in time to catch my door, then he held out a hand to help me out of the car. As I stood, he pulled me against him, and I felt his claws shifting against my stomach and chest. He gave me a kiss that left me in no doubt that we would likely be too late for the matinee if we continued touching each other like this.

We managed to make it to my door, and I fumbled in my clutch for the key, my fingers chilly from the morning air. Vincent took the bag from me and withdrew my phone to hand it to me, then plucked the key free and stuck it in the lock.

He held open my door for me and followed on my heels as I rushed inside my neatly kept two-bedroom apartment. The place smelled of winter candles and air fresheners that I used to try to cover up the musty scent of old carpeting. No matter how many times I'd had it cleaned or how much I vacuumed, I could never get rid of that odor.

"I love your home," he said as he eyed my shelf of painted and carved skulls in every material but bone. "I had a collection of skulls in my room when I was growing up. My mother hated them but let me keep them anyway."

I beamed at the compliment and wondered why I'd worried that he would dislike this aspect of me when Valerie had already told him about my interests. "I'll bet they were little animal skulls rather than ones made of wood or stone or clay."

"Some weren't so little," he said, though he'd nodded at my guess. He gestured to my shelf. "I should have thought of having someone paint them. My brother Samuel is an artist. I'll bet he could make something beautiful out of even the most fearsome of them."

"Samuel is your little brother, right?"

He returned his attention to me, looking pleased that I had remembered. "Yes, you're right. Though I would hardly call him 'little' anymore. Not without expecting a fight. You've been listening to all my rambling about my family."

I shrugged. "Of course! Why wouldn't I? I would love to meet them someday."

His expression sobered as he studied my face intently. "Would you, Gabby?" Then he gestured with one hand to my home. "Would you leave all this behind to travel with me to meet my family?"

I glanced around my apartment, noting that despite my best efforts to decorate it, I couldn't hide how boring and boxy the rooms were. Even the kitchen lacked character, being a basic galley kitchen with Formica countertops and white appliances that I kept spotlessly clean.

"I mean, leaving here wouldn't exactly be much of a sacrifice." Again, his hints about being from somewhere different and far from here drove me wild with curiosity, but I suspected he wouldn't answer my question about where he was from if I asked it directly.

"What if you could never return?" He swept his arms out to indicate the living room. "What if you could only bring one bag with you, carrying only the things you couldn't bear to part with, and you knew that you would never see this place again, and that you could never speak to your loved ones again? Would you still make that sacrifice?"

His tone had grown serious, any playfulness or teasing stripped from it. I realized that he wasn't speaking hypothetically.

"Where are you from, Vincent?" I asked, whispering the

question as if the men in black had bugged my apartment for some inexplicable reason.

He stepped closer to me and took my hands in his, his head bent to look down at me, never breaking eye contact, as if he wanted to will me to give him the answer he wanted to hear. "I come from a place that is difficult to reach without risking discovery by the authorities of this world, and it is dangerous to attempt to return here for the same reason. When I leave this world, I must leave it for good." He lowered his head until his lips hovered just above mine. "I want to leave it with *you*, Gabriella."

My own lips felt so numb that it was difficult to shape the words to respond. "You're from a different world, then?"

Shit just got real! This was going well beyond a fantasy or a dream. He was asking me to leave Earth with him. Not just for a family reunion, but forever.

I would have to say goodbye to everything I had ever known, including the people in my life, to return with him to a world that would undoubtedly be unlike anything I'd ever experienced in my twenty-six years.

I would never see my mother again, and while that thought actually brought a bittersweet feeling of relief, the thought of never seeing Valerie again made me sad.

"I'm from a different dimension, not just a different world," he murmured against my lips as if even he thought the men in black were listening in.

I hadn't even considered that, and I should have with my imagination. The revelation shocked me, stealing my breath for a moment.

He lifted his head rather than kissing me, as if he sensed I needed oxygen. I wanted to clutch his fingers to stop him when he released my hands, but I felt paralyzed with shock.

"I'm rushing this." He lifted a hand to rub the back of his neck, looking away from me like he didn't appreciate the expression on my face. "You don't have to give me an answer now. I know it's a lot to think about."

"Vince," I said as my breath rushed out of me, "I-I just... I don't know what to say. It's... I...."

"It's too early." He turned his back on me to regard my cryptid figurine collection. "Forget I mentioned it for now. I don't want to ruin the rest of the day for us."

I wanted to push it aside and focus again on how good it felt to spend time with him, but I felt like this great big bomb had dropped onto my happiness, blasting me back into reality. It felt even worse than an alarm clock going off and awakening me from my dream.

My dream lover remained, but he wanted me to take a leap into the unknown without any safety line to pull me back into the familiar. He wanted me to do that knowing that there would never be any going back.

And it was technically still only our first date!

What a way to begin the New Year.

19

Vincent

I was frustrated by my own impatience and impulsiveness. I wanted to roar in anger at myself for once again rushing things. I knew I should have held off speaking of my origins, and of the sacrifice Gabby would have to make to be with me. I'd been lulled into a feeling of anticipation for her answer by her excitement and interest in my family.

I also had to admit that even speaking of them to her was only increasing my homesickness to painful levels. That likely had played a part in my hasty proposal to Gabby.

I had completely botched what I'd planned to be a gradual reveal with a dramatic proposal at the end, possibly with a ring made just for Gabby to signify my desire to make her mine forever. I knew that was the human tradition, as my mother had explained it all. She even wore three custom-made rings that fit together to form a larger ring on her ring finger to signify her union with my fathers.

I'd learned that a lot of human females desired a grand

proposal, with all manner of pageantry and pomp. Instead, I'd clumsily asked her to leave this lovely home she'd created for herself that spoke of Gabby in every object and fold of fabric. I'd told her she could never come back, and she couldn't even take much of what she possessed with her.

That was gray-father's rule. Everything had to be approved before he allowed it to leave a dimension, because some items might have significance that would make critical changes in their home dimension if taken from it. This significance wasn't always obvious from the appearance and status of the item. Thus, he'd made the rule that only small personal parcels could be brought back to the Fall by immigrants seeking a new home there. Usually, just one suitcase or bag per person that the anchor could quickly scan and process.

Many residents seeking a mate outside our dimension objected to the strict rule because it could often become a sticking point for their mate. Gray-father pointed out that a female unwilling to abandon mere objects in the name of love wouldn't be likely to appreciate leaving her entire dimension behind forever for love.

Still, some things had significance to people beyond their practical value. Even large things.

Like my Chevelle that I would have to leave behind.

The rule seemed unfair to me, and I could guess that Gabby didn't appreciate it either. She looked stunned and not in the least bit happy that I was asking her to become my mate and join my family.

Gabby still wore my oversized shirt on her petite frame. She still smelled of my lust and her own and had not even had a chance to rest since she'd met me. In fact, no doubt she'd worked a full day prior to her evening out.

She was probably tired, overwhelmed, and in need of some time alone to think about everything.

Despite knowing this and accepting it, I still felt rejected and hurt. I knew that was irrational and unfair to Gabby, but I supposed I had wanted her to jump at the chance to be with me without a moment's hesitation. She seemed so excited about the thought of being in a new place, surrounded by wonders she could never see in this world. I had taken that to mean that she would want to leave here. I had fooled myself into believing that I would be enough to convince her that it was worth the sacrifice even if she had doubts about leaving here.

Now, she remained silent behind me as I stared sightlessly at her walls. I could hear her drawing in her breath, then making sounds like she struggled to find words.

"Vincent."

I turned as she touched my arm hesitantly.

When I looked down at her face, I saw that her beautiful eyes were wide. She nibbled her plump lower lip. "I *do* need to think about it. It *is* a lot to take in right now."

When I nodded abruptly and turned towards the door, she tightened her fingers on my sleeve. "Wait! I'd still like to spend the rest of the day with you. We don't have to talk about this right now, do we? There's not a deadline, is there?"

I turned back to her, slowly shaking my head. "Not a ticking clock type of deadline, but every day that I remain here runs the risk that someone will get curious enough to discover the truth about me. Maintaining a low profile can be difficult sometimes."

I looked down at my bound claudas ruefully.

She smiled uncertainly at my expression, but it didn't reach her eyes, which were now shadowed with doubt and some other emotion I couldn't read.

Sometimes, I envied Sherakeren his empathetic abilities. Then I got a reminder of what living with them did to him and I thanked Cold Mother that I didn't suffer from such a curse.

"How long have you been here?" she asked, releasing my

sleeve to twist her hands together in front of her like she felt nervous asking me questions about my origin.

I didn't want to see her uncomfortable with me like that, but I wasn't sure what to do to unsay my proposal. "A few months. I've had a couple of close calls where humans began to grow suspicious, but not enough that I have had to completely leave the area or resort to full camouflage."

She sighed, lifting a hand to run it through her tousled hair. "It would be really bad if anyone figured out the truth, wouldn't it?"

Her tone made it sound like a rhetorical question, but I answered anyway. "I am alone here, Gabby. I am trained as a warrior. My blood-father saw to that, and I have fought enough battles in the Fall to be confident in my abilities, but I would be quickly outnumbered by the authorities in this world if they even suspected the truth."

Her eyes sharpened with interest, even as she returned to nibbling her lower lip with concern. "The fall? Is that what your home is called?"

Perhaps mentioning that people actually called it the *Dead* Fall wouldn't be conducive to convincing her to go there. "My home is actually called New Omni. It's a beautiful city surrounded by a grove of sentient trees that keep us safe. Beyond my home is a world that is slowly growing less dangerous thanks to the expansion of the Grove, but it still poses some challenges that keep the less combative citizens staying safely within the boundaries of New Omni."

"*Sentient* trees?" She forgot to bite her lip, and I took that as a positive sign that her curiosity was overcoming her doubts and concerns.

"Not *just* trees." I shrugged, searching for the best way to explain the ancilla. "They have blood pumping through their veins beneath their bark. They were once mobile life forms, and very powerful ones at that. They are still incredibly powerful, but they're benevolent now and use their gifts to help the people of New Omni. Some worship them even though they don't seek to be treated as above any other living creature in the Fall."

"They sound fascinating," she said in a wistful voice. "I've always loved trees, and forests. I sometimes thought the trees could understand me when I spoke to them and pretended maybe one day they would answer back."

"The ancilla—the trees—are telepathic," I said, hope burgeoning that she might decide to accept my proposal if I told her more about my world and the wonders within it.

Now that she knew the truth, I didn't have to watch my words. I could describe all the beauties of New Omni, and even the wonders of the Fall. "They can speak inside your mind if you touch their bark. They can also understand anything you say around them. They are remarkable. There are so many remarkable things about my world, Gabby."

I swept my arms out to my sides to take in the space surrounding us. "Just by looking at your home I can tell you would love my world."

I pointed to her shelf of creature figurines. "There are beings like all of these in New Omni and the Fall. Our world is connected to countless dimensions and people from all of them come to New Omni to make new lives within the grove."

I saw the excitement in her expression as she glanced at her collection, then back at me with wide eyes. "Really? I can't even imagine...."

I took her hands again, feeling how chilly her fingers were and how clammy her palms had grown. She was nervous and dealing with a lot at once, and I still wasn't giving her time to process any of it.

"You *can't* imagine it, Gabby. Even my family is unique. My Fayi blood-father is considered a giant compared to most New Omnians, especially when he is engorged. My wing-father is like a huge humanoid bird, and gray-father... you have a figurine that isn't far off from what he once looked like." I pointed to a little figure of a slender, big-headed gray alien on her shelf. "You must see them, see all of the wonders of my world, in order to truly appreciate it, and I know you would. I know you would love it there."

"But I would have to leave Earth forever. I would never see my mother again. I'd never see Val again."

"Your mother doesn't appreciate you," I said, not mentioning Valerie, because she would be a true loss in Gabby's life, and I didn't want to draw her attention to that.

It was a pity Valerie couldn't come with Gabby. I knew there were males in the Fall who would appreciate her—garrulous, dominating personality and all. However, Valerie already had a male she was quite fond of, and she didn't have the same open-minded appreciation that Gabby did for the unusual and strange. She probably wouldn't be convinced to leave Earth and would likely try to convince Gabby to remain.

Doubt clouded her eyes again, but she didn't pull her hands back, instead, lacing her fingers with mine. "Can we not discuss this today, Vince? I still need to think about it, but I love being with you, and I want to spend more time with you, just having fun."

I nodded, grateful that she didn't immediately reject the idea of going with me. I loved being with her too. That was why I was so determined for her to join me in the Fall. I didn't like the thought of living without her now that I'd experienced what it was like to have her in my life.

Her shoulders sagged with relief, and she hugged me around the waist, resting her cheek against the binder on my claudas, which shifted beneath it in a desire to clutch her close to me.

"I'll go change." She pulled away, looking up at my face with a happy smile, even though her eyes remained uncertain.

I lowered my head to kiss her, but a knock at her door gave me pause.

She glanced at the door in surprise. "Who is it?" she called, her tone curious.

"Gabby?" a male voice said from the other side of the door. "Are you okay, baby? I've been so worried about you since I received your text! Open up the door."

Her eyes widened until the whites showed around her irises. "*Charles*!" she said in a tone of complete disbelief.

She glanced at me, her eyes widening even further, then again looked at the door, her expression panicked. "What are you doing here?"

"Gabby, open the door," the male said, and I clenched my fists at his demanding tone.

I knew who this "Charles" was. Gabby's loser ex-boyfriend, or "Chucky" as Valerie called him. I didn't like that he had the nerve to call Gabby "baby" like it was an endearment. I didn't like that at all, and venom dripped from the tips of my claudas as my lips pulled back in a scowl.

"Go away, Charles," Gabby said, her tone sounding desperate as she shook her head at me. "I'm busy, and besides, I have nothing to say to you."

A pounding on the door followed that statement. "Gabby, you open up this door right now! I need to see for myself that you're safe after that bizarre text you sent me last night. The one where you said some guy named Vincent wasn't human and that I should call the FBI or the military. I want to know what drugs you were taking last night!" He pounded again. "And if you have any more of them. And who the hell is 'Vincent' anyway?"

Gabby's face went pale, and her jaw dropped open as she stared at the door. Then she slowly looked up at me, her pulse throbbing in her throat as she noticed my expression.

Betrayal stabbed through me like a spear, and I felt like it had struck a mortal blow as I stared down at the face of the woman I had been so certain was my mate. The one I was meant to be with forever.

She'd sold me out to her loser boyfriend. He couldn't possibly be an "ex" since she'd texted him last night and told him about me. She'd sold me out! Because she wanted to become a billionaire from my blood perhaps? How much would she and her loser male make from turning me over to their authorities? I felt sick that I shown her so much of myself, allowed her to get so close, when she was just like the humans who were invading my father's homeworld and stealing away Fayi males to drain their blood for profit. How could I have been such a fool to trust her?

She held up both hands defensively as if I would ever hurt her physically. "Vincent, I can explain! It's not what you think!"

I lifted a hand to cut off her words and even in my despair and rage I disliked that she flinched away from it. "It seems I can thank *Chucky* for inadvertently letting me know what kind of woman you really are, Gabriella." I said her name with all the anger and disdain I could put into my tone. "I would say you're a snake, but I've known too many good serpents to insult them like that. You're a vile, treacherous creature, *Gabriella.* I can see why your mother despises you so much."

Ignoring the way her face crumpled and tears rose to her eyes at my cruel and biting words, I turned on my heel and strode to the door.

I jerked it open as the boyfriend lifted a hand to pound on it again. He froze when he caught sight of me.

I bared my teeth and roared in his face, and he staggered backwards so fast that he fell onto his backside on the gravel outside Gabby's apartment entrance.

Then I stalked past him, my coattail snapping in his face as he pushed himself further away from me with his feet churning up the gravel in his panic.

"Vincent!" Gabby called after me, racing out her door as I strode to my car, my steps heavy with my pain and rage at her betrayal. "Please, let me explain!"

I heard nothing but the roar of my own blood in my ears after that as I unlocked my car and jerked the door open.

Then I climbed inside and started it up. I didn't flinch as she reached my car and pounded desperately on the driver's side window, shouting for me to listen. She was only trying to delay me. No doubt the human authorities were on their way to capture me, and she had to keep me in one place long enough for them to arrive. I wouldn't let her fool me again.

Putting my car into gear, I backed out of the space, even in my anger careful not to knock Gabby off her feet as she waved her arms at me and screamed for me to stop and let her explain.

Then I pulled away in a cloud of exhaust and a roar of the 454 that couldn't come close to the roar going on inside my head at the pain crushing my heart.

20

Gabby

G***abby's New Year's Resolution # 7:*** *Always double check my texts before I send them. Always, always, always!*

My heart was breaking into a thousand pieces as I watched the Chevelle speed down the street after I chased it to the entrance of my apartment complex, still waving my arms and shouting like a crazy woman.

He didn't look at me once, his jaw set and his profile hard. He'd completely shut me off, and I couldn't even blame him, because I'd made a horrible mistake and ruined the best thing that had ever happened to me.

I walked slowly back to my apartment, Vincent's jacket not nearly enough to warm the chill inside me. I knew that my destiny had just left me in a cloud of exhaust, all because I couldn't take half a second to double check that I was sending my text to the right person. Sure, I had been in a hurry last night when texting Val, but one quick glance at the recipient before I pushed send would have saved me all this grief.

When I returned to my apartment, I discovered that Charles had entered it and made himself at home at my kitchen counter, plopped on one of my black stools chowing down on a container of my leftover fried chicken as if he lived there.

I shook my head, glaring at him. "Oh, hell no you don't! You get out, Chucky. Right now!"

He had the nerve to look outraged at my words and tone, and all I wanted to do was pick up one of my painted skulls and smash it against his to wipe that look off his face.

"Gabby, *you* texted me. I came here to rescue you, and it's a good thing I did, too." He waved a hand towards the door. "That guy was a freak. What the hell were you even doing with him?" Then he glanced at my shelves and huffed, returning his cold gaze to me. "Never mind, that was a stupid question."

"Listen, you *asshole*," I marched up to him to snatch my fried chicken away, slapping the lid back on the container to put it back in the fridge, "I had no intention of texting you last night."

He couldn't even make the effort to heat it up first!

"Those texts were meant for Val. The 'not human' text was a joke that she would have understood. I never asked you to come here, and I never wanted you to be here!"

I held back the urge to cry at the memory of seeing Vincent leave in such a rage. He would probably never forgive me. First, I'd rejected his proposal—because I could tell that was what it was. Then, I'd betrayed him by texting *Charles*, of all people, to say that Vincent wasn't human. Given the danger of discovery for Vincent, he must have thought I was an absolute cretin for selling him out. His harsh words had definitely hit their mark.

Valerie had his number, I hoped. I needed to get ahold of her as soon as possible. I had to get Vincent to just listen to me and let me explain. It had probably been wrong of me to even text Val to say he wasn't human, but I'd still been cautious then, and I didn't want to blithely march to my own death without at least warning somebody. Surely, he would understand that Val would give him the benefit of the doubt and wait until the prescribed time to contact the authorities?

But not Charles. I couldn't blame him for being angry that it was Charles who got that information texted to him.

Now, I had to deal with the idiot in my kitchen before I could contact Valerie and tell her all about what had happened.

He was looking at me with a wounded expression, his hands still hovering in the air after I took the food away from him as if he couldn't believe I wasn't going to put it right back and maybe cook him up some more. His surprise wasn't completely misplaced, since I'd been such a sucker when I'd dated him that I had done that very thing on multiple occasions even after he'd treated me like shit.

"C'mon, Gabs," he said, lowering his voice in a way he knew I'd thought was sexy.

His voice had nothing on Vincent's. He couldn't even come close.

"I'll forgive you for going out with another man, especially since he's obviously a crackpot."

My brows lifted as I pulled back in shock. "Excuse me? You'll *forgive* me?" I crossed my arms over my chest, grateful now for the extra material of Vincent's jacket covering my body. "I'm not dating you! You have absolutely no say about who I do date, and screw you anyway, because Vincent is a thousand times better a man than you." I narrowed my eyes on him, noting the marks on the collar of his button-up shirt that looked like foundation. "Besides, you no doubt had your own date, or was it *dates*, last night."

He shook his head, his hand lifting reflexively to cover the evidence of his sexual encounters. "I was just hanging out with a friend, Gabs. You're the only woman for me."

"Well, guess you're without a woman then, because I want

nothing to do with you, *Chuck*." I pointed to the door. "Out. *Now*."

He slouched on my stool, and I recognized that he was entrenching himself in the hopes that if he resisted long enough, I'd give up and let him stick around until he could weasel his way back into my good graces.

Those days were over! Vincent had shown me what it felt like to be with someone who lifted me up instead of tearing me down. Even if I never saw him again, and I didn't want to give up on that just yet, I would never settle for less than the way Vincent had made me feel.

And Charles was much less. So much less that he wasn't even in the same dimension as Vincent.

I felt a wave of panic as I had that thought. What it if turned out to be true? What if Vincent left this dimension entirely?

I needed to get rid of Charles and get ahold of Valerie!

Charles grabbed my hand in an attempt to tug me closer to him, but I snatched it back, curling my fingers into a fist to keep myself from slapping his smug smirk off his face. He thought he would win this time, as he had so many others.

"Get out," I said in my coldest voice. "Right now. Or I call security and have them escort you off the premises."

Charles flicked his long hair over his shoulder, giving me a crooked smile. "Gabs, you're overreacting. I came here because I was worried about you, and now you're acting like I did something wrong by chasing off the nutcase." He waved to the door. "I did you a favor."

I turned my back on him and made my way to the couch where I had tossed my phone. When I bent to pick it up, Charles slipped off my stool. "Wait! You aren't seriously planning on calling security, are you?"

I straightened as I unlocked my phone. "You have until the count of ten. One."

Charles rushed towards me, and I counted faster as he

neared, holding the phone up between us while I held my free hand out to keep him from getting too close.

"Gabby!" he said, falling to his knees in front of me. "Please! I need you! My roommate kicked me out and I need a place to stay. When I saw your text last night, I knew you wanted me back, and I want you too, Gabby! I do." He tried to take my extended hand again, and I jerked away from him.

"Five, six, seven." I used my thumb to open my contacts. "I'm a good friend of the security guard here, Charles. I'm sure he'll respond quickly when I call him."

Charles jumped back to his feet, holding up both hands. "All right, already!" He backed towards my front door, reaching behind him blindly for the handle. "Listen, I know you're a little worked up right now, Gabs, so I'll give you some time to think about it. But I can't wait forever. There are other women lining up to be with me."

I scoffed at his words. "Like you ever made them *wait* in line, you unfaithful piece of human excrement." I pointed to the door. "Now get!"

His expression shifted from pleading to angry, and he opened his mouth to say something I knew would be vicious. Then he snapped his lips shut when I pushed dial and put the phone to my ear, giving him a smug smile. I flipped him off with my free hand as he threw open the door and rushed through it.

"See ya never, you loser!" I shouted at his retreating back, pushing end on my phone before the security guard, Bill, could pick up.

I sagged in relief as I closed the front door, then I collapsed on my couch, feeling the panic at losing Vincent return now that I no longer had getting rid of Charles to distract me. I quickly brought up Val's number and called it, screaming at the phone in frustration when it went to voicemail.

"Damn you, Val! Answer the phone!"

I needed a way to contact Vincent, as soon as possible. I was so afraid he would decide to just abandon this dimension altogether, and he'd told me he could never return. I realized that I didn't even have a car to go to his house. I vaguely recalled the directions.

I brought up my rideshare app on my phone and ordered a car, then rushed into my room to throw on a change of clothes while I waited for my ride to arrive.

Ten minutes later I got a text that my driver was waiting for me outside and I hurried to the door, every minute that passed seeming like one more minute too long.

The driver took me to Vincent's house without questions and I appreciated that. Sometimes, the drivers could be a little chatty, and I didn't think I could handle making conversation at the moment, my mind too focused on the fear that I would lose the best thing that ever happened to me for good.

Fortunately, my subconscious must have picked up the directions because I was able to backtrack to his house. My driver waited while I hopped out, in serviceable tennis shoes this time instead of bunny slippers. I raced to the door hoping vainly that it would open automatically at my approach. That would be a sign that Vincent wanted to see me again. Maybe if he did see me, he would let me explain what I'd done.

It didn't open, so I knocked on the door, calling his name, just in case he couldn't figure out it was me, despite the doorbell camera filming every second of me standing there like a desperate stalker.

"Vincent! Please, let me just talk to you. Hear me out!" I turned to face the camera directly, in case he was watching this all play out on his phone. "I accidentally texted the wrong person last night. I never meant to say anything to Charles. I should have taken that bastard out of my contacts altogether. I swear, I wasn't trying to get you in any kind of trouble by contacting Val, either. I was just trying to be cautious because I still didn't know exactly who I was dealing with at the time I sent the text. Please, Vincent!"

I pressed my palms together in front of me in a supplicating gesture. "*Please* forgive me for that terrible text. I want to be with you." I sucked in a deep breath, feeling lightheaded as I considered the ramifications of my next words. "I'll go with you, back to your home. I'll give up everything in this world to be with you." I blinked back tears as I leaned closer to the camera. "I don't want to live in this world without you, Vince."

Nothing. Not even a response back from the speaker of the camera.

It was as clear a rejection as I could get, since I had no doubt Vincent had been alerted to my presence and was now watching me pour my heart out and plead for him to forgive me.

Still, despite that assurance, I remained standing on his doorstep, bouncing a little as the chill settled in even though I wore his jacket over a sweater and jeans. My breath fogged and my nose grew so cold I couldn't feel it anymore, and even beneath the knitted cap I wore, the tips of my ears turned icy.

I continued to wait, knocking a few more times and calling his name. Just in case he was in the shower and hadn't yet seen the video footage.

Recalling his shower, and what we'd done in there, and how wonderful and beautiful and sensual he'd made me feel, I wanted to cry all over again, but I feared my tears would freeze on my cheeks.

My driver honked impatiently after I waited so long that even the most hygienic person would have finished their shower. I bowed my head in defeat. Short of trying to break into his place to confront him directly, there wasn't much I could do.

Still, I wasn't entirely ready to give up on him. "I know you're very angry, Vince." I held up both hands as I spoke to the camera. "I don't blame you. I would be too if I was in your situation. I just want to ask you to consider my words and try to understand the situation I was in last night, before I really got to know you. I also hope you'll believe me when I say I would *never* contact someone like Charles, even if I thought I was in danger." I made a face, shaking my head. "*Especially* if I thought I was in danger. The texts were meant for Val, and you *know* Val. She would have been cool about everything. She would have waited to see what I had to say for myself."

Another honk had me growling in frustration as I shot the driver an irritated glare. "Vincent, just know that I want to be with you. I need you! You made me feel happier than I've ever felt in my entire life. You gave me the best first date ever and started my New Year off in the best possible way. I'm so sorry this happened, and I'm afraid I'll never see you again." I tapped my chest as I looked into the camera lens. "I just don't want that to be because you wouldn't give me a chance to explain."

A flurry of impatient honks caused me to sigh, realizing it was over for now. My driver would probably take off in another minute if I made him wait any longer. "I have to go, but please call me." In case he didn't have my contact information, since I hadn't given it to him and I wasn't sure Val had, I rattled off my number.

Then I turned to go, my shoulders hunching as I waited for the door to open behind me.

When it didn't, hope died.

21

Gabby

Still not completely ready to give up on getting Vincent back, I had the driver take me to Val's place. I had to retrieve Phoebe anyway, and I really needed to talk to Val. She would know what to say to Vincent to get him to forgive me. She'd known him longer, and she'd been the one to set all this up.

Val would have the answers.

When Valerie opened the door to me, I could tell that she was still drunk. She swayed in the doorway, the mess behind her indicative of a New Year's Eve party gone wild. Fortunately, someone had kicked out all the guests.

"I need your help," I said, though I frowned worriedly at the sight of her swollen eyes surrounded by running mascara that streaked her face like warpaint. It looked like she'd been crying. "Let me tell you about it while I pick up the place."

She stepped aside, holding the door open, gesturing to the trashed apartment with one hand as she staggered backwards. I noticed that she held a whiskey bottle in the other hand. As I stared at it, she lifted it to her lips and took a healthy swig.

"V," I entered her apartment, looking around for Ben, "maybe you should take a break from partying for a while and get a little sleep."

"Why bother?" she said in a bitter tone, her lips wet with whiskey. "I wanna party all the time, party all the time, party all the—"

She dropped the bottle and it fell on its side and spilled across the entryway tile. Then she rushed to her kitchen and vomited into her trash bin.

Putting aside my own problems for the time being, I focused on Val. "Sweetie, this needs to stop!" I bent to pick up the whiskey bottle and joined her in the small kitchen, setting it upright on the counter.

When she lifted her head from the trash bin and swiped one hand over her lips, she reached with the other for the bottle. I snatched it away, then carried it to the sink and dumped it out.

"I'm not gonna stand here and pretend you don't have a problem anymore, Val," I said firmly, turning back to her as she slumped dejectedly on a kitchen stool. "Where's Ben?"

"Probably with that two-dollar whore he fucked last night," Val said with a scowl. Then her face crumpled, and she laid her head on the counter. Her shoulders shook as she sobbed.

"Oh no!" I brushed my hand over her hair in commiseration. "I'm so sorry!"

"I walked in on them screwing on *my* bed!" she said, her voice muffled. "He said he was drunk and didn't know what he was doing."

My lips tightened in disapproval. "If that's the case, then he needs to get some serious help." I looked around the room at all the discarded beer cans and empty liquor bottles. "You both do."

Val lifted her head and it fell back on her neck, so she looked upwards towards the ceiling rather than at me. “I don’t believe him, Gabby. He knew exactly what he was doing. The woman he was with told me they’d hooked up before while we were together, right before I kicked her skanky ass out.”

She lowered her bleary gaze to meet mine, her expression shifting to one of irritation, even as tears streaked her cheeks. “Where *were* you? I needed you last night! I texted you!”

I shook my head, pulling my phone out of Vincent’s jacket pocket.

Sure enough, there were multiple texts from Val that I had totally missed—first, so focused on my time with Vincent, then on losing him.

“I’m sorry,” I said sincerely as I set my phone on the counter. “I didn’t see them until just now. I had a crazy night, and a rough day.” I sighed heavily as I pulled open a drawer to withdraw a new kitchen trash bag and shake it out. Then I picked up the beer cans that littered the countertop and tossed them into it. “I wish I had been here for you. I’m so sorry about Ben!”

She laid her head back on the counter again. “Never mind. You’re here now.” Then she lifted her head quickly, as if she’d just thought of something. “Hey, why are your eyes red, Gabby?” Even through her alcoholic haze, she narrowed her eyes thoughtfully on me. “What do you mean your night was crazy?”

I swept paper plates, crumbs, and discarded utensils off the counter and into the trash bag. “I want to tell you all about it, but you don’t look so good. Maybe you should sleep first.”

I desperately wanted Valerie to tell me everything she knew about Vincent, including how to contact him, but she really did look like hell. I couldn’t believe Ben had cheated on her, since he’d always seemed to treat her so well and so lovingly. Compared to how Charles had treated me while we were dating, Ben had seemed like a dream come true for Valerie.

I wondered if it was just inherent in men to cheat, then wondered if half-human hybrids like Vincent would cheat if that was the case. Was there any hope for a faithful, happy relationship with a man? I supposed the question was irrelevant given that Vincent had left my life as quickly and dramatically as he'd entered it.

She rubbed her hand over her face sloppily, moaning as if she were in pain. She probably was, though it wasn't physical. I knew the feeling of betrayal far too well. It never got easier, either. No matter how many times I had braced myself to discover that Charles had cheated on me, it still hurt just as much as the first time I found out about his infidelity.

"I can't sleep," Val said with a clumsy shake of her head, "not in that bed we shared, where he *fucked* that other woman!" She opened her eyes wide as she studied me, blinking like she had to bring me into focus. "Tell me your problems, Gabby. Let me forget about my own for a while."

I set down the bag and opened the cabinet where Valerie kept her OTC medicines. I dug out the aspirin, then searched for a clean glass. Finding none in the cabinet, nor anywhere on the counters, I washed out a dirty one, then filled it with water and handed it along with two aspirins to her.

"Take these, then start drinking some water. If you won't get some sleep, at least you can rehydrate."

Valerie smirked, her lids lowering over her eyes like they were too heavy for her to keep them up. "You're always mothering me."

I didn't tell her she needed a mother, because she already had one who was under the mistaken impression that her daughter was perfect and lived a dream life, thanks to Val never being honest with her parents when she contacted them. They expected too much from her, and she'd struggled under the pressure they put on her. Though they hadn't been as oppressive in their expectations as my mother had, they still didn't let

Valerie just be the person she wanted to be and live the kind of life that she wanted to live.

Her coping mechanism had been to fake an entire life, even going so far as to rent a house for the weekend when they last came to visit her so she could pretend it was hers.

"Tell me what happened last night," Val said after swallowing the pills.

Unable to stand still as I told her about my first date with Vincent, I puttered around the kitchen, picking up the trash, putting all the dishes in the sink, then cleaning off the countertops.

"I sent a couple of texts that I thought were going to you." I sighed heavily as I looked at her face.

She was still with me, though I could tell the alcohol dulled her faculties. Now was the time to drop the bomb on her about Vincent. She had to know the truth, because I needed to impress upon her how important it was that we get ahold of him before he left this dimension. She might be more inclined to believe me when she was inebriated. It did sound like the kind of story a drunk person would tell or believe.

"They went to Charles instead."

"Ugh," Valerie said, her gaze following me as I moved into the living room to pick up more trash and empty bottles.

"The thing is, I learned something about Vincent last night," I said carefully, picking my way around the topic like I picked my way around the living room where even the furniture had been kicked around and knocked over.

Definitely a wild party.

"You learned he was perfect for you, right?" Val gave me a satisfied smirk as she leaned on one elbow on the counter, still slumped on the stool.

I nodded. "Yes, he's perfect for me. The problem is that I might lose him forever if I can't figure out a way to get him to forgive me."

Valerie sat up straight, her gaze sharpening. "Forgive you for what, exactly. What happened, girl?"

I exhaled on a long sigh, then poured out the whole story to my best friend in the world.

Valerie stopped me several times with disbelieving exclamations, and then she realized I was being dead serious, her eyes widening with shock and awe. She knew I wouldn't pretend about something like this, especially not when she was in her current condition.

"He had *claws* wrapped around his stomach?" She shook her head, her gaze looking at nothing as if she tried to picture it.

"He said they were technically more like tails because they originated from his spine, but yes, they looked like crab legs. That's what I thought when I first saw them. But they were really cool," I hastened to add, lest she think I was freaked out by any part of Vincent.

Her focus returned to my face as if still seeking some sign that I was pulling her leg. "Wow, I had no idea about any of that. I just thought he was really into vampire stuff. He seemed quirky, like you. That's why I knew you two would be perfect for each other. I never imagined he'd actually be from another dimension." She laughed shortly, running a shaking hand through her straight blond hair. Her gaze shifted to my neck, looking sharper than it had when I'd first entered the apartment. "And he actually bit you and drank your blood? And you *liked* it?"

I exhaled on a longing and wistful sigh. "Liked it is an understatement, V. It was incredible. I guess his saliva has a quality to it that makes his bite euphoria-inducing. It felt so good!"

She regarded me thoughtfully, still looking like hell herself, her makeup almost all worn away save the mascara smudged around her eyes and steaking down her cheeks. "Damn, girl! I asked you to distract me from my own problems, and you actually made me almost forget about them entirely for a while."

"Mission accomplished," I said with a smile I didn't really feel, any more than Val probably felt the small smile she wore that didn't reach her tired eyes.

She held out a staying hand as I opened the tiny kitchen pantry and pulled out the broom and mop. "You don't have to clean up my place. I'll get to it later."

I snorted, noting that she still wore her party dress, though her hose looked a lot worse for wear, especially over her bare toes. Her thick, blond hair was as silky as ever, but more from genetics than from maintenance at this point. "*You* need to get some sleep. I don't mind picking up around here. You know cleaning relaxes me." I gestured to the living room. "It's also satisfying when I get to clean up a real mess like this and make it all sparkly and neat again."

She chuckled weakly. "You're the best, Gabs. I don't deserve a friend like you." Her smile faded even as I shook my head at that statement. "I'm so sorry about Vincent. I wish I had his number, but I never got it. He came into the station every day and that's when we spoke. I'm such a space cadet that I didn't even think to ask for it." She pounded her fist on the countertop. "Why am I *such* a loser? I can't do anything right! I can't even keep my own man, much less set my best friend up with one."

I set the broom and mop down and went to her to hug her close as she broke down again, even my wild tale not enough to fully distract her from her own heartache. "You're too hard on yourself, Valerie." I patted her hair. "You're amazing and Ben didn't deserve you. You'll find someone who does."

Valerie snorted soggily against my chest. "And then he'll eventually cheat on me too."

I didn't want to say that would never happen again, but then I thought about Vincent and how devoted he'd seemed to be towards me even on our first date. "Maybe you just need to meet the right man. The one you were always meant to be with."

"I thought I already had," Valerie said on a low wail, then started crying again as she clutched me.

"I know, sweetie." I petted her hair again, holding her tight as her sobs shook her. "I'm so sorry."

Tears prickled at my own eyes because I hated to see Valerie unhappy like this, and I realized that I was also destined to be unhappy in love now that I had no other way to get ahold of Vincent beyond camping on his front doorstep, which I doubted he or his neighbors would appreciate.

After Valerie's tears dried up a bit, she pulled away, swiping impatiently at her eyes. "Sorry about that. It's the alcohol making me emotional."

I sighed, studying her ravaged makeup. "Can we finally talk about that now?"

Valerie regarded me warily through swollen lids, her dark brown eyes watery. "Do we have to do this now?" She held up both hands like she was surrendering, but her words belied her pose. "I can't take this conversation right now, Gabby. Let's table it for later, okay?"

I huffed, crossing my arms over my chest, my shirt wet from her outburst. "Fine. We'll discuss it later. But we *will* be discussing it, Val."

Valerie nodded tiredly, finally looking like she might be ready to crash. "Thanks, Gabs," she said in an exhausted tone. "I know you care. I do." She smiled weakly. "You're like the sister I never had."

"V, you have three sisters." I had always been envious of that, even though Valerie didn't seem to have a close relationship with any of them.

They were all very successful in their lives and very busy

and lived scattered all over the world, so it wasn't surprising they didn't get together often.

She chuckled. "Right, but you're like the sister I actually wanted."

That was an unexpected insight, though I should have realized that Valerie's relationship with her sisters wasn't as good as she always pretended it was. Valerie worked hard to maintain the illusion that everything was perfect in her life, even with those who were close to her. At least, until she reached a breaking point like this.

"Hey, V, there's something you should know," I said slowly, deciding to put aside that revelation to examine it later.

She regarded me through wary eyes that were growing sharper as she sobered. "I'm afraid to ask after everything else you told me."

"I, uh... I borrowed your bunny slippers." I chewed on my thumbnail after that confession, watching her expression.

It took a moment for her to process my words, and I could almost see the wheels churning back into life behind her eyes. Then she narrowed her eyes on me. "Which ones?"

"The pink ones."

Her eyes widened as she straightened on the stool. "You stole Little Bunnies Foo and Foo?"

"Stole is such a loaded word," I said defensively, fighting a grin at the silly names she had for her slippers.

She gave me the side eye. "Did you expose my innocent little Foos to anything indecent?"

"They'll never be the same again, I'm afraid." I couldn't keep my grin hidden anymore.

"*Gabriella*! You shameless, naughty slut, you!" Despite her words and mock outraged tone, a genuine smile answered my grin. "They'll need therapy after you traumatized them!"

I nodded, my expression unrepentant. "I'll pay for their treatment. They saw some wild things last night."

She slowly shook her head, the smile still playing around her lips. "You are such a goober, Gabs. I love you, girl. Thanks for cheering me up, even though you snaked my poor bunnies."

"I'll get you some new ones."

She waved away my words. "Consider them a gift. No need to replace them. I still have Flopsy and Mopsy."

I laughed at that. "You know, V, you're a little bit quirky yourself."

She smiled, and it got a little closer to reaching her eyes this time. "I suppose I am."

We had our moment to pretend that we'd be okay. Then I helped Val get into bed and returned to cleaning the apartment, no longer distracted enough to feel anything but despair at losing my dream man on day one of the New Year.

Way to kick things off with a bang, Gabby!

22

Vincent

New Omni had lost its charm for me. I couldn't appreciate its beauty anymore. Nor could I appreciate all the wonders that surrounded me. All I could think about as I walked the streets of my home was what Gabby would have thought about everything she would have seen here.

Gabby was the only thing I could think about. She dominated every minute of my days, and they seemed to drag on endlessly, no matter what I did to make them go by faster. Nothing distracted me from my heartache for long. Not even fighting in the arena.

"You've lost your focus," my uncle Kisk said in disapproval as I sat in the anteroom waiting for my wounds to heal, which happened rapidly enough that I didn't require the services of the healers that worked over the other fallen combatants.

He crossed his scaled arms over his furry chest, his brow furrowed with genuine concern beneath his spiral horns, despite the gruff tone of his voice. "You aren't fit to be in the arena when you're distracted like this. We want fair fights out there, not beatings."

I shrugged, wincing in pain even as my lacerations knitted together. "He was a better fighter than me."

Kisk snorted in disbelief. "I've seen you take down more skilled fighters than that one. You should have held your own, at least. Instead, you went down like you were throwing the fight." He regarded me with goatlike eyes. "All this moping over a female who is unworthy of you serves no purpose."

I glared at him, despite the fact that I respected him and looked up to him. "What if Aunt Alice had betrayed you? How would *you* feel?" My tone bordered on offensive, and Kisk had pummeled far larger males than me for speaking to him in such a way.

He growled, the sound rumbling from his chest. "Do not bring your aunt into this, youngling. The female you chose did not deserve you, and you learned that early enough to avoid bringing her to this world and finding out the hard way that she doesn't love you enough to remain."

Frustrated with this conversation, and oddly angry at Kisk for criticizing Gabby, I shot to my feet, standing eye to eye with him. "I don't need this right now!"

"Then leave," he snarled. "Do not return to my arena until you are capable of fighting again."

Hurt by the dismissal, I scowled and walked away from him, my claudas twitching with my anger.

"Vincent," he said, causing me to pause, his tone softer than before. "I do this for your own good. I don't want to see you getting hurt out there because you can't focus."

I kept my back turned to him but bowed my head in shame at my disrespectful behavior towards my uncle. "I know."

He didn't say anything else, so I continued on my way, leaving the arena behind without another word.

As I walked through Old Market, which surrounded the

arena and had been the very first marketplace in New Omni, blind to all the goods spread out like a treasure hoard on either side of me, I heard a familiar voice call my name. My jaw tightened and I sped up my steps, seeking a convenient alley to duck into.

"Bro!" Alex called, and his voice sounded closer. "Hold up, Vin! I want to talk to you."

I made a quick turn at the nearest corner, not paying any attention to where I was going, and nearly slammed into Sherakeren. His telekinetic ability froze me in place to keep that impact from happening.

Since when do you flee from your brothers?

His voice seemed intrusive in my head, and I scowled at him. "Use your outside voice, Eren," I snapped.

He shrugged, his telepathy releasing me. "My apologies, brother." He studied me with his unnerving black eyes, so much like gray-father's, although his other features appeared human. All but his three-fingered hands and three-toed feet.

"You know you can't go on like this," he said gently, even as Alex caught up to us.

My clutch-mate slapped me on the shoulder hard enough to sting, a broad grin on his face that revealed his fangs. "Sherak always knows how to find you, bro."

I crossed my arms over my chest, my claudas twitching beneath them. "Maybe I don't want to be found."

Alex snorted. "When has that ever stopped us?"

I rolled my eyes, growling in irritation. "I dream of the day when my own siblings take my feelings into consideration."

"It is your feelings that I am most concerned about, Vincent," Sherakeren said. "You haven't been the same since you returned."

"You *know* why!" I spread my arms wide, my claudas spreading as well. "Gabriella! I thought she was the one, but she betrayed me for her loser ex-boyfriend."

Maybe I didn't have a soul mate. I couldn't imagine ever feeling as strongly for another female as I had for Gabby. I'd been so drawn to her that I couldn't think about being with anyone else. I still couldn't, even after what she did. That was one reason I hadn't bothered to remain in her world, seeking another female who could make me feel even half as blissful in her company as Gabby had. I knew I would never find one.

"You should have torn that worthless male to shreds," Alex said dismissively, as if that was something I could do while hiding in another dimension.

"It was Gabby who betrayed me." I *had* wanted to rip Charles to shreds, but not more than I wanted to flee the pain the sight of Gabby caused me once I realized the extent of her treachery.

I'd wanted to flee so badly that I'd gone straight to the anchor and activated it, leaving that world behind for good.

Without Gabby.

"Maybe you were wrong about her intentions," Sherakeren suggested, his tone thoughtful as he regarded me.

"Yeah, what Sherak said." Alex clapped a hand to my shoulder. "You do tend to jump to conclusions, bro."

"Impulsive." Sherakeren nodded his head, his long, black hair pulled back in a neat ponytail as usual. I often wondered why he bothered to let it grow to the middle of his back when he never allowed a stray strand to break free.

I jerked my shoulder away from Alex's grip. "What other conclusion could there be when her loser ex knew that I wasn't human. Something Gabby only discovered after I'd brought her into my home and trusted her with my secret."

Sherakeren shrugged. "I cannot know without reading her mind, but you did not even give her the chance to explain. That was unwise."

"No," I flicked my claudas in irritation, "it was *wise* to leave as soon as possible, before that scrawny, worthless blood bag of a male went to the authorities and had them asking dangerous questions about me."

"You were not concerned about discovery when you activated the anchor in emergency mode, which poses a far greater risk than waiting for it to cycle to safe mode," Sherakeren said in a tone that reminded me I couldn't ever lie to him.

"What is this, a family reunion?" another familiar voice piped up. "Why am I never invited to these things?"

I cringed at the sound of that voice. Then I sighed heavily as I heard Samuel's chuckle at my sister's question.

Alex and I turned to see my siblings standing behind us at the mouth of the alleyway. Little Lily stood beside Samuel, her three-fingered hand clasped in his talons. Ria stood on the other side of him, just beyond the arc of his raven black feathered wing, one hand propped on her hip, her other hand resting on the sword that she always wore, despite our blood-father's refusal to let her battle anything more powerful than the other combative females in New Omni.

Lily broke away from Samuel to come to me, placing her hand on my forearm.

I don't like when you're sad, Vinnie. Her little voice in my head felt less intrusive than Sherakeren's.

She looked up at me with enigmatic black eyes, her silvery skin, eye shape, small, barely-there nose, and thinner lips closer to gray-father's than to my mother's appearance.

I knelt to bring us closer to eye-level, though she didn't need it to read my expressions, since she was learning how to read thoughts very well. "I know, sweetie. I'll stop being sad soon. I promise."

She shook her head, looking far older than her six years. "You don't believe that," she said aloud, her narrow lips pulling into a small frown. "You will miss Gabby forever. You should go back and get her."

Sam made a trilling sound in his throat that made him

sound a lot like wing-father despite his lack of a beak, stepping forward to reclaim Lily's hand. "Lily, what did mother say about intruding on someone else's private mind-space?"

She turned to look up at Sam, attempting to school her features to look contrite, her eyes wide and innocent. "She says don't do it?" she asked as if she wasn't sure of the answer.

She's a menace, Sherakeren said in my head, but I detected the amusement in his mental voice.

I chuckled, cheered by their interaction despite myself. It wasn't the distraction I was hoping for, but once in a while, my siblings came through for me.

"Vin," Ria brushed past Sam and Lily to approach me, "let's go back to that dimension and grab the girl. She'll come around once we get her here." She regarded me with a thoughtful expression. "I mean, you're not exactly the biggest prize in the game, but she's only human anyway, so beggars can't be choosers."

Alex laughed aloud as I growled at my "loving" sister. "Better not let Mom hear you say such condescending things about humans," I snapped, the threat that she *would* hear about it most definitely implied in my tone.

Ria shrugged. Now an adult, she didn't fear being grounded anymore, and she was an impetuous, fiery female who clashed frequently with our mother, because she was desperate to strike off on her own and write her own legend to rival that of our mother's. I had to admit that Evie's shadow would be a deep one to stand in. Only gray-father had a more impressive reputation in New Omni, but he wasn't nearly as beloved by the people as Evie was.

"Let's go *get* her," she said instead of responding to my threat. She gestured to Sherak. "'Rak can get NEX to open the portal without Gray Daddy finding out until it's too late to stop us. We'll go there, snatch her up, bind her so she can't escape, and then bring her back here before anyone's the wiser." She glanced at Sherak. "NEX will keep our secret. As long as 'Rak asks it to."

I glanced at my eldest brother, and he avoided meeting my eyes. "I won't be a party to this, Ria," he said in a chilly tone that he rarely used with family.

"You can't conceal when the Nexus opens," Sam interjected in a tone that implied he thought her suggestion was as ridiculous as I did.

"'Rak says you can." She smirked at our brother.

His face blanked of all expression, which was a warning sign for anyone with sense. My sister tended to lack that. "What I *said* was that NEX had upgraded the Nexus generator to decrease the energy release when it opens so it would be undetectable in *anchored* dimensions. *Not* in this one. The ancilla will still detect it."

Ria's smile didn't fade as she returned her focus to me. "The mother tree will help us, Vin! She'll keep what we're doing from Daddy until we have your female in hand and back here in the Fall. She *loves* a good love story, and you have always been her favorite, so she'll want to see you get a happy ending to yours."

Alex huffed, his claudas flicking outwards. "Pavdan is her favorite, which should be obvious."

Ria rolled her eyes, then gestured to herself and the rest of us. "I meant her favorite of *our* family, you brainless nit."

I didn't bother to remind her that Pavdan was part of "our family" just like our aunts and uncles, because she was referring specifically to Evie's children, and we all understood that. I regarded my brothers and sisters, noting how eager they were to help me, even if some of their plans were terrible.

I had been so focused on my own troubles with romance that I hadn't stopped to consider what was going on with the rest of my family.

Thus far, our generation had not been lucky in searching for love, and for my siblings' sakes, I hoped that would change.

Poor Friak hadn't returned from his quest for his "spark" in years, and my aunt waited desperately for word of his fate, but even NEX struggled to track him through the dimension he was in. It was the one where gray-father's people proliferated—his home dimension as well as the dimension where my aunts and mother came from, though all they had known when they were in their own dimension was Earth, whereas gray-father had traveled the galaxy when he was there. The other Lu'sians posed a greater threat of discovering the Nexus anchors because of their knowledge and technology. Gray-father didn't want them to learn about NEX. He feared they would try to use that knowledge in their own dimension to make their own Nexus.

There were many powerful beings in that dimension, and I feared that Friak had fallen afoul of one of them and that was why he hadn't returned with his spark.

Other than him, I was the first to really go in search of a mate. Alex had only ever expressed a desire for an entire nest of Fayi females to keep him sated. Ria was... well, *Ria*, and therefore would sorely test any male foolish enough to sniff around her. Samuel was "too young" to find a mate, according to my mother, though Sam would probably beg to differ, but he'd said he was content to wait until his Veraza training was complete before seeking out his bride.

Lily, Anunakeren, Nathan, Mikey, and Daria were all still children. Aunt Lauren and Uncle Asterius's youngest, Asterion, was only a teenager, his horns still growing in, as were Sekhmet, Sobeka, and Iyaren Junior. Only Omni, Pavdan, Alastor, and Sherakeren were old enough to truly start looking, other than myself and my clutch siblings.

Alastor hadn't yet expressed a desire to find a mate, though he was popular among the unmated females in New Omni, but he had only just turned eighteen.

Omni was unpredictable and often unreadable. I had no idea what he would decide to do when it came to finding love—or if he would even bother. He spent most of his time in the most dangerous parts of the Fall, seeking battles in order to prove himself the strongest warrior in this dimension or any other. Aunt Alice had learned to temper her concern for him, knowing it would change nothing. I still saw the strain her worry for her sons put on her, as well as on my uncles.

Sherakeren was—

Not interested in seeking a mate at this time, his voice said inside my mind.

I glanced at him, realizing he'd read my thoughts about what my kin were doing about their own love lives.

First, Friak's quest is a disaster that leaves us with no news of his fate, and now, my own quest has failed. I sent the thought rather than speaking it aloud. *Is there any hope for us to find the kind of love our parents enjoy, brother?*

Sherakeren sometimes had visions of the future, though he had not learned how to control them or guide them as his sire did. Even gray-father couldn't tell us everything that would come to pass.

He shrugged, his expression solemn as my other siblings got into an argument about the best way to sneak back into Gabby's dimension and kidnap her to drag her through the anchor portal without being stopped by gray-father.

Only Lily watched us curiously, her little head cocked to one side, her black hair tied in short pigtails that stuck out on either side of her teardrop shaped face.

I don't understand the ways of love, Sherakeren said after a long pause that I assumed he used to consider my question. *I don't think I inherited the desire for it from my human blood. I am more like my father in that regard.* His expression softened. *Before he met our mother, of course.*

My own sire hadn't understood the ways of love either, but he'd certainly proved capable of it when he met my mother and their keys activated, drawing them together and eventually binding them with an unshakable loyalty and devotion that few people, even in New Omni, got to enjoy.

I had been reared on tales of legendary love affairs, and I had seen the proof of them with my own young, impressionable eyes. I'd believed in them and had faith that I would one day find my soul mate the way my parents had found theirs.

But gray-father always said that not all paths lead to a happy ending. Friak's path might even be the proof of that, though Aunt Alice would never give up hope that he would return.

Nor will I, Sherakeren said, his mental voice tinged by the grief he felt at the disappearance of his cousin. They'd had a closer relationship than any of the other children in the family, and they were more like brothers than cousins. *NEX continues to search tirelessly for him. I won't give up on finding him again, even if it is dangerous to look into that dimension.*

Does gray-father know that you use NEX for this? That you take the risks you're taking?

Sherak shrugged, his expression pulling tight. *My sire doesn't know everything, even though he thinks he can predict life like it isn't constantly changing. NEX has learned to circumvent some of his controls and conceal its actions from him.*

Alarm widened my eyes as I stared at Sherak, the argument going on between my other siblings devolving into noise with my distraction. *Eren, gray-father needs to know this! NEX cannot be allowed to operate autonomously!*

I have it under control. It cannot conceal its actions from me. Sherak's mental voice held the sharpness of irritation and a darker tone I didn't want to acknowledge.

My brother's words and tone deeply disturbed me as I feared something underlay them, some secret that could spell catastrophe for our dimension. NEX wasn't something anyone should toy with—for any reason. My brother thought NEX could find Friak and bring him home, and he was likely obsessed with that goal. Perhaps to the point that even he might act rashly, despite his normally calm and logical demeanor.

"So, it's decided then!" Ria grabbed my arm to get my attention.

I turned my head towards her, my gaze still fixed on Sherakeren for a moment longer before I reluctantly let the subject of NEX drop.

"What's decided?" I asked impatiently as Ria smirked up at me.

She looked almost completely human save for her fangs and her pointed ears. She didn't have claudas, much to her frustration. Her eyes were the same color as my mother's, as was her hair. Only Alex had inherited the Fayi-white hair of our sire.

"We're going to abduct Gabby and bring her back here, so you'll stop moping around all day and maybe be a little less boring for once."

"You will do no such thing!" I said, only feeling a little twinge of panic at the suggestion, because surely our elders would stop such nonsense before the plan ever got off the ground.

There was no way the mother tree would allow the portal to open without informing gray-father. That was even if my idiot clutch siblings could convince Sherakeren to secretly activate the Nexus generator, which would mean NEX would be in on the secret—a dangerous prospect for sure. Sherak was far too intelligent for that.

I glanced at Sherak, because he didn't comment when I had

the thought, and I knew he had to still be reading my mind. He smirked at my questioning expression.

"That's an insane plan," he said aloud to my siblings, causing me to sag in relief.

"Good to know one of my siblings still has some sense." I smiled triumphantly at Ria and Alex.

"Hey, *I* told them it was a bad idea," Samuel insisted, his wings spreading briefly before folding tightly against his back again.

"I think it's a good idea," Lily said with big, liquid eyes that served her better than her telekinetics to convince others to give her whatever she wanted.

Sherak was right. The child was a menace. Far too cute for anyone else's good.

"You're six," I said patiently. "You don't understand how this world works, nor any other. Especially Gabby's world. You can't just pop in there and snatch up a human and then disappear again. All those actions have consequences and there are a lot of authorities in that dimension who have weapons that you can't always defend against."

I slashed my hand through the air, my claudas snapping open to reinforce the gesture. "No more talk of going to fetch Gabby. Besides, she betrayed me. What even makes you think I would ever want to see her again?"

They all looked at me with the same expression, as if they could read my mind as easily as Lily and Sherak could.

23

Gabby

Life went on for me and Valerie, but it felt like it had lost all its flavor. Not that there had been much of that to begin with for me. My time with Vincent had shown me how good life could be, how exciting, how happy, and made me realize what I'd been missing for my entire life before him.

I now measured my time as B.V. and A.V. Before Vincent, and After Vincent.

Then he'd left me, and I had to assume he'd gone back to his home dimension, because his house had been rented to someone new, and I never saw the Chevelle around town again. Valerie also never saw him come back into the station.

He was gone from my life for good, and I would never be as happy as I had been with him.

As summer dragged on, the heat and humidity punishing, I moved back into Val's place. It was good to have a roomie again, especially after the loneliness of my empty apartment began to weigh heavily on me. I spent most of my nights crying into my pillow, my stomach aching from the feeling of having lost something life changing.

Poor Valerie wasn't doing much better. Ben had tried to make up with her, but she couldn't forgive his betrayal, and I didn't blame her. I'd been there. I'd forgiven. And I had paid the price for it by being betrayed all over again. Maybe there were people who could cheat once on a person and then realize what a terrible mistake they'd made, but the way I saw it, if Ben didn't respect Valerie enough to remain faithful to her the first time, why would he respect her more after she took him back.

Of course, I didn't say this to Val. I didn't want to be the one to suggest what she should do about Ben. It needed to be her decision, and she'd made it, possibly coming to the same conclusion I had. Or maybe just unable to ever see him naked again without picturing him going at it with another woman on her bed.

Charles tried to contact me a few times, but I blocked him on my phone and all my social media. I wanted nothing to do with him. I knew he was only trying to use me, and I'd finally gotten a backbone and wouldn't tolerate it anymore. I knew now what it felt like to be desired for myself and not for what I could give someone.

I would never again settle for anything less.

That probably meant I would remain forever alone, because no human man could ever live up to Vincent. It wouldn't even be fair to try to date because I would always compare the person I was with to an impossible dream I'd had for far too brief a time.

In fact, sometimes I wondered if it wasn't all an elaborate, lucid dream. As time went on, I started to fear it had been, though Valerie reassured me that Vincent had been very real and that everything up until I left the party with him had happened just the way I remembered it. Charles had also verified it was real, though unknowingly. He'd asked me where my "freak lover boy, Vincent" went in one of his texts before I'd blocked his number.

My text messages also still showed that I'd sent those fateful messages to Charles. The ones that had ruined my life just when it had finally started to get good.

I went through my own personal transformation though, making new resolutions about how I would treat myself from now on. It was time to love myself enough not to ever accept someone like Charles into my life. It was time to open up to opportunities to make friends by talking to strangers once in a while, and it was time to stop worrying so much about what those strangers might think of me.

Like Valerie said, I was quirky. An oddball. Strange, but in her words, "in the best possible way."

I had let too many people bully me into resenting that weirdness in myself. Now, I embraced it.

I got a new job as an office manager that paid significantly more than the apartment management job. Though it could be boring, I made some friends by allowing myself to relax and accept that they were genuinely interested in talking to me when they did, and not just looking to get something from me or look for an opportunity to make fun of me.

Valerie, on the other hand, struggled for the first time since I've known her when it came to socializing. She started spending all her time outside of managing the gas station drinking. I would come home to find her passed out, despite it being only five pm. She would drink herself to sleep at night, then wake up and start drinking again.

She had no interest in any of her vast friends' list anymore. She said she couldn't bear to talk to people who knew both her and Ben—and the woman he'd cheated on her with. That made up the majority of her friends.

I worried about Valerie as summer moved into fall, and though it provided a distraction from my sadness over losing

Vincent, it wasn't a welcome one. I wasn't certain how to reach her. Ben's betrayal had hit her harder than even I could have predicted. Not only was her heart broken, but her faith in herself was gone. Her life was falling apart around her, and I was the only one there to help her keep the pieces together.

Sometimes, I think she hated me for that, but if I hadn't lived with her, she would have been unable to pay the bills. Especially when she lost her job at the gas station after one too many call-ins because of her hangovers, and she sank deeper into despair. A gas station manager hadn't been the kind of job her family had expected her to have anyway, she'd bemoan. She was supposed to be using the graphic design degree she'd earned after a very expensive four years in college. She was supposed to be living the life she'd pretended to be living for her parents' sake.

My focus on Valerie allowed me to get through each day, but those days dragged on endlessly, and I felt the struggle weighing on me without anyone to turn to. I kept having the stray thought that Vincent would have helped me pull Valerie out of the terrible spiral she'd fallen into.

Then I remembered that Vincent hadn't even waited around long enough to give me a chance to explain myself.

It was at that point that my sadness over losing him turned into anger directed at him for being so damned impatient and too stubborn to stick around and listen to my side of the story. If he had truly cared about me the way he said he did, he should have stuck around long enough for me to explain. After all, he'd wanted me to literally give up everything to follow him to another dimension, never to return again, after *one* freaking date! I had even been considering it, too. Then he couldn't have even the ounce of courtesy to give me a chance to apologize for my screw-up?

He may have been perfect in many ways, but his abandonment of me over one simple misunderstanding was proof of one of those flaws he had insisted he possessed. The worst part about it was that his flaw had kept us from being together, and I knew we could have been happy together, if he had only given things a chance.

As fall continued into winter and the holiday season loomed, I managed to sober Valerie up a little. At least long enough for her to get a new job managing a retail store. I hoped she would be too busy during the Christmas shopping rush to get wasted every night.

She still avoided her old friends, but Valerie couldn't remain indifferent to people for long once she got around them. She was back to chatting with everyone she met during her work, and she was already making a new circle of friends, though she told me I would always be her bestie.

My own new circle of friends had taken to coming over and hanging out with us, so we ended up having a nice little group to celebrate on Christmas Eve, and the white elephant gift exchange brought lots of much needed levity.

Still, even with the laughter and the jokes and the copious egg nog—which Val was still too fond of—I couldn't shake the lingering bit of depression at the thought of what it could have been like if Vincent was here. Nor could I stop wondering what the holidays must be like in his home dimension.

He'd said something about orgies!

At night, I dreamt of a sentient forest of trees, and me strolling through it, talking to each one fondly as if they were all my best buddies. Vincent would be at my side, shirtless, his claws spreading open as he gestured at something. I never could see what though. Everything in that surreal forest was blurred like it was seen through petroleum jelly smeared over a camera lens.

On Christmas day, I called my mother like a dutiful daughter. I listened to her bitch at me for half an hour, then I made an excuse to get off the phone. My calls to her were less frequent this year than ever before, and the saddest part about that was that she didn't seem to care. She had her own life, her own friends, and a new fiancé with adult children of his own whom she doted on, if her words were any indication.

She'd demanded I attend their wedding in February—a Valentine's Day wedding—and I'd reluctantly agreed, wondering who I would take with me as my plus one. She didn't want me in the wedding party, of course. Her fiancé's daughters would have that honor, because, as my mother insisted on pointing out, they had the right "look" for her wedding photos. In other words, they were all blond and beautiful and built like fashion models.

I didn't need her approval anymore, but I felt obligated simply because I was her daughter to continue to try to earn it. Just like Val tried so hard to live up to her family's high expectations that she'd crashed and burned and now struggled to rise again.

Not everything had changed for us, despite our New Year's resolutions.

With another New Year rapidly approaching, Val and I decided not to throw a party at our own apartment, but to go to a big bash held at a local hotel as each other's date, since she couldn't bring herself to trust another man enough to date seriously after Ben's betrayal, and the handful of dates I'd gone on over the last year had all ended without anything but a polite thank you and goodbye, even when the men had been kind and interesting.

They just couldn't compare to Vincent, and I didn't want to lead anyone on. After those failed attempts to move on, I regretted even attempting to date until I got over this obsession with a guy I had only had a single date with—the most fascinating man I had ever had the good fortune to meet.

On New Year's Eve, I came out of my room in a t-shirt that said, "I'm ready to drop the ball," and a pair of fitted jeans that hugged my toned lower body. The gym had been my refuge over the last year, allowing me to burn off my restless energy when nothing else seemed to work, and the payoff had been an even fitter physique than I'd had when I'd met Vincent. The extra skin that hung on me after losing even more weight had only gotten worse, but a body lift procedure was out of my price range for the time being. I was saving for it though, as a gift to myself.

Valerie was looking fluffier than she had last year, but the extra weight looked good on her. The aged appearance her face had taken on from heavy drinking and extended depression did not, and I hated to see how much Ben's betrayal had ravaged her. I recalled when I had first caught Charles cheating being a very difficult time for me too, and could see myself having fallen into the same spiral she did if I had turned to alcohol or drugs to escape the pain.

Now, it wasn't even about Ben anymore. She was dealing with an addiction that had honestly begun even when she and Ben were supposedly happy. Ben himself was doing even worse when it came to alcohol abuse, from the rumors I'd heard through the grapevine.

Val wore a sparkly golden dress in the same cocktail style I'd worn last New Year's Eve, and the sight of it made me wistful for what could have been. She had layered on the makeup and barely looked recognizable, her dark eyes surrounded by long, thick fake lashes, her long, wavy hair flowing loose around her shoulders. She tottered on six-inch heels, and the way she swayed a bit told me she had started the party early.

"That's what you're wearing?" she said in surprise when she saw my outfit and my simple ponytail and clean face. "No makeup either?" She ran her hands down the sequined material of her dress self-consciously. "Now I feel overdressed."

I smiled and shook my head, my tight, mud-colored curls bouncing with the motion, giving her an admiring look.

"You're beautiful, V, and trust me, I'm pretty sure you're dressed properly for this party. They'll probably think I'm a member of the janitorial staff at the venue." I shrugged, glancing down at my casual wear. "I just didn't feel like getting all dolled up this time around. I want to ring in the New Year looking the way I do every day, because Gabby's New Year's Resolution number one for this upcoming year is to love Gabby, just the way she is."

Val's smile looked a little watery. "I didn't make any resolutions yet. I feel guilty."

I patted her on the shoulder. "Don't worry, girl. We can come up with some together, if you'd like."

She nodded, eyeing me with uncertainty. "I want to quit drinking, Gabs. I've tried so many times this year, but it always seems too hard, and then I fail, and then I hate myself for failing at yet another thing in my life, and that makes me just want another drink!"

I sucked in a deep breath, wondering what the best way to address this topic would be. I had gone to AA meetings with Val, but she could never stick with the program. I had read a bunch of pamphlets and self-help books on dealing with addiction. I had done plenty of research.

Yet the best I could say was, "I'll help you, V. We'll take it one day at a time. Hell, we'll take it one *hour* at a time if we have to."

I knew what it was like to turn to something for comfort that ultimately ended up hurting me. I had used food the way Valerie was using alcohol. It had been a struggle to break out of the cycle of overeating, then hating myself for overeating, then eating again because I felt bad, and food had become the only thing that made me feel any better.

If I could break what had been a lifelong habit for me, then I had to believe me and Val could work through this together.

She smiled hesitantly at me, blinking her false lashes

rapidly as her eyes sheened with unshed tears. "Okay, from now on, I'm only drinking virgin drinks!"

"That sounds like a plan, V. Getting a head start on your New Year's resolution makes it more likely to succeed."

I could see the doubt in her eyes, but she put on a brave smile, and so did I. Then she tucked her arm into mine and we headed towards the door. "C'mon, my date, it's time to party!"

When we reached the venue, vehicles of every make and model packed the parking lot, and I had to park Phoebe in a neighboring lot near a sketchy alleyway that made both Valerie and me nervous. Still, I had no choice other than to just abandon the idea of attending this party. Since Val and I were meeting our friends here, we didn't want to leave just because it felt like eyes watched us from the deep shadows of the alley.

I had my bear spray, and this time, I was carrying a tote bag of a purse with a Chupacabra sucking the blood of a goat painted on it, rather than a tiny clutch.

Val and I climbed out of Phoebe and looked around at the nearly empty parking lot, wondering if more cars would be forced into this overflow parking as the night went on. We still had several hours before the ball dropped.

We made our way to the venue, arm in arm, talking and laughing as if we didn't have a care in the world, even though we both covered up our own heavy burdens.

24

Gabby

Valerie was actually doing it! She hadn't drunk a single alcoholic beverage since we got to the party. I had been watching her like a hawk the entire time, despite my gaggle of friends surrounding me as they discussed the past year and their resolutions for the future.

Maybe she would succeed this time. I wanted to have faith that she'd turned a corner, but I would remain vigilant, because she could backslide again. We'd been here before.

I got distracted by one of my coworkers and had turned to listen to her chatting about work for a few minutes when I heard one of my other friends suddenly whistle.

"Who is that hottie talking to Val?" she said as I shifted my attention to her.

My gaze returned to Val to find her smiling at a tall, very attractive man with unusual platinum blond hair, cropped short on the sides and left longer on the top so the silky bangs framed his handsome face.

Since they stood a distance away in the crowd, I couldn't get the best look at his features, but he had a strong and nearly flawless profile.

It reminded me of someone, but my coworker continued to speak, distracting me.

"She looks like she's smitten," she said, admiring the large, bulky shape of the man, who wore a tuxedo that seemed well fitted even on his heavier frame. "Can't say I blame her. Where did she even find that guy? I searched this entire crowd when we arrived and didn't see him anywhere." She toyed with her thick braid that lay over one shoulder. "I don't think I would have missed *him*."

"Girl, you are engaged," my other friend said as I returned my gaze to the crowd, seeking out Val and the mystery man again.

"Doesn't mean I can't enjoy the scenery."

Both of my friends laughed at that while I continued to look for them in the crush of a crowd.

Something about him niggled at my memory, but I couldn't figure out what it was that was bothering me. Then I realized I couldn't see either of them anymore and alarm filled me, though there was no real reason why it should, since we were in a very public and crowded place. It wasn't like he could just drag her off and axe-murder her.

Then it hit me.

The man's profile had not only looked nearly flawless, but also familiar. Familiar enough to be related to another man whose profile I had admired, right around this very time last year.

"Oh, *hell* no!" I said, pushing out of the circle of my friends to head towards where I had last seen Val.

Concern warred with excitement at the thought that Vincent might have returned to this dimension with his brother. The man *had* to be his brother. The one he called Alex.

I remember Vincent telling me had the same white hair as their father, and this man was around Vincent's age. His tuxedo also concealed a bulky frame, with a waist on the thicker side. A waist that could have bound claws around it.

Why was a man who was potentially Vincent's brother chatting with Valerie?

And where the hell did they go? I wondered as I scanned the crowd, growing more worried than merely concerned now as I didn't see Valerie anywhere.

I shoved unceremoniously through the crowd, seeking some sign of Valerie's sequined form. Then I saw her heading out the door with him, hanging on his arm as though they were old friends. The way she leaned into him as if she needed his help to hold her up made my heart sink. Maybe she'd been sneaking drinks when I wasn't looking, because she certainly appeared to be under the influence.

I had to stop them! I also had to speak to Alex and find out if Vincent was here too. I needed to know why the heck Alex had shown up out of the blue on New Year's Eve to lure Valerie out of this party.

It took too long to make it to the door, and it seemed like everyone and their brother who wasn't an alien hybrid from a parallel dimension made it their personal mission to get in my way. When I had finally woven my way through the milling partiers, ignoring the curious calls from my friends at my back, I found that Valerie and Alex had already left the building.

I rushed outside, looking around and seeing no sign of them. I called Valerie's name, running further away from the hotel where the party was taking place, then down the wide marble steps, nearly knocking into a few stragglers still making their way into the venue.

"Valerie?" I called out again and again.

I saw no sign of her in the hotel parking lot, nor any sign of the difficult to miss white-haired head of her companion. I pulled out my phone and texted her, demanding she contact me as soon as she saw the text and let me know just where the heck she was going without letting me know that she was even leaving the party.

My tote bag that I had refused to surrender at the coat-check vibrated, and I groaned as I reached inside it and pulled out Val's little clutch purse, her phone still inside it.

Damn it! I'd offered to hold onto it for her so she wouldn't have to check it at the door or risk losing it during the party. I sighed and rubbed my forehead as I tossed my own phone into my tote along with her clutch.

Maybe I was wrong and that wasn't Alex. Maybe it was just some cute guy Valerie had found at the party and decided to go home with. Regardless of what the case might be, I needed to stop her from doing something she might later regret. If she was inebriated, she didn't have her full faculties about her, and who knew how a strange man might take advantage of that. If she still wanted to be with this guy when she was sober, that was one thing, but I'd be damned if I'd let her stumble drunkenly into a situation that she wouldn't be happy about in the morning.

I felt guilty now that I'd let her stray so far from me in the crowd. I'd mistakenly believed she was keeping her resolution, and it wasn't like she was a child, but I knew she had a problem. I'd allowed myself to get distracted while poor Val was surrounded by temptation. Hell, the wait staff were bringing around trays of champagne constantly. That would be difficult for her to resist. For all I know, she could have snagged a few and threw them back whenever my attention was distracted.

We probably shouldn't have even come to this party, but neither of us thought sitting at home alone in our jammies to ring in the New Year would be the best idea. Now, given her disappearance on the arm of a stranger—potentially an interdimensional one—staying home and watching a documentary about the mantis shrimp and pigging out on Chinese food sounded like the best possible way to ring in the New Year.

"Valerie!"

I wandered all around the parking lot, even looking inside all the cars in case the man had taken her outside to get in a quickie in the back seat of his vehicle. I clutched my tote, wondering if I would need the bear spray inside it to free Val from the clutches of the mystery man.

It had to be Alex. No human man would have a profile that perfect. But Vincent did.

"Val, where are you, girl?" I said aloud, peeking into the backseat of a BMW. "I need to have a chat with you about your new friend!"

I was growing desperate as my searching turned up nothing. I returned to the hotel and walked around the entire huge building, raced around the parklike grounds, and then returned hopelessly to the parking lot.

Finally, I made my way to Phoebe, planning to drive around the area in the hopes of spotting Valerie with the stranger, even though I didn't have much hope of finding her like that. I didn't know what else to do until she contacted me.

As I left the hotel parking lot and crossed the street to the overflow parking, fireworks went off overhead, signaling the new year. I shook my head, realizing that I had once again missed the ball dropping.

As I neared my car, I heard a feminine voice call my name from the alley.

"Val?" I rushed towards the alley, pulling my bear spray out of my tote. "You okay, girl?"

"Hi," a woman who was most definitely not Val said as she stepped from the shadows just as I reached the alley.

She was stunningly beautiful, but that wasn't what froze me in place with shock. She grinned at me, and two fangs framed her perfect, white teeth.

"This is gonna hurt," she said, "but I hope you'll forgive me when we're family."

Then she swung a fist that connected with a solid and agonizing thud against my jaw, the pain causing my fingers to go nerveless so the bear spray dropped back into my tote. My head rocked back, and I staggered backwards several steps.

"Wow, you're tougher than I expected," she said, following me with an anticipatory grin. "I really don't want to hurt you—too much. Even though you kinda deserve it after what you did to Vin." Then she swung her fist again and it connected with my eye.

This time, I blacked out as I went down.

25

Gabby

"I told you, *this* one says she knows Vin!" a deep male voice said as I struggled to open my eyes, my head aching and one side of my face throbbing. "She fits the description. Sparkly dress, overdone makeup, curvy body, long, wavy hair. You grabbed the wrong one, Ria! That one doesn't look at all like Vin's description."

I sensed someone moving closer to me where I lay on a hard floor that felt like concrete beneath my back.

"I don't know who this one is, but she's not the one we're looking for. Why did you beat her up anyway? You were supposed to drug her to knock her out."

"She hurt Vin," a female voice said, and I froze as I recognized it, my body trembling with fear that the crazy vampire bitch would hit me again if she realized I had regained consciousness. "I figured she deserved at least one or two little hurts in return."

"This quest is turning into a root tangle, Ria," the male

voice said in obvious frustration. "You should have listened to me and stayed hidden. I had everything under control. Now we have *two* humans who have seen us!"

I couldn't see anything because I kept my eyes closed, one of them helpfully swollen shut from what I could feel. Still, I suspected that the male's voice belonged to Alex, given the similarity of his accent to Vincent's.

Obviously, Ria was Vincent's sister. It figured I would be abducted by the two most mischievous of Vincent's siblings. Why couldn't I have encountered the nice one—Eren—instead.

"Just activate the anchor already, Lexie. I'll slap this one awake and verify she isn't the girl we're here for, then we'll take the other one."

I tensed as I heard the scrape of Ria's shoe moving closer to me, then sagged a little when Alex seemed to block her path.

"No, you little menace!" Alex snarled. "We're already in huge trouble here. You can't go beating on humans without leaving an impression! Besides, she already saw your fangs. She knows you're not human. We can't just leave her here, even if she isn't Gabby. She'll tell somebody. Somebody who might track down our trail and discover the anchor."

"Like anyone in this mundane dimension would believe her." Ria snorted in disdain.

Then I heard a slight scuffle as if she tried to push past her brother to attack me again. Thankfully, he seemed successful at stopping her.

"I'm telling you, Lex, this girl is the one, not that other girl! Let me prove it to you by asking her. Then we can leave the drugged one behind. You concealed *your* fangs, so she won't have anything unusual to describe other than that a human man took her from the party, even if the ridiculously clueless authorities in this world pulled their heads out of their waste holes long enough to believe a tale about a vampire."

"I'm not activating the anchor until we get this figured out, but we'll wait until one of them comes around on their own, Ria. No more hitting people!"

"Oh, like injecting humans with drugs is so much better?"

Ria did have a good point. I hoped Val was okay after getting a shot of alien sleep juice. These two seemed a bit incompetent, seeing as they couldn't even decide which one of us was the correct Gabby.

If Vincent had told them about me, which he must have, then he hadn't described me in enough detail for them to figure out whether it was me or Val they wanted. We didn't look that much alike in the face. Val had thinner lips and a completely different hair and eye color. Still, given the way she was dressed, maybe the confusion could be understood. I wondered how much Vincent had told his siblings about me.

I realized that I could save Val if I just let them know I was conscious and cleared up the confusion. I opened my one good eye, just as Alex cursed and Ria laughed.

"Too late, Lexie. Looks like NEX got impatient waiting for us to activate the anchor."

I saw a strange gyroscopic spinning device on a pedestal nearby, symbols flashing on the front of the pedestal in a wild display. Then it lit up with a blinding flash of light.

"We'll just take 'em both. 'Rak can wipe the memory of the wrong girl and send her back."

"Wait," I said weakly as Alex strode to Val and bent to grab her and Ria approached me. "I'm Gabby! Leave Valerie here!"

They didn't seem to hear me as a loud "whoosh" sound filled the concrete room we were in.

Ria did notice that I was conscious though and grinned, snatching me up as I struggled to rise into a sitting position.

"Vin is going to be so pissed when he realizes what we've done," she said in my ear as if she relished the thought of her brother's anger. "He'll get over it though, and then you can make him stop being such a miserable squirmer all the damned time!"

Then something sucked me and Ria through a portal, and it felt like being pulled by an irresistible, invisible force that I had never experienced before, though it felt a bit like a roller coaster plunge. My vision grew disoriented as I went from sitting up to falling backwards with Ria laughing in glee the whole way, her grip hard on my upper arms.

We passed through a huge ring of clouds in the sky that suddenly replaced the concrete room, though the portal we came through was only a tiny circle in comparison to the rest of the ring, which appeared to contain a huge, black void in its swirling cloud vortex center. Then I saw Alex holding onto Val as they passed through after us. Then flashing lights emanated from within the cloud ring, and Alex and Val suddenly disappeared out of thin air.

As I opened my mouth to scream, more lights flashed just as we began to fall faster, and my vision went black.

26

Vincent

The number of deadly areas in the Fall had decreased significantly—too significantly, in my opinion, at least aboveground. My mother would be angry to hear me speak such a thought aloud given how hard our families had worked to bring peace and safety to the Dead Fall, but then again, she was worried about me right now, so she probably wouldn't express that irritation towards me.

Now, she watched me closely whenever I was around her, her eyes pinched with worry and her lips tight with words I knew she wanted to express but wouldn't out of respect for my wish to never hear about or discuss Gabby again.

I knew she felt conflicted about the woman I had believed was my mate. She'd expressed outrage that Gabby had betrayed my secret, especially to another man she had a relationship with, but she was also concerned that Gabby had been the woman for me and had even suggested I was too quick to abandon that dimension, without first getting answers about why Gabby did what she did.

My mother feared that I didn't have the necessary "closure" and that was what was tearing me up inside to the point that I had joined my cousin Omni in seeking out the deadliest battles in the Fall, both of us growing frustrated at the dwindling opportunities to fight a truly challenging opponent.

Most of the deadliest beasts had fled underground as the ancilla forest spread along with the reclamation of the ruins to expand New Omni. The ancilla roots didn't run as deep as some of the tunnel havens of the monsters that had thus far avoided gray-father's sensors and spies.

In fact, the old "subway" tunnels of the city had been expanded even below the barrens, spreading away from the Dead Fall ruins like a contagion, creating a series of extremely dangerous "settlements" formed of scavengers and dissidents unwilling to live by the rules of New Omni, nor willing to leave this dimension to return to their own dimensions, for whatever personal reasons they might have.

As much as we craved a good battle, my cousin and I weren't foolish enough to enter the underground without an army at our backs. For now, gray-father forbid such a measure, saying that as long as the violent creatures remained underground and kept away from the city and its residents, he didn't want to start another war in the Dead Fall. His flesh worms did their best to keep an eye on those areas in case the creatures ever decided to foment an organized rebellion that would demand a forceful response.

Thus, we were relegated to fighting the occasional pocket of monstrous resistance or resilient predators that we could find aboveground, and those skirmishes didn't do enough to satisfy the bloodlust within us.

For my shapeshifting cousin, Omni, those battles were meant to prove his worth. For me, they were meant to distract me from the question that had wormed its way into my heart and soul. The question of why I couldn't forget Gabby, no matter how much I tried to turn the obsession I'd felt for her into hatred over her betrayal. I just couldn't do it, even though I constantly reminded myself of how she'd sold me out to her boyfriend.

It was also best to stay away from the city as much as possible. My mother grew more worried about my mental state as months passed, and I only seemed to grow sullener and more taciturn. I just couldn't hide my misery from my family. I had overheard her confessing to blood-father that I didn't even seem like the same person anymore.

All my family were growing worried and exhausted with what my "loving" sister Ria called "my moping." Gray-father was the only one who didn't make the pointless effort to distract me or talk me out of my misery. When I had asked him why he didn't worry like the others, he'd given me an unusually sad look and slowly shook his head.

"I *am* worried," he'd said. "You have a genetic key, and the human woman activated it with her own that matched. Leaving her behind holds severe consequences for you." His black eyes had then taken on a silvery sheen, which let me know he was seeking what he called the "flux," the shadows of the future that he could somehow view. "It also has consequences for our world, though I cannot see through the tsunami ahead to predict what those will be or when they will happen."

His words had bothered me the most, especially since they had confirmed that Gabby had been meant for me. It made her betrayal hurt even more.

I had grown tired of all their concerns. Tired of enduring their attempts to shake me out of my misery. Tired of seeing my mother's strain as her worry for me grew.

She had other worries to weigh on her as well. In fact, I shared at least one of her worries myself, and that concern was the first time I had been pulled out of the depression I'd fallen into since Gabby betrayed me and I returned to the Fall.

Gray-father had left our dimension for the first time since NEX had brought him and his crew here against their will. The AI had finally picked up Friak's trail, and Sherakeren had threatened to travel to the other dimension himself to retrieve his cousin. Since gray-father's objection to that fell on deaf ears, gray-father took it upon himself to bring Friak back, to keep my brother from doing something foolish and impulsive to reunite with our cousin.

After all, gray-father knew his home dimension better than anyone else and would know best how to navigate within it. Unlike the dimension where I had found Gabby, gray-father's old dimension was filled with powerful species capable of intergalactic travel and possessing technology almost as advanced as NEX itself. Gray-father's own species, the Lu'sians, had even learned to fold space-time using space stations in order to travel instantaneously across the galaxy. They likely weren't too far off from creating their own interdimensional portals, but gray-father didn't want to help them speed up that research by handing over any part of NEX, even an anchor. He knew the dangers of interdimensional portals, and the consequences of blindly opening them to uncharted dimensions. He had impressed that upon all of us while we were growing up.

NEX's ability to scan and navigate new dimensions was inexplicable and thus far even gray-father had not been able to replicate it.

Not long after he had left through the Nexus, NEX had lost track of both Friak and gray-father, and we were all feeling unnerved by its inability to detect them the way it detected beings in so many other dimensions. Something in that particular dimension interfered with NEX's astral scanning abilities.

It had been several weeks since gray-father had disappeared into his home dimension, and Sherak was going close to insane with worry over both his sire and his cousin now, and since his erratic emotions caused problems with his telekinesis, he spent most of his days in the lab with gray-father's inhibitor on to block his mental acuity from causing dangerous collateral damage to the rest of the family. He was even sleeping in there now.

My mother also seemed to be barely holding it together, and blood-father and wing-father spent most of their time with her, soothing her and reassuring her, though I could see the signs of worry in their expressions too.

All my siblings, even the youngest, were worked up about our father's disappearance, and my aunt and uncles were no better off. They had gained some hope for the return of their son when NEX found him again and gray-father had agreed to go after him. Now, they were despairing as if they had lost Friak all over again.

Perhaps their sadness over Friak's loss was another reason Omni spent so much time in the Fall rather than at home with his parents. I could understand the desire to escape the oppressive atmosphere of a household waiting for news of a loved one that never seemed to come. Though it might be selfish of us to want to get away from it all, we knew that our own problems and feelings did nothing to help the situation.

"Ah, if it isn't the whelp of the bloodsucker!" a harsh voice growled when I strolled past a broken ruin on the edge of the Fall, lost so deep in thought that I had foolishly ignored my surroundings and missed the presence of another creature.

I turned just in time to meet the charge of a massive male built like a tank and armed from head to toe with sapphires that sprouted from his flesh. When his body hit mine, those sapphire spears impacted my skin hard enough to impale it in several places.

I grunted in pain, my claudas spreading and slamming the tips home into his body as he tackled me, pumping venom into him reflexively, even though I knew it wouldn't work on this particular beast of a male.

Kuru had come to the Dead Fall during NEX's reign but had decided not to leave when gray-father gained control of the Nexus. He had remained in New Omni for some time, but eventually killed another male during a violent altercation. He'd been asked to leave, or more accurately, dragged out by my own sire, who had left him in pieces in the Fall when he'd fought to protest his exile.

Doshakeren had gifted the sapphires he'd taken from Kuru to my mother, and had some of them set in a ring that had become one of three intertwined wedding rings she always wore now.

Kuru had apparently survived his dismantling by my father, and now he wanted a little revenge. I had no doubt he'd tracked us since he recognized who I was.

He was tough. I would give him that. I didn't have my father's size and strength, my body not growing to the lengths his did when he was engorged on blood. At most, I could increase my height by a half foot, whereas my father's size, as far as we knew, could increase indefinitely, depending on how much blood he drank, though he never went beyond twelve feet, simply because he didn't have a need to drain the blood of so many living things to reach that point often.

Kuru stood at nearly eight feet to my seven-foot two-inch current height, and he outweighed me by several hundred pounds, much of it in a hard, crystalline form over a skin so thick and resistant that it might as well be stone.

To make matters more difficult, he was immune to my venom.

He jerked out of my claudas' hold and slammed me to the ground. Then he dropped his elbow onto my gut between my claudas, the spear of crystal on the end of it impaling my stomach.

I punched him repeatedly as he dug his crystal into my flesh, my body trying to repair the damage around it but unable to fully heal until I got the sapphire spear out of me.

A roar split the air that had Kuru looking up as a shadow fell over us. Then he smirked, the sunlight flashing on his sapphire-armored face right before Omni's winged form blotted out the sun. "Breathe your fire, beast," Kuru shouted, shaking his free hand in a fist at Omni. "You'll not burn my flesh." He looked down at me pinned beneath him. "But you will roast your companion."

Omni growled as his leathery wings kept him hovering overhead. Then he dove, his scaled body crashing into Kuru hard enough to knock him off me.

I struggled to my feet, pressing one hand to the gaping wound in my stomach so my blood wouldn't be wasted on the ground as my body healed. I made my way towards where Kuru and Omni wrestled, Omni's razor-sharp teeth snapping at Kuru's fist as he raised it to slam into Omni's horned head.

Fire wouldn't destroy or even slow Kuru down, just like my venom wouldn't. The only thing that could harm him was crushing force.

I sought a more effective weapon against Kuru to help my cousin out, though Omni was holding his own despite the impact of Kuru's crystal studded fists against Omni's scaled hide. Omni roared again, digging all four sets of his claws into the gemstones studding Kuru's stony flesh.

Kuru got his hands around Omni's serpentine neck, keeping Omni's teeth away from his face after a fierce bite broke off some sapphire from his cheek.

Finally, I spotted a column of concrete that I could lift and heaved it off the ground. Then I charged at Kuru. He heard me coming and turned his gaze away from Omni, his eyes widening as I lifted the column over my head, my gut still spilling my blood from the shrinking hole his elbow crystal had made.

"I need a sapphire for my mate's wedding ring," I snarled. Then I glanced at Omni, who pinned Kuru down with his weight, his tail wrapped around the stone man's body to constrain his struggles. "And I'm sure this dragon would prefer some of your 'flesh' for his hoard."

Kuru shouted in rage as I brought the column down on his head. Parts of the column broke away, along with chunks of sapphire. I brought it down again and again, paying little attention to my own weakening body as I slowly crushed the head of the screaming Kuru.

When he finally fell silent and stopped moving in Omni's relentless grip, I tossed the remnants of the column aside and collapsed on the ground beside Kuru's corpse. I heard Omni chuckle through my heavy panting. Then he uncoiled his tail from Kuru and folded his wings, his body shifting into a more bipedal form.

He regarded me with serpentine eyes as his tail flicked a chunk of sapphire in my direction from where it had fallen on the ground beside Kuru's destroyed face.

"For your mate, eh? You still haven't given up on her?"

I shrugged weakly, reaching for the sapphire that was nearly as large as my fist. "In my mind, yes. In my heart...." I turned the sapphire in my hand, imagining the set of jewelry I could make for Gabby from the gemstone.

Then I glanced at Omni, who still crouched on Kuru's corpse as if he really was claiming the gemstones for his hoard. I jerked my chin towards the fallen enemy. "What about you? You could create an entire jewelry store for your future mate? Any plans on looking for one?"

He laughed aloud, his sharp teeth gleaming in the sunlight. "After what you and my brother have been through? Are you kidding?" He shook his head, the shape closer to human now that his shift was nearly complete. "From what I've seen, all the quest for a mate does is bring misery." He narrowed his eyes as the scales melted from his face and golden fur replaced them. "Not just for the male, but for everyone who cares about him."

I sighed heavily, shifting with a grimace of pain from my stomach wound as I moved to stow the sapphire chunk in the pouch hanging from my belt. "Maybe you're right, Om. Maybe our generation is doomed to fail in our quest for love." I turned my gaze to the ruins bordering the wasteland called the barrens. "I wanted to find someone who could give me the kind of love and devotion our parents have for each other. I didn't realize it would be so difficult."

Omni laughed so hard he nearly fell off Kuru's body. "You didn't think it would be *difficult*? Have you not *heard* the stories our parents tell?" He leapt off Kuru, landing lightly on taloned feet. "That is why I told my brother he was a fool to go in search of a mate. He wasn't equipped for such a challenge." He shrugged feathered shoulders that rippled to fur, then scales, then back to feathers. "Who among us is? Even the mighty Gray was brought low in his quest for Aunt Evie. Who are we to think we are so much stronger than our fathers that our love would come easily?"

I regarded Omni closely, noting the flicker of grief in his expression rather than paying attention to his dismissive words about his brother.

Omni had confessed to me that he believed Friak dead, despite his mother's insistence that her son still lived. Naturally, he never told her that, knowing how difficult it was for Aunt Alice to accept the loss of her child. Then NEX had confirmed that Friak was alive, and Omni had regained hope, along with the rest of the family. Only now, he was wrestling with the dying of that hope all over again.

I searched for something to say that wouldn't bring more attention to the fact that Friak had been gone for years in our dimension, having spent an unknown amount of time in gray-father's home dimension. I opened my mouth to speak of Gabby instead, because the thought of her never strayed far from my mind, regardless of what other thoughts plagued it.

Above us, the ring of clouds surrounding the Nexus crackled briefly with energy that lit them up. Then it went dark again. If we hadn't both turned our attention to that gateway, we wouldn't have noticed the pinhole portal that opened in the dark void of a sky that always remained within the vortex of clouds when the portal was in standby mode.

More lights flashed in the ring, and those I recognized as coming from the teleportation drones that hovered within the cloud cover around the Nexus. Those drones teleported people who came through the Nexus directly to New Omni's welcome center, so they didn't have to fall to the ground like the victims of NEX used to.

I rose to my feet, clutching my gut with a low groan as my gaze remained fixed on the sky. "Did the Nexus just open?"

"That's what I saw." Omni's stance was tense as he also stared fixedly at the portal.

"You think it was gray-father?" I looked away from the portal long enough to meet his eyes.

I saw the brief flash of hope in them before he schooled his features into a blank mask. "Who else could it be? Only gray-father and Sherak are authorized to command NEX."

The portal was too far away for us to have recognized the figures that came through, but it hadn't been open long. "Let's get back to New Omni. We can hit one of father's nearby relays to teleport to the welcome center and see what's going on."

Omni's wings jutted from his back in a rending of flesh that sounded painful to me, but he swore he barely felt it anymore. "I'll fly us to the relay."

27

Vincent

We arrived at the welcome center to find it in chaos. Apparently, we weren't the only ones to notice the opening of the portal, even though it had been very brief. Brief enough that none but the mother tree might have noticed it if we weren't all on edge, constantly searching the sky for signs of the portal opening.

My mother and Aunt Alice were in the green room, the first stop for arrivals that lived up to its name by being a plant-filled paradise of a space, thanks to Chloro—the most expert of our plant experts in New Omni, being one himself.

Doshak and Veraza flanked my mother, one hand of each on her shoulders as if they held her back. Uncles Kisk, Iyaren, and Tak surrounded Alice, who leaned back into Iyaren's four-armed embrace, her face pale around eyes shadowed with worry, as Tak and Kisk held her hands.

If gray-father had returned, my family didn't seem in the least bit happy about it. My mother was hollering up a storm at someone. When we moved further into the green room, I saw that she was yelling at Sherak, Ria, and Alexander, and she appeared to be sharing her ire equally among my siblings.

"What did I miss?" I asked, startled by her obvious fury.

My mother rarely lost her temper with her children, even my idiot clutch mates, and I never saw her yell at Sherak, who would always know when she was upset even without her raising her voice. As they all turned to look in our direction, I asked the obvious question, not seeing any sign of gray-father or Friak.

"I saw the Nexus open. Did father return?"

Aunt Alice gasped and left the embrace of her mates to rush to Omni, holding her arms out to him. Though he found the atmosphere in his home often constricting, he didn't hesitate to hug his mother close as if he had missed her, his arms folding around her as he towered over her.

"Oh, Omni-kins!" she said in a tearful voice, "I worried about you! You need to come home more often to visit!"

"Yeah, Omni-*kins*," Ria said with a snicker.

Then she fell silent, and her grin faded as my mother glared at her, holding up a hand for her to be silent.

Omni ignored Ria as he usually did, looking up from his mother's face to greet his fathers'. "Friak?" he asked in a tone I could tell he wanted to be neutral, but I heard the hope in it.

Kisk shook his head slightly, as Tak lowered his. Iyaren joined Omni, slapping a hand to his son's shoulder, the expression on his furred face solemn. "We need you here at home, Omni."

My cousin slowly nodded, acknowledging the unspoken command from his father. It seemed I would be out in the Fall on my own now. I looked away from them, turning to study my own parents and siblings with a question in my eyes.

"What's going on?" I asked, holding my arms out at my

sides. "I know I saw a pinhole portal in the Nexus. I've seen it enough times to recognize that it opened."

My mother was the one to answer as everyone else looked at me with unreadable expressions. "Your siblings," she ground out the word, "just used NEX to abduct two human females and bring them here to the Fall."

My eyes widened as shock filled me, and my gaze shot to Sherakeren, who was the only one who could make NEX do what he wanted now that gray-father had left. "Were they in father's old dimension? Does this have something to do with Friak?"

I was still confused about what was happening. Then Alex enlightened me just as I heard a feminine shout from the other side of the door that led into the teleportation chamber.

My mother moved towards the door that Alex stood blocking, but he knew better than to stand in her way and quickly sidled out of her path, his gaze looking guilty and contrite, even if Ria's didn't.

"We brought Gabby here, bro," he said in a small voice, lifting a hand to rub sheepishly at the back of his neck. "Well, we... uh... didn't exactly know which one was Gabby when we tracked her car down, and so me and Ria kinda both grabbed the woman we thought was her, and we... uh, just brought them both here, figuring gray-father could wipe the mind of the extra one and send her back home."

"You'll be sending them both back home!" Evie shouted, pointing a finger in Alex's direction. "And there will be *no* mindwiping." She shot a glare at Sherak, who looked surprisingly defiant towards our mother, which was also very rare.

He also looked pale and haggard, like he hadn't slept in weeks. Not since gray-father had left. Much of his long hair had broken free of its usual neat ponytail, like he'd been running his hands through it, and it now framed his face. Despite his ragged appearance, his expression was calm but hard. He was in control of himself at the moment, but for how long before he had to retreat back to the lab?

I should have been here, helping my family deal with grayfather's absence—especially Sherak.

Evie pulled on the door handle and growled when she found it locked. She shot another look at Sherak, and he flicked his fingers, causing the door to open just as someone pounded on the other side of it.

My mind still struggled to process their words, but the meaning of them clicked into place the moment I saw Gabby stumble out of the teleportation room, her fist raised in the middle of thumping on the door with all her might.

Behind her lay another woman in a sparkly dress that looked very similar to the one Gabby had worn on our first date.

The woman had her back turned towards us and appeared to be out cold. I didn't spend much attention on determining who she was, though I had my suspicions. I was too focused on Gabby.

"Gabby," I whispered, feeling a pain in my gut that had nothing to do with Kuru recently impaling it with a sapphire.

Despite my low voice, her gaze shifted to mine as her mouth gaped in shock and her eyes rounded with fear at the sight of the strange people surrounding her.

"Vincent!" she cried, panic in her voice that had me rushing towards her, oblivious to our audience.

"Told you that she was the one, you idiot," I heard Ria mutter to Alex as I reached Gabby.

"You hush your mouth, young lady," my mother snapped at my sister. "You're in so much trouble right now, you'd better not smart off to *anyone*, even your brother, who is in just as much trouble for this debacle!"

Ignoring them, I reached for Gabby, unable to help myself, even though I'd spent the last four months trying to forget her, and when I couldn't, trying to hate her for her betrayal.

She flung herself into my arms, clinging to me and pressing her face against my bare chest as if she didn't want to look around again and see the crowd of tall and—compared to her—very alien people surrounding us.

Her arms wrapped around my waist between my top two claudas and the rest, and she hugged me tight against her. My claudas closed over her as I inhaled deeply of her scent, which I hadn't been able to forget, no matter how much I'd tried.

I lifted a hand to stroke her ponytail, reveling in the softness of her hair beneath my calloused palm. It looked different from when I'd last seen her. The curls were tighter, and the color was a soft, warm brown. I liked the look of it, and thought it suited her better than the color she'd had before.

"I can't believe you're here, Gabby," I said, bending to nuzzle her hair and inhale again.

She pulled away just far enough to look up at me. That's when I noticed that her left eye was swollen, and a bruise was forming both on her eye and on her jaw. "What happened to you?" I gently touched the darkened flesh at her jaw.

"Your sister beat me up," she said in a thin voice that sounded like she was on the verge of losing herself to hysterics.

I growled, shooting a furious glare at Ria, who got another sharp reprimand from my mother and a promise of extended punishment.

"She'll pay for that," I said with a snarl at Ria, who bared her fangs at me with a snarl of her own.

"I did you a favor." She huffed, crossing her arms over her chest. "She wouldn't have come quietly, so I just gave her a little love tap—or two." She shrugged. "Not like she didn't deserve it after betraying you."

"*I* only drugged the other woman," Alexander said as if that was somehow better. He realized the folly of that when Doshak grabbed him by the collar of his formal suit and jerked him off his feet to bring him up to eye level.

"We'll be having a nice long *discussion* about your behavior in the arena," blood-father said in a voice tight with fury towards his son as he scowled in his face.

"I think I'll join in on that discussion," Veraza said with an angry caw, the feathers of his crest quivering with his outrage. "After we see to the care of both our new guests."

Evie nodded fiercely, turning towards Sherak to gesture to the teleportation room. "Take the other woman to the medical ward and flush the sedative from her system." Then she turned her searching blue gaze to me and Gabby, who had tucked her face back against my chest again as if she didn't want to look at the others. "Vinnie, escort your... uh, guest to the medical ward. I'll be there shortly to speak to them both and hopefully put them at ease."

The way her gaze hardened as it shifted to the back of Gabby's head told me my mother would have to struggle to put human decency above her own anger at how Gabby had hurt me. I didn't worry. I knew she would do what was right. She was as honorable as any of my fathers and would treat both Gabby and the other woman with care. Especially considering how they were brought here against their will.

I couldn't believe my siblings had been so foolish. Not even those two, and definitely not Sherak. Gray-father's absence must truly be weighing on him for him to even consider such a mad plan.

"Gabby," I said softly, stroking my hands down her back as my claudas kept her close to me. "Come with me and I'll get those bruises healed up."

I could have let her drink my blood to speed her healing right then and there, but I didn't want the inevitable result of feeling her lips on my skin to be visible to everyone in my family who currently stood staring at us with varying expressions, but all of them held curiosity. It would be best to wait until we could be in semi privacy in the medical ward before I let her feed from me.

She tried to pull away from me, craning her neck to look back at the teleportation room. "Wait, Vince! I need to make sure Val is okay!"

I frowned, glancing back at the other woman's prone form as Sherak approached her. "Valerie's the other woman?" I shook my head, shooting another furious glare at my idiot clutch mates. "You brainless nits! She looks *nothing* like Gabby!"

Alexander shrugged. "I asked her if she knew you. She said yes, she knew you *well* and demanded to know where you'd been hiding for the last year. I figured that meant she was your woman."

"It's been a year since I left Earth?" I returned my surprised gaze to Gabby.

She nodded, her beautiful gray eyes still looking stressed even as her full lips compressed into a tight line. "We were at a New Year's Eve party when I saw this...," she cast a glance at Alex, "*person* talking to Val, and then he took off with her. I followed, and she," she flicked one hand towards my sister, "leapt out of an alley and attacked me!"

Ria gasped in outrage, propping her hands on her hips. "I didn't *leap* out of the alley! I just walked out, like any normal person would."

"I'll deal with you later, Ria," I growled. "You will *never* lay your hands on my mate again."

"Didn't she betray you though, Vin?" Omni asked from behind me.

I heard my aunt shush him. "I think it's time for us to return home," she then said in her melodious voice. "It's been a long day, and a long time since we've had our Omni home for a visit. We should let Vinnie and his... friend reconnect."

Val's body floated out of the teleportation room followed by

Sherak, who stalked in her wake, his gaze fixed on the unconscious woman, but the expression on his face telling me his mind was elsewhere.

Of all my siblings who'd taken part in this travesty of a plan, Sherak's motivations confused me the most. He'd rejected the idea of abducting Gabby months ago, having the good sense to see what madness it was. Yet now that gray-father had left the Dead Fall, giving him the opportunity to use the Nexus without alerting our father, he'd done so to bring my mate back to me.

Had I really caused that much pain for my family that my own brother would act outside his conscience to help me? I could expect that kind of wild behavior from Ria and Alex, but Sherak? How far gone was I that he'd felt compelled to do this?

28

Gabby

When Vincent had told me about his family, I had tried to picture them, but never imagined how bizarre they would be in real life. It was one thing to imagine an almost cartoonish caricature of his giant of a blood-father in my head or the feathered bird man of a wing-father. It was another thing altogether to see them in person.

Vincent really was the most mundane in appearance to his non-human family members, whom I assumed included the menagerie of creatures standing around the other full-figured human woman who wasn't Vincent's mother. A four-armed lion man, a four-armed lizard man, and a creature that seemed to be a bit of both, only with two arms and spiral horns jutting from his brow.

And then there was the second largest of the creatures besides the giant—a scaled, feathered, furred, horned humanoid with an almost human face but skin that kept shifting in texture like it couldn't decide on one look.

My mind struggled to process all this strangeness, as fascinating as I found it to be. It also struggled to process that Vincent held me in his arms—and claws—again, and I felt like I fit perfectly there. He smelled delicious, even if there was an overtone of something less pleasant lingering around him, like he'd been somewhere that held rotting, reeking things.

As his claws released me so I could follow Val's levitation out of the room with my gaze, nervous about the dark-haired, human-looking male who appeared to be controlling Valerie's floatation, I glanced back at Vincent and noticed that blood covered his belly.

"Vincent! What happened to you?" I cried, my attention shifting fully back to his stomach, where I could see the remnant of a wound rapidly healing before my eyes.

This was enough to cause everyone still in the room to freeze and then turn back towards us. A cacophony of concerned voices suddenly rose around me, many making sounds I couldn't understand.

Vincent rolled his golden eyes as he covered his stomach with one hand, shaking his head at his family members. "I'm fine. It's just a flesh wound."

"Vinnie," his giant of a father said, striding closer to us, "you should feed before you do anything else." His gaze shifted to my face, and I noticed his eyes were golden like Vincent's. "Including giving your mate your blood to heal her. Her wounds are minor. You have taken serious damage."

I appreciated that the giant spoke English, likely for my sake, and noted that his accent was much like Vincent's and Alex's.

My head bobbed in a nod of agreement. Though my face throbbed from where crazy Ria had punched me, I hadn't been impaled through the gut. I could certainly wait until Vincent was taken care of.

Vincent took my hand, twining his fingers with mine. "I'll grab some blood when we get to the med—"

His words were cut off when a flash of light appeared in the other room. The one where we'd suddenly appeared after falling through the sky.

Everyone turned towards that room just as two new people appeared.

One of them was a scaled male as large as Vincent. He wore a futuristic suit of armor—all sleek lines with no extra adornments. A gray alien stood beside him, wearing a similar suit of futuristic armor. The gray appeared bulkier than the slender creatures from our human urban legends and not just because of the heavy armor he wore. He was certainly more built than the figurine I'd had on my shelf at home. His unnerving eyes and distinctive face shape left no doubt what he was though.

He and the scaled man rushed into the room we were in, the gray alien's gaze sweeping past me without seeming the least bit surprised to see me standing there.

"Where is Sherak?" the gray said in a voice that somehow managed to be intimidating even though it wasn't as deep as the voices of the other males.

"I'm here, father," the dark-haired man who had floated Val out of sight reappeared in the room from the door he'd exited, his eyes black and close in appearance to the gray's, if significantly smaller. "What do you—"

"We have to destroy the Nexus generator," the gray alien said with a raised hand that seemed to paralyze everyone in the room, even though I felt nothing other than nervous to see that hand lifting and the three extra-jointed fingers straightening. "As quickly as possible."

Sherak's eyes widened until they looked closer to the gray's in size as he shook his head sharply. "What are you *saying*? NEX is still *linked* to the generator!"

"Do what you can to disconnect the AI, but we have no more time to waste!"

Then he tapped a silver badge on his armored chest, even as Vincent's mother called his name.

He disappeared in a flash of light and pop of air without responding to her.

Sherak's expression looked panicked and pale as he ran both hands through his long, wild hair that had broken loose from the tie at his nape. "NEX is still *linked*!" he cried out as though his father still stood there to hear him. "He'll destroy it if he destroys the Nexus generator! I can't isolate it without cutting it off from its databanks. Not in such a short amount of time. Without it, we can't navigate dimensions!"

The trees and potted plants around him whipped like a strong wind suddenly blew through the plant-filled room, some of them bending nearly in half, before the scaled newcomer said Sherak's name sharply.

He jerked like he'd been slapped, and then his entire demeanor grew eerily calm as he nodded to the stranger in unspoken acknowledgement, the sudden movement of the plants around him falling still. He seemed to realize that he was only wasting more time and ran to the teleporter to stand atop it. He promptly disappeared in a flash of light without another word, his jaw tight and his expression blank and masklike.

"Friak! What's happening?" Vincent's mother asked the strange, scaled man as the other human woman rushed to him, crying out "Friak!" as if she couldn't believe her eyes.

Friak caught his own mother in a fierce hug, looking down at her tearful face with obvious love and affection. The kind I'm sure never crossed my face when I looked upon my own mother. Then his gaze hardened as he lifted his head, though he didn't release Alice.

"We have an Iriduan on our tail—the deadliest one I've ever faced. Somehow, he managed to remotely hack the anchor when we activated it. Uncle Gray was able to deactivate remote mode long enough for us to open a portal back here, but he couldn't lock the Iriduan out completely. He insists that destroying the generator is the only way to destroy the anchor. If we don't, the Iriduan will follow us here, and Gray seems to think he's far more dangerous than even I suspected." His brow lowered to cast his eyes in shadow. "With NEX, that creature could invade any dimension he wanted. Gray says he would be like the ancilla before the infection." He shook his head. "Or possibly worse," he growled.

The feathered man squawked in an alarmed sound as everyone else gasped, except for the clueless abducted human. I had no idea what Friak meant, even though he was speaking English. In his case, probably not for my sake. It hadn't escaped me that Evie and Alice spoke with American accents and English was probably their first language. Maybe their children defaulted to English when speaking around them.

Friak nodded as if the feathered man had spoken—he probably had, but not in a language I could understand. "If we destroy the generator, the Nexus is gone. We know. There's nothing we can do about that. The Iriduan is too powerful and possesses an uncanny skill with technology that Gray could only mitigate temporarily. The longer it takes to destroy the generator, the more time he has to reactivate the anchor and take control of it from his side."

"Without the gateway," Evie said, glancing from Vincent to me, "everyone will be permanently trapped here."

I realized that she was speaking more to me than him. Then I realized what she was saying. "You mean me and Val can never go home?" I asked, my heart thudding harder than it had at any time since Vincent's siblings had abducted us.

Vincent pulled me close, and I looked up to meet his eyes, noting that his lips had tightened in a hard line. "You want to leave already, Gabby? You don't want to be here with me, do you? You'd rather be with Charles, then?"

I shook my head quickly. "No, Vincent! It's not that! This doesn't have anything to do with Charles."

My whole life on Earth, gone! And it wasn't my choice to come here. I didn't have the time to even prepare myself or process the extent of the loss I faced. It wasn't that I didn't want to see Vincent again. It wasn't even that I wouldn't have chosen him and his world eventually, even knowing that I would have to give up mine.

He couldn't seem to understand how monumental such a decision was, nor how traumatic having the choice ripped away from me felt, no matter how much I cared about him and wanted to be with him.

Friak sighed heavily as he nodded once in agreement. With his mother, I assumed since my words had to mean nothing to him. "I trust Uncle Gray in this matter. If this Iriduan is dangerous enough to concern him, then I believe that such a drastic measure is necessary."

"Why was this person chasing you?" Alice asked, pulling away from her son to look up at his face with concern.

Friak sighed and ran a hand over the crocodile-like ridges on his head, then scrubbed his palm over his humanoid face. "Halian was a target of mine when I worked as a bounty hunter for the Iriduan Empire. I tracked him to a hole of a city on the Rim of settled space and found him running with okihan pirates. He is a brutal bastard, and difficult to kill, much less capture alive, but I managed to corner him and collar him. He slipped my leash by tricking me into believing he was the harmless scientist I thought I was dealing with, and I learned too late how ruthless he truly was. When I returned to the empire emptyhanded, the woman I thought was my spark—the one I was serving the empire for in the belief that once her mission was complete, she would become my mate—told me that she had no more use for me, because I was a failure. It was only then that I realized she had been using me the whole time —for *years* as measured in that dimension—and lying about her intentions towards me."

Alice gasped, squeezing her arms tightly around her son again. "Oh, Friak! No! I'm *so* sorry, sweetie!"

Friak's expression didn't look sad. It looked terrifying, as if an inner rage burned inside him over the betrayal of the woman he'd thought was his 'spark,' whatever that meant.

"I decided to return to the anchor, but Halian and his pirates had turned the tables on me and tracked me down to capture me," he continued after a long moment where he schooled his expression, wiping away all sign of emotion. "I think he figured out that I wasn't from his dimension, because he seemed obsessed with finding out what world I came from when he was interrogating me. Uncle Gray helped me escape, but Halian was hot on our tails as we made our way to the anchor."

He sighed, his shoulders slumping. "And I've already told you the rest. Now, we lose the Nexus because Gray says this Halian is someone we should all fear—and I never thought Uncle Gray feared anything."

"My Gray is capable of fear," Evie said slowly, her eyes wide as she stared at Friak, "but it's for the ones he loves, not for himself. If he would destroy the Nexus generator and risk destroying NEX itself, then this Halian creature is as dangerous as he believes him to be."

She turned her attention to me, her blue eyes holding sympathy as if she knew how difficult it was for me to realize that I would never see Earth again. I would never walk among or speak to the people I had known there. Not my mother, nor all the friends that I had made in the last year.

"I'm so sorry, Gabriella," she said softly. "I know what it feels like to lose your home suddenly and against your will.

We will try our best to make you and Valerie feel welcome here."

"Can't this Nexus generator be fixed?" I asked, still not ready to completely give up hope. Surely, if it could be built, it could be rebuilt.

"Maybe." Vincent's tone sounded chilly even though he kept an arm around my shoulders, holding me close to him possessively. "Though it would take a significant amount of time for such an endeavor and all the anchors linked to the generator will be destroyed along with it, so the generator would have to make another connection by phasing with a parallel dimension. And if NEX itself is destroyed, then there will be nothing to interface with and control the Nexus generator, and it will randomly phase with dimensions or open on anchored ones, causing massive chaos in the Dead Fall, like it did in the old days when NEX was our enemy."

He lowered his arm from my shoulder and stepped away from me, his expression closed as I met his eyes. "The likelihood that you could return home even if the generator was rebuilt would be slim, and it would be many years from now at best."

I knew what he was thinking. He believed I was asking because I didn't want to be with him. After all, he probably thought I had betrayed him because I wanted to be with Charles. The very idea made me shudder, and unfortunately, that didn't go unnoticed by him either.

He stiffened, a scowl creasing the skin between his brows and pulling his lips back to bare his fangs. "There isn't much that can be done about this now. I need to visit the medical ward, Gabriella. I can escort you there," he glanced at his mother, "or ask one of the other humans to do so, if you'd prefer."

"Vincent," I said, hastily grabbing his hand, feeling a flush of embarrassment as he pulled it out of my grasp in front of his entire family, his rejection of me obvious. "Please," I swallowed thickly, "I need to talk to you," my gaze darted from him to everyone else in the room, noting how Friak watched us with genuine curiosity, "in private."

My voice had dropped to a whisper as I inched closer to Vincent, my humiliation increasing as I noted the hard gazes of Vincent's siblings—Ria glaring narrowly like she debated punching me a third time.

"Take me to the medical ward," I said nearly under my breath to him, "so we can talk about this!"

I felt exhausted, stressed, and still processing my shock. I just needed a chance to recoup, and hash this all out with Vincent without having his family members bear witness to my vulnerability.

I also really wanted to check on Valerie, because she was gonna be so pissed when she woke up and realized that her New Year, like mine, had started with one hell of a bang.

29

Gabby

The medical ward turned out to be high-tech and futuristic, with fancy handheld scanner thingies, one of which Vincent passed over my face, checking for any additional damage his sister might have inflicted on me. I sat still, waiting for the verdict, feeling the swelling in my face throbbing as my shock wore off to be replaced by a mixture of nerves and intense curiosity about this world in which I now found myself.

And also, depression over my uncertain future and my lost past.

"It looks like Ria pulled her punches, at least," he muttered, his tone darkening when he mentioned his sister's name.

As cold as he was being to me, I was surprised he still expressed anger at his sister for hitting me.

"It sure didn't feel like she was pulling them," I said with a huff of disbelief.

He lowered the scanner, setting it aside on a nearby cart

before returning to tower over me as I sat on an examining table.

I noted that his stomach wound had completely healed after he drank the entire contents of a large container that I assumed held blood. I was both awed by his regeneration and relieved to see that he was well again.

Despite what he might think, I still cared about him. Now, I just had to convince him of that, which seemed to be difficult since he was misinterpreting all my reactions, not taking into account that I might be a little overwhelmed by the sudden and dramatic shift in my circumstances.

"Trust me," he said slowly, his gaze unreadable as it roved over my face, "Ria may look human, but her strength is far beyond that of any normal human, male or female." He lifted a hand as if to touch my face, but quickly lowered it, his claws drumming their tips on his abdomen, which was still stained by his own blood, as were his rugged, suede cargo-style pants. "She could have really hurt you. I can't believe even *she* would do something so reckless as to abduct you though!"

"I'm surprised she did." I watched his expression carefully. "I figured you would have forgotten about me by now."

He scoffed, his claws spreading to his sides, then folding up to disappear behind his back, like they lay against his spine, leaving his belly unguarded.

Was that a sign that he was leaving himself open and vulnerable to me, or was I just reading too much into his body language?

"As if I could ever forget about you, Gabby," he said softly, looking at the far wall instead of meeting my eyes.

Then his golden gaze sharpened as it returned to my face. "Nor could I ever forget about your betrayal."

Frustrated and at the end of my rope, I couldn't hold back my own anger any longer. "Oh, *come* on, Vincent! You're being so damned unfair! You didn't even give me a chance to explain what really happened! You just heard Charles say some shit and immediately jumped to conclusions and then ran away like a coward!"

The way his big body tensed made me fear I had gone too far with that last statement. I saw the joints of his claws reappear on either side of his body as if he was barely containing their reflexive movement. His jaw tightened and a muscle ticked beneath the skin.

"A coward?" he said in a forbidding tone. Then he gestured with a sharp slash of his hand towards the door that led out into the rest of the medical ward. "Do you see what happens to our family when we are betrayed by the ones we believe to be our mates? My cousin had to run for his very life, and now we have lost the most fundamental part of our world, all because he was tricked by a woman!"

I rubbed my aching head, feeling like the throbbing of Ria's punches had only increased instead of lessening over time. "I meant to text Valerie, not Charles. It was an honest mistake, that's all! I know it wasn't cool that I was telling Val your secret, but I knew that she wouldn't expose it to anyone without double-checking with me first. I figured it was an insurance policy, in case you turned out to be dangerous to me. You can't blame me for taking some precautions! It doesn't mean I intended to betray you!"

He stared down at me, his hands shifting to settle on his hips, his stance defensive even as his claws twitched and then spread to wrap around his waist again, lacing over his stomach where his wound had disappeared.

"Vincent," I wrung my hands together in front of me in a pleading gesture, "this has been an extremely stressful day for me, after a really shitty year where I struggled to get over you after you just disappeared out of my life without even the courtesy of a text message. I missed you every single day of the last year, and I spent that entire time kicking myself for my mistake." I blinked away the tears that felt coming on. "I would have come here with you willingly, Vince," I said in a voice that shook with unshed tears, "if you had just given me a chance. I only needed time to grow accustomed to the idea. To grow accustomed to you. It was a first date, for crying out loud! Cut a girl some slack!"

My voice rose at the end of my words with the anger and frustration I'd felt at how Vincent hadn't even given me a chance, just leaving without another word other than the ugly things he'd said to me at the end.

For the first time, I saw a flash of uncertainty cross his face as he looked away from me, his broad shoulders slumping and his hands dropping from his hips. The tips of his belly claws clicked together as they shifted with what might be nervous energy.

Then he lifted a hand to run it through his mussed and tangled hair that still somehow looked silky even though it had dirt and debris sticking to it. The wound to his stomach told me he'd been in some kind of fight, but it was only now, after all the other shocks had faded, that I really had time to assess his appearance.

In my dimension, he'd looked more civilized. Here, he looked a little wild, and I could swear he was larger and broader of shoulder and chest than he had been when I'd last seen him. In fact, he seemed to tower over me even more as I'd stood beside him earlier, but I'd been too preoccupied to notice.

"You're pretty impatient, Vince," I said softly, reaching a trembling hand to stroke one of his claws. It stretched towards me as if it wanted more contact with my skin. "I've heard of whirlwind romances, but it isn't all that common to run away with a guy on a first date where I'm from, especially a blind date."

He smiled ruefully, his expression softening as he watched

my fingers touching him. “I *have* been called impatient on more than one occasion.”

I cocked my head, meeting his eyes as I curled my fingers around his claw. More of them stretched towards me, even as he stepped closer. “That impatience isn’t always a bad thing. It makes a girl feel wanted.” My hesitant smile faded. “I just wish you had wanted me enough to give me a chance.”

He stepped even closer, his hands settling on my shoulders, his thumbs brushing my neck, the tips of his belly claws trailing along my arms. “I’m sorry, Gabby. I shouldn’t have been so quick to jump to conclusions. I really wanted to crush your ex-boyfriend between my claudas, so I had to get out of there, but I shouldn’t have assumed the worst and left you for good. I’ve been miserable ever since then.” He glanced around, then returned his gaze to me.

“That’s why my siblings brought you here. My misery has been making everyone else miserable too, and I guess they just grew tired of it and thought they could fix it by snatching you out of your own dimension and bringing you to mine.” He cradled my face gently between his big hands, his palm barely skirting my swollen and bruised cheek. “They knew that if things turned out badly, we always had the Nexus and could send you home. I’m angry at them myself, but I know they didn’t expect this to happen, so I hope you’ll be able to forgive them someday.”

He lowered his head, his lips hovering above mine. “I hope you can forgive me someday too. I made both of us miserable by leaving without waiting for an explanation. I regret that.”

I lifted a hand to grab the nape of his neck and tugged his mouth closer to mine, pressing my lips to his with a low moan at how good they felt.

Then I gasped when I moved my mouth, the pain in my jaw shooting through my face. He lifted his head, shaking it when he saw my free hand gingerly probing my jaw.

"I shouldn't have made you suffer for so long," he said guiltily. Then one of his top belly claws dug into his own flesh, cutting a line into it so his blood welled out. "Drink from me and your bruises will fade quickly."

I didn't bother to argue because I had already experienced the power of his blood. Instead, I leaned towards him and closed my lips around the cut, sucking hesitantly.

He groaned with pleasure as he cradled the back of my head with one hand, his other stroking down my back.

"Gabriella," he said with a long, satisfied sigh, "I missed the feeling of your lips against my flesh. I missed the taste of you on my tongue. I never forgot how good it felt to bury my stem inside you. Not once in all the months that have passed since I left you have I been able to forget how good it felt to be with you."

I wrapped my arms around his waist, lacing them between his belly claws as I sucked more of his blood, the taste of it still strange to me, but the feeling it caused in me making up for that. I felt the strength and enhanced senses fill me and the throbbing ache in my face faded rapidly the more I drank.

Vincent lowered his head, keeping my mouth pressed to his chest as he nuzzled my hair. He inhaled deeply, his fingers delving into my hair. "You smell so good, Gabby. Nothing in this world smells as compelling as you. *Especially* not the Fall, where I've spent the last two months almost exclusively."

I finally pulled my lips away from him, though I gave his cut one last, long lick before lifting my head to smile up at him. This time, when he claimed my lips in a kiss, I felt no pain.

Only pleasure.

30

Vincent

Speaking to Gabby, finally, after months that had felt like centuries, made me realize how foolish I had been to leave her the way I did. I couldn't make up for that lost time, not really, but I wasn't about to waste any more.

After she drank my blood, I could tell she was soaring, and her hands fell to the catch of my pants. I broke our kiss long enough to eye the open door of the examining room, then shrugged my shoulders, unwilling to break out of her embrace long enough to shut it. The room was situated at the very end of a corridor. I doubted we would be disturbed.

Then all rational thought fled my mind as she undid my fly and slipped her hand into my pants, stroking questing fingers over my tattooed slit. My stem pushed several inches out of my slit, the hard casing splitting open, eager to feel her fingers caress the tip.

She obliged without me making the request, seeming to

know exactly what would please me most as she stroked a soft touch over the flaps on my stem. Then she broke our kiss and lowered her head to drag her tongue along those same flaps, leaving me moaning and shuddering, my claudas vibrating with my excitement and pleasure.

"Oh, Gabby," I said on an exhale as she took my tip in her mouth, her hand encircling my shaft, "the things you do to me!"

It was a struggle to keep my seed from shooting into her mouth just at the sight of her head bent over my stem, bobbing up and down as her lips pulled on my girth and her tongue teased my sensitive tip. I stroked my hand over her hair, grasping hold of my stem at the base of the extruded portion to keep it from twitching in her mouth, not wanting her to stop because I lost control of it.

Though she gave me pleasure, it wasn't this that I had missed as much as just having her near me and knowing that she was there for me. It felt selfish to be happy she was here in my dimension, especially given that she hadn't come here of her own free will and couldn't leave again. Those were all things we would have to work through and deal with eventually, but for now, I could just revel in being with her again.

She was right that I had been impatient, pushing her too far, too fast. Demanding and expecting too much from her on what really had been only the first date, though it had felt by the end of the night that I had known her all my life. I knew that wasn't how humans did things, but I also knew that what existed between us was more powerful than a regular love affair. It was something that we felt right down in our DNA.

"Gabby," I said on a note of panic as her mouth brought me close to climax, "I'm going to come if you keep doing that!"

She lifted her head, licking her lips as she eyed me with a wicked smile. "That was sort of the point." Then she captured my tip again and sucked my stem as deep as she could.

I tried to tug her head away from me as I felt my stem tightening and the rush of fluid through it towards my tip. I didn't want to give her a mouthful of my seed, but she was relentless, her cheeks hollowing as her tongue teased my flaps.

I shuddered as every muscle in my body tensed, my claudas spreading and then clenching on air as I fought my impending climax, not wanting to jerk away from her for fear of harming her but also determined not to spill inside her mouth, even if she thought that was what she wanted.

I feared she would think differently if she realized just how much seed I would spill after so long without doing so. I hadn't even wanted to pleasure myself during the last four months, because the only one I could think of that would bring me to the point of coming was Gabby, and thoughts of making love to her only depressed me more.

Now, my overfull seed pouch was ready to burst because of her talented mouth, and she seemed determined not to release me until I did.

"Gabby, I need to taste you! Let me taste you before you make me come."

I could scent that she was aroused, and she only grew wetter at that suggestion. Relief filled me when she released my stem and lifted her head to meet my eyes.

Then she grasped the bottom edges of her shirt and pulled it over her head, revealing her beautiful body to me. It had changed since I'd last seen her, growing smaller and tighter, but her pleasingly soft flesh remained over toned muscle.

My mouth watered as she bared her top, then undid her pants and slid them down her thighs. I grabbed ahold of the waist of them and tugged them off her legs, growing impatient for that sweet nectar I could already scent.

She shifted her hands to her panties, but my hands beat her there, and I slowly peeled them down, groaning at the tension in my stem as it jerked towards her wet heat, extending further from my slit. The sight of her plump, slick folds caused a fountain of seed to spurt from my tip, spattering the side of the examining table, some of it dribbling down the shaft of my stem.

"Cold Mother's Nest, Gabby!" I said with another groan, then bent over the examining table, wrapping my hands around her thighs to tug her the end of it as I knelt between them. "You've undone me!"

I buried my head between her thighs, lashing her sensitive flesh with my eager tongue.

The sounds of her moans and soft cries as I licked her blended with the rush of her blood through her veins to play a beautiful and erotic music to my ears. I slipped two fingers inside her soaking channel, thrusting them in time to each stroke of my tongue over her swollen nub, until I felt her inner muscles convulse as she shuddered with her orgasm. She cried out so loud that I was certain someone elsewhere in the medical ward would come to check on us.

I didn't care as I felt her cream slick my fingers inside her. With a hum of anticipation, I withdrew my fingers and replaced them with my tongue, lapping up the evidence of her climax, the taste of it exciting me like a drug.

After I drank my fill, I rose to my feet, staring down at her lying on her back, her bra still wrapped around her body, but her hands clutching the breasts she had freed from it, her fingers toying with her own nipples as she'd reveled in the pleasure I'd given her.

Without preamble, I thrust my stem into her slick opening, rocking my hips to bury it deep inside her, both of us moaning as each joint sank into her hot, tight flesh.

I spilled more of my seed from that act alone, before I even had a chance to thrust, but Gabby didn't seem to notice, or perhaps she didn't care, as it bathed her womb and slipped out of her body when I began to pump inside her.

I lowered my body over hers, capturing one of her nipples between my lips as her breasts bounced and jiggled with each of my hard thrusts. Her inner muscles clenched around my shaft with each pull of my mouth on her hard bud. I caught her wrist to tug her hand away from her other breast, enjoying the sight of it bouncing from the corner of my eye as I moved inside her.

Gabby's sounds of pleasure urged me on, making me move faster, chasing another orgasm inside her. When I released her nipple and shifted my lips to her neck, she clutched the nape of mine, her fingers digging in. I felt her tense just before I sank my teeth into her throat. As I sucked her blood, feeling its warmth in my belly, her inner muscles convulsed in another orgasm around my stem.

I came hard at that feeling, pumping all my seed into her, my flaps fluttering to push it closer to her womb, though I was already driving as deep as I could go without causing her discomfort. This time, I shuddered along with her as we climaxed, my teeth still buried in her neck.

"Gabby!" a familiar voice called out from the hallway. "Gabby, where the hell are you? Where the hell am *I*, for that matter?"

"Shit," my mate said, propping herself up on her elbows as I withdrew my fangs from her throat, my stem still deep inside her.

Then Valerie appeared in the doorway. "Gab—oh! Uh, oops! Sorry!"

Gabby's eyes met mine, her face flushing bright red.

Then we laughed as we heard Valerie speaking from the hallway. "I'll, uh, be in the next room, Gabs. You just, uh, finish what you were doing and all. Then you can come in here and tell me where the hell we are!"

Gabby's embarrassed smile faded along with mine as the realization that Valerie was going to be just as unhappy as

Gabby had been to discover the truth of her situation—perhaps even more so—washed over me.

This wouldn't be a pleasant discussion, but I wouldn't make Gabby speak to her friend alone. From now on, we would take on these difficult challenges together.

31

Gabby

Vincent stood at my side, one of his heavy arms lying like a comfortable weight over my shoulder, making me feel more grounded as I faced Valerie, who sat on an examining table staring at us with eyes so wide that I saw the ring of white surrounding her brown irises.

She'd been completely silent during my halting explanation of our abduction and subsequent stranding here in a parallel dimension. Vincent had fleshed out the details that I still wasn't sure about during my explanation, but as Valerie remained speechless, looking completely shellshocked, I worried about her mental health.

I knew how hard it was to process such a thing, and poor Valerie didn't even have someone like Vincent to provide a bright side to her unexpected circumstance. I glanced up at Vincent, who was watching Valerie with a worried frown. It made me happy that Vincent also cared about Val's wellbeing.

She needed as many friends as she could get in this alien world. One neither of us had yet had an opportunity to explore.

"V?" I asked after a long moment of silence followed my final words where she simply stared from one of us to the other as if she were watching a tennis match. "Are you okay, girl?"

She blinked as if coming out of a trance, her gaze narrowing in on Vincent's belly claws, which twitched nervously at her fixed stare. "So, I'm stuck here?" she asked, "with a bunch of aliens and monsters?"

"There are over a thousand humans from different dimensions in New Omni," Vincent said in a reassuring tone, and I blessed him mentally for not taking offense to Valerie's implied insult. She was speaking out of shock, not maliciousness. I understood the feeling completely, not entirely over my own shock.

I glanced up at Vincent again, surprise returning to my own expression. "There are other humans here besides your family members?"

He smiled softly as he looked down at me, then returned his focus to Valerie, who was still staring at his claudas, which rippled against his abdomen at her steady regard.

"Most of the humans live in a part of the city called Human Town—not very original, I suppose." He shrugged. "Out of all the different species we've brought into this dimension, humans seem to be most comfortable surrounded by their own kind, though many are mated with nonhumans who live with them in that sector of the city."

"How many of those humans are hot guys?" Val asked curiously, her question surprising me.

I had expected something a little more pertinent to her current situation, but then I realized that she was already thinking about the future, unlike me dwelling on our past.

Vincent huffed out a surprised laugh, his claw tips clicking together. “I couldn’t speak to the attractiveness of the human males as my interests don’t lie in that direction,” he shot me a heated glance, then returned his attention to Val, “but the ratio of unmated human males to unmated human females is about even. There are also many other species that appear very similar to human, save for a few minor differences.”

Val raised her brows, her gaze sharpening. “Like you, you mean?” A sly smirk tilted her lips. “Or your hottie of a brother.” She glanced at me, grinning broadly. “Alex, wasn’t it?”

Vincent appeared suddenly uncomfortable, lifting his hand to brush through his hair, dislodging some debris that drifted to the floor between us. “Alex is… yes, I suppose he would qualify, and he’s unmated, but….” He shot me a desperate look as if he needed me to intervene.

“I’m sure there’s no shortage of dating options, Val,” I said quickly, “but is that really your biggest concern at the moment?”

She wasn’t a shallow person, and she had been reluctant to date again ever since Ben screwed her over, though she’d had more than a few one night stands and casual encounters. I knew the sight of Vincent’s shirtless body was impressive, but I was startled that it had put her in mind of thinking about hot men when so many other questions and problems had to be weighing on her.

Val shrugged her shoulders, the sequins on her dress sparkling wildly with the motion. “Why not? Earth sucks. My family will never be proud of me the way I am. My job is miserable. Our apartment was cramped, and the booze was expensive and always tasted like shit.” Her gaze slanted back to Vincent. “Are there good bars in this city?”

I held up my hand before Vincent could helpfully supply a list of them. “V, remember your resolution.” I sounded like her mother more than ever with that comment, but I couldn’t help it. The last thing she needed right now was to turn to alcohol as a crutch to deal with her changed circumstances.

She laughed bitterly. "Fuck that shit! The New Year happened in my old dimension. If I can score some alien inter-dimensional liquor, then there's no way in hell I'm giving up drinking right now!" She made a hand it over gesture with her fingers towards Vincent. "So make with the tourist list of best bars in the area, Vincent." She patted her dress at her hips in an exaggerated way, looking down at herself as if she was startled to see herself in a fancy party dress. Then she looked back up at us and smirked. "Oh, and can you spot me some cash, or help me set up a line of credit, since I've just lost everything I own but this shitty, clearance-rack cocktail dress I don't even like?"

The way her voice rose at the end made me realize that Val was barely holding it together. She wasn't unaffected by the realization that she was trapped here. She was just trying to blow it off like it was no big deal. Then she would go out to some alien bar and get wasted on liquor that could end up killing her or end up hooking up with some guy she would never trust while sober.

"Valerie," Vincent said in a gentle tone that told me he had picked up on her near hysteria too, "I promise you we will make sure you are well taken care of, and we'll supply you with whatever you need to feel at home here." He pressed his hand to his chest. "My family bears the sole responsibility for taking you from your world without your consent, and we will do all we can to make amends, and to make you feel welcome here."

I wanted to hug him tight and give him the biggest kiss at how gentle and soothing his tone was with Valerie, but I didn't because she needed my full attention. I could see now how fragile her mental state was as she glanced from one of us to the other, her chin trembling. Her expression twisted for a moment as she fought back tears. Then she sucked in a deep breath, blinking rapidly.

"If you want to make me feel welcome," she said to Vincent, not meeting my eyes, "then hook me up with a good, stiff drink." She smirked, but I noted the tension of her expression that made it look more like a wince than a sly smile. "And send your bro to keep me company." She winked at us, then waggled her brows exaggeratedly as she eyed Vincent's claudas.

32

Vincent

I left Gabby with Valerie to hopefully help calm her down, because even though she tried to play off her emotions, it was clear that her mental state wasn't good.

I felt anger rising in me at the way Valerie had been left alone to wander the medical ward with no one to guide her or help ease her into being here. I was partly responsible for that myself, having been so focused on Gabby that I had completely forgotten about the other abducted human who had just lost everything.

I also had to cut most of my family some slack because losing the Nexus would be traumatic for the entire city, and no doubt riots would break out once people realized it was gone, possibly for good. Though many families had formed over the years as New Omni grew, plenty of people remained without mates who had counted on eventually seeking them through the Nexus.

Now, their opportunities would be limited to the other citizens of New Omni, and there remained a surplus of males overall, though the ratios weren't nearly as bad as they used to be when my parents were first building New Omni. More females were born every day as families either benefited from genetic engineering to hybridize or the keys that still popped up between disparate species over generations, leading to natural born fertile hybrids.

Gray-father believed the keys were the result of some ancient race of interdimensional travelers who meddled in the genomes of countless species in an effort to achieve some unknowable goal. Those travelers could have possessed a persistent interdimensional portal like the Nexus or something similar. Perhaps they hadn't even intended for the keys to replicate themselves into the descendants and mutate to accommodate new pairings.

Regardless of why they existed, they made unlikely pairings fertile and led to offspring who usually also possessed dormant keys of their own that continued the cycle of reproduction.

That meant that there was still hope for New Omni as new generations would be born throughout the years with a genetic diversity far exceeding the requirements to grow a healthy population. The loss of hope for the future would have been the biggest cause of civil unrest. There would probably still be a significant amount as citizens realized they wouldn't necessarily find the loves of their lives, but it wouldn't be as much as it could have been had the Nexus been destroyed twenty years ago.

Still, I knew all my parents would be busy as they explained the situation to the city and calmed the populace. My aunts and uncles would have their own headaches to deal with. As the leader of the city, Uncle Asterius had a challenge ahead of him to maintain control without resorting to brutal methods that could backfire, and Aunt Lauren, as head of the city's security force, would undoubtedly be helping him maintain order in the most peaceful ways possible. This wasn't the old days. The population was integrated now, with no walls separating families from the unmated males, and compared to only hundreds of citizens back then, New Omni now boasted tens of thousands, which meant a rebellion in the masses could end up being catastrophic for the peace and safety of the city.

The current population size honestly wasn't even close to what the original city of the Dead Fall had once held, which wing-father claimed had been in the multimillions before it was destroyed. The very idea boggled the mind, but the Veraza kept all the lore and taught our history to every new generation. He wouldn't make something like that up. Keeping the truth alive so the next generation could learn from the past was important to him.

No doubt Aunt Alice and my uncles would be focused on the return of Friak, as well as helping to calm the citizens. My aunt put most of her efforts into improving morale in the city, and she had founded and currently headed up most of the social programs meant to help newcomers integrate more comfortably, as well as help those who had fallen on hard times to improve their situation.

Valerie would likely need Aunt Alice's help at some point soon, but right now, my aunt must be preoccupied. Otherwise, there would be nothing that would keep her from fussing around Valerie and Gabby until she helped them choose homes, clothes, jobs, or whatever hobbies they wanted to pursue, and had them signed up to take part in a million charitable or social programs.

Of course, Gabby would make her home with me. When I had left this dimension to go in search of my mate, I made sure I had a home of my own to bring her back to, leaving the overcrowded family apartment complex that still sat closest to the heart of the ancilla forest, in order to purchase a townhome of my own in the modern, more artistic sector of the city bordering Human Town. I hoped Gabby liked the home I'd chosen, but if she didn't, I could arrange to trade it or resell it for another that better suited her.

She might want to live closer to the Heart Grove where the mother tree was, but those residences had been the first to be filled up when the city was founded, and it would be difficult to find a place there. I wouldn't ask any of my family members to pull rank to make it happen. My mother was determined not to abuse her status as an elite citizen of the city that came from being one of the founders—and a living legend to boot, given her role in defeating Jagganata to save the Grove twenty years ago. Nor would she allow any of her children to do the same because of their parentage.

Alex and Ria should really be the ones who helped Val acclimate, seeing as it was entirely their fault she was here. I supposed it was also Sherak's fault, but I knew he would be busy with gray-father dealing with the technological aftermath of destroying the Nexus generator.

Though I also worked with my father and brother on the technology used in New Omni, anything related to the Nexus was restricted only to gray-father and Sherak, and I had been completely okay with that. NEX itself had grown less antagonistic over the years of its captivity and more willingly helpful, but from all the tales I'd heard told about it, I didn't think I could ever trust it, nor feel comfortable interacting with it any more than I had to.

Although I wasn't certain that mattered anymore, since I didn't know if they had been able to save it from deletion when they destroyed the generator.

I would leave Sherak alone for now, though I certainly intended to have some harsh words with him later, once everything had settled down, about bringing Gabby here against her will. I knew it was my own stubbornness that had driven my siblings to such desperate measures, but they should have pulled me aside and had a discussion with me first.

Or beat some sense into me to make me agree to return to Gabby's dimension and try to get her back in a more acceptable way. Like actually talking to her and finding out the truth that I'd been too hurt to wait around to find out from her own mouth. I had acted like a jealous, ignorant fool. It was true that I had wanted to kill Charles in that moment as I'd stalked out of Gabby's apartment, so perhaps it had been best that I didn't hang around while trapped in that enraged mindset, but I should have stuck around long enough to calm down and then hear Gabby's side of the story.

I resolved to make up for my mistake for the rest of our lives together. I wanted Gabby to be happy here. Far happier than she had been in her own world. I didn't want her to look back and think about all that she'd had to give up to come here, nor how it had all been taken from her against her will. I wanted her to look back and realize all that she'd gained when my idiot siblings abducted her. I wanted her to love me so much that it felt like a worthwhile trade.

I found Alex and Ria in the main recreation room on the bottom floor of the huge main building of the extensive family complex. All my younger siblings were there along with Lauren's and Alice's children, save for Omni and Friak. Even Pavdan had left his usual haunt in the ancilla forest to join the family members in a vigil as we waited for word from our parents about how to proceed in this changed world of ours.

I had already confirmed that the Nexus ring was gone when I'd left the welcome center's medical ward. The sky looked so empty without that yawning black void and ever-present ring of clouds. Without them, the teleportation drones stood out obviously, like debris left behind in the aftermath of an explosion as they hovered above the Dead Fall.

It had pained me to see such a dramatic change to the

world I'd known all my life. The Nexus had been such a permanent fixture in my existence that it felt like I had lost a limb with it gone. I wasn't the only one struggling with our changed circumstances.

Many of my siblings and cousins had counted on going off to seek their own adventures—and future mates—through the Nexus, and like the wider population would undoubtedly be feeling, they were mired in depressed feelings of loss and grief at missed opportunities.

Alex and Ria both looked up at me, Alex's expression guiltier than my sister's, though he tried to hide it once he realized I'd taken note of it. He tried for a nonchalant shrug as I glared at him.

"I don't know why you're trying to glare holes into our heads," Ria snapped, straightening from her leaning stance against one wall where she'd been watching my youngest siblings coloring on the floor near her feet. She pointed to herself, then flicked a hand towards Alex. "Thanks to us, you have *your* mate. If we hadn't brought her here, you would never have seen her again."

She had a point. One it pained me to even consider. I had been so close to losing Gabby forever. I couldn't even imagine how I would have felt if my siblings hadn't abducted her and then the Nexus had been destroyed. Even though I had tried to put Gabby out of my mind, unsuccessfully, the Nexus had always been there as an option. One I knew I would eventually have to use to return to her, as being away from her had only made me feel more miserable with each passing day.

"That's right!" Alex said, nodding firmly as he also straightened to square his shoulders. "The rest of us will never have the chance to seek out our destinies, but you got lucky, thanks to us."

He flung his arms out to indicate the crowded rec room, and I felt the eyes of all our young family members shift from him to me, the looks in some of them resentful at my good fortune and the loss of their own chances.

Then he pointed to his chest, bare now of the ridiculous tuxedo he'd been wearing when he'd abducted Val. "I will never know what it feels like to be part of a Fayi nest, nor even *see* the world of our sire with my own eyes and look upon the fallen bones of Cold Father for myself."

"And I will never escape this stifling world where our fathers won't let me join real battles!" Ria said with a frustrated stomp of one booted foot. "I will *never* have the chance to build a legend like Evie's!"

"And I will never find my spark," my eighteen-year-old cousin Sobeka said in a sad voice, rubbing her chest, where I could see the glow of her internal flame flicker beneath the fabric of her shirt at her words.

Her sixteen-year-old sister, Sekhmet, growled at that, her ears folding close to her furry skull, her four arms crossing over her chest. "I wanted to return to my sire's world to learn the magic of the priestesses, and maybe find my own kanta to guard me and become my mate."

I had heard that she'd wanted that, but only secondhand. Uncle Iyaren did not think highly of the Sari'i priestesses, so he'd been opposed to his cub becoming one, but none of our parents would actually keep us from pursuing our greatest dreams. Well, except for Ria, but that was because she would get herself killed and everyone knew it.

Alastor rose from his crouch next to my ten-year-old blood-brother Anunakeren, lifting his horned head. His humanoid face, a male version of my aunt Lauren's features, creased in lines of anger. His tufted tail flicked behind him, slapping the cargo pants that concealed his furred and hooved legs. "My brother and I planned to return to father's world to destroy the so-called gods who made him a monster in the eyes of the humans."

My youngest Fayi-blood kin, Nathan, Daria, and Anunakeren, all now ten, watched everyone around them with wide eyes. They didn't appear to have any complaints of their own about the loss of the Nexus. Perhaps because the truth of what that meant for them hadn't impacted them yet.

Lily also seemed unconcerned by the loss in regard to her own hopes and plans, but it was clear from the sad and scared expression on her silvery gray face that the feelings of the others in the room were impacting her. She really shouldn't be here among all these negative emotions, but I imagined there wasn't anyone else to take care of her at the moment, other than the ancilla forest itself. It was possible even the ancilla were dealing with some backlash from the destruction of the Nexus. I still wasn't certain how they always knew when to respond to its opening. Maybe they were connected to it in some way, in tune to its energy, which meant the impact of losing it could be even greater on New Omni than I already feared it would be.

Samuel perched beside Lily on a huge horizontal bar installed specifically for that purpose. He also remained silent about whatever his future dreams might have been, though he'd glanced at our fourteen-year-old brother, Michael, perched beside him, who had expressed a desire to return to our wing-father's world and soar the skies beneath the watchful gaze of Veraza's gods and meet the Tears of the Dawn. Mikey kept his lips shut, but they were tight with disappointment as his black eyes met mine briefly, then lowered to study his own talons clutching the perch. His wings shifted, some of his black feathers bending as one of them brushed against Samuel's wings. Samuel put his arm around Michael's shoulders in silent commiseration.

Twelve-year-old Iyaren Junior opened his mouth when my gaze found his, after I felt his eyes on me, then he closed it again without speaking, a frown pulling his brows together over amber eyes. His humanoid nose, the mirror of Aunt

Alice's, crinkled as he looked away from me, but not before I saw the flash of resentment in his expression. Like his sister, Sekhmet, he crossed his four arms across a narrow chest, not yet filled out with the strength he would one day possess when his mane fully grew in.

I didn't know what his dream might have been, and I'd foolishly believed him to be too young to have one fully formed, like my own youngest siblings, but it was possible I had been wrong. I realized that it likely had to do with finding a mate, despite how young he was to be thinking of such things, since he'd looked as if he felt it unfair that I had mine here when no one else had the same luxury.

I turned my attention to Pavdan, whose grayish-green skin, armored with roots and bark, and branches that extended from the wooden portions of his head, began to glow softly.

"What of you, Pavdan?" I asked curiously, since he was usually a taciturn one with an almost unknowable mind. At least a mind I had never truly gotten to know, though perhaps Lily and Sherak understood what went on behind the wooden armor covering that head of his. "What dream did you have for the future that is now lost?"

Pavdan shrugged shoulders already as broad as my own, even though he was still growing, despite being twenty now. No one knew how big he'd get, but he was an ancilla, technically, though a mobile one, now immune to the disease that had turned the others into the towering giant trees that guarded our city.

"The Dead Fall is my home. I have no desire to leave it. I will miss the Nexus, but I believe I can find my future in this world without it. Mother says that we should not despair. Change often brings discomfort, but it can also bring growth."

Unlike the rest of us, Pavdan had two mothers in addition to multiple fathers, both of whom he loved dearly. Aunt Alice had raised him as her own, but the mother ancilla tree had given of her own unique flesh and the heart wood—the last pure part—of Jagganata to bring him to life, before asking Alice to raise him so he would learn to live as someone who could move about the world freely, unlike the ancilla trees that must remain forever rooted in their ever-expanding grove, reliant upon their tenders to come to them. When he said 'Mother' he meant the mother ancilla tree, because Aunt Alice was still 'Mom' to him, or 'Mommy' if he was feeling particularly affectionate. Taciturn he might be, but when he cared about someone, he didn't let them doubt his feelings.

"Bro, you should be paying us for the service we did for you," Alex said defensively as my focus shifted back to him and Ria. "You're the only one of us who got your future."

Though I couldn't argue with that assessment, I still bared my teeth at him. "You should not be speaking out of turn, Alex. You abducted not only Gabby, but Valerie too. You have taken Valerie's future away from her."

Alex snorted in disdain that made me want to plant my fist in his face. I barely resisted the urge, but only because Lily made a little peeping sound and then jumped up from her cross-legged seat on the ground and rushed to stand between us.

Alex took note of Lily's stance too, and the tension melted out of him as his guilty expression returned. "I swear, Vin, I didn't think it would matter if we just borrowed her for a bit. I really thought we could easily return the wrong girl once we verified it."

"And now you can't," I growled, my voice tight with my anger, even though I tried to tamp it down, for Lily's sake. "And Valerie has *nothing*, her entire life and family, save for my Gabby, left behind in her world. Lost to her forever."

I swept my gaze over the room. "All of you are hurting. I know that. I am too, despite my gratitude that Gabby is here with me. The Nexus has been a part of my life since I hatched.

It is the very reason I stand here at all. We all owe our existence to it, and now, it's gone. We can dwell in our misery, or remember that others are also suffering, and reach out to help them get through this loss."

I speared Alex with a narrow glare. "Valerie needs friends right now. I'm not sure if she'll actually forgive you for abducting her, but you need to go to her and make it up to her."

I turned that glare on Ria. "*Both* of you."

"Hey, Sherak better have to make up to her, too," Alex grumbled, even as he left his spot by the wall and strode to the door, his claudas curling tight against his abdomen with his guilt.

"I'm sure he will, but he's busy right now," I said to his back as he jerked the door open and stalked through it.

Ria sauntered past me, shrugging her shoulders at me when I met her blue eyes. "I'll take the woman under my wing," she shot a wink at Sam and Mike, whose wings shifted at her phrasing, "and show her what New Omni has to offer." She stroked her chin. "Maybe she'd like a trip to the arena. Lots of...," she paused, glancing down at our younger siblings, "uh, good scenery there."

Lily cocked her head curiously at Ria, blinking her black eyes as a little crease appeared between them. "RiRi, why are you thinking of—"

I held up both hands, cutting off Lily's question, because I had no doubt Ria's thoughts were inappropriate for a young audience, though her idea of "good scenery" was more likely to be lots of blood and gore, rather than half-naked males. "Just be gentle with Val, Ria. She's a good person, and she's in a very bad place right now." Then I grabbed her arm as she made to continue to the door. "And don't even think about laying another hand on Gabby," I growled in warning.

I didn't hit my sister. Ever. I wouldn't get my revenge via

physical abuse, but there were other ways to get back at Ria, and she knew I could be creative.

She scoffed and shrugged off my grip. "Relax, Vin. I'm happy I'll be getting my first sister-in-law. I'll be nice to her from here on out. I swear by the Grove and Cold Mother's icy teat."

"What's a teat?" Anu asked, having never been breastfed, since that wasn't part of our development cycle, which always made me wonder why Cold Mother might have one.

Unless my blood-father picked that curse up from my mother, which was entirely possible.

"I'll tell you when you're older," I said quickly to Anu as Ria chuckled and strolled through the door.

Her leaving didn't remove the tension from the room, and my siblings watched me with varying expressions, most of them holding sadness. I didn't know what I could say to help them deal with their grief, and all I really wanted to do at the moment was return to Gabby. I still needed to take her on her very first tour of her new home, and I wanted to introduce her to the mother tree.

It might be some time before things settled down for my family enough for formal introductions, but until then, I could show her our home and see her settled into it. For now, I should probably bring Valerie along and set her up in one of the spare rooms that I hoped one day would be for mine and Gabby's children.

At least five, Gabby had said. I could give her that. My mother had ten, and though she insisted she was done, blood-father's blood kept her young and fertile, so she could have more if she wanted. Gabby would have my blood to keep her in the same fertile state, and we could hopefully have as many children as she wanted.

But first, I had to extricate myself from this room, though I felt a responsibility to my family, being the oldest there now that Ria and Alex had left.

Samuel leapt lightly from his perch, tucking his wings tight against his back, his eyes on me. "Go take care of your mate, Vin. I can handle things here."

I wanted to hug him tight, but he hated that kind of constriction, claiming I was crushing his light bones, though I knew better, since they were far less fragile than one would expect.

"Thank you, Sammy," I said instead, backing towards the door. "I owe you one."

Samuel chuckled with an odd trilling that reminded me of his sire. "You're going to have a lot of repaying to do if you don't stop assuming debts."

33

Gabby

Valerie and I sat in the waiting room of the medical ward, noting that it was empty of all but a few robots that rolled past us on tracked wheels, without seeming to pay attention to us.

"At least it doesn't look like there's much violence or illness in this city," Valerie noted, sniffling as her puffy-eyed gaze followed the latest robot to roll past us on its journey towards the corridor to the examining rooms we'd left behind.

"Not unplanned violence," a feminine voice said before I could respond, and I stiffened as I recognized it.

Valerie and I both turned towards the owner of that voice as Vincent's sibling kidnappers strolled up to us, Alex towering over his sister, his short-cropped white hair a stark contrast to her raven black long ponytail.

"Huh," Valerie patted her hair, which was mussed into a hopeless tangle after her ordeal, "I didn't think Vincent would actually send you." Her expression took on an angry cast as she glared at Ria and Alex. "Not sure I really want to see you right now, you bastard!"

Alex's handsome face took on an apologetic expression. "Hey, I'm sorry," he held his hands out to his sides, his claudas clamping so tight over his stomach that I wondered how they didn't cause him pain. "I never meant to strand anyone here. I just figured whoever wasn't the right girl could be put back in your own dimension before you even realized you'd been taken from it."

"Oh, that makes it better then?" Valerie snapped sarcastically, crossing her arms over her chest.

Alex's golden gaze dropped to the floor. "No," he muttered, scuffing one booted foot against the tile.

"Hey," Ria glanced at her brother, "we can dwell on past mistakes, or we can try to move forward." She stepped closer to us, and I flinched back in my seat.

She held up both hands in front of her. "Easy! I'm sorry for hitting you. I thought you screwed my brother over. I figured I was bringing you back here so you could show him what a bitch you were, and he would finally get over you and move on with his life."

"Way to move forward," Valerie said before I could speak, rising to her feet to square off with the other woman. "Unless you plan on moving right into a fight, *bitch*."

"Whoa!" Alex inched closer to the two women. "This was definitely not what Vincent intended to happen when he sent us to apologize, Ri!"

"I'm not the one lobbing threats," Ria said, baring her fangs as she glared up at Valerie, who stood about two inches taller than Ria.

I jumped to my own feet, crowding Ria and forcing her to back away from Valerie. I could tell my girl was itching for something to punch, and Alex and Ria totally deserved it, but this wasn't productive. We couldn't change what had happened. All we could do was move forward.

"Let's all just calm down here," I pleaded, placing a staying hand on Valerie's arm to draw her away from Ria.

I angled my body between the two women, glancing meaningfully at Alex, who jumped to grab Ria by her arm and drag her behind him, much to her annoyance as she huffed in outrage.

"We really are sorry," Alex insisted, his claudas shifting behind him to poke at Ria when she made a disagreeable snort. "I know we can't take back what we did, or fix it the way we'd planned to, but we want to make amends."

He held out a hand. "I should probably formally introduce myself. Although I did tell... uh... Valerie that I was related to Vincent."

I regarded his hand suspiciously, and he slowly lowered it, looking uncomfortable as Valerie crossed her arms over her chest again and smirked at him.

"Should've told me you were a no-good kidnapper," Valerie said. "I thought Vincent was better than that. I hope it doesn't run in the family."

"Vincent *is* better than that," I insisted to Valerie. She knew he hadn't had any part in this crazy plan hatched by his siblings. Still, I suspected she would take some time to get over her anger at being dragged from her own world as the "wrong girl" for Vincent.

"Hey, my bro had nothing to do with this," Alex said, adding to my own defense of Vincent. "Me and Ri planned this, and Sherak helped us use the Nexus. Vincent had no idea what we were doing. Trust me, he woulda stopped us."

Well, that didn't sound very flattering when Alex said it like that. Still, I wouldn't take it the wrong way. I knew what he meant. Vincent wouldn't have done what Alex and Ria did because he knew it was wrong. Vincent had more honor than they did.

"Well, I don't know who this 'Sherak' character is, but quite frankly, I don't care. I think you're all assholes." She pointed at Alex. "And you *owe* me, buddy. You told me you were going to take me to get the best drinks I've ever tasted."

So, that was how Alex had lured Valerie away from the party. It was probably also why she hadn't told me she was leaving. She didn't want me to know she was going with someone to get drunk. I sighed softly, but she still shot me a narrow look, lifting her chin as if to tell me not to judge her. Like I had no right.

Maybe I didn't. She was in a bad place right now. Who was I to tell her how to get through it?

Alex pointed to his naked chest, which while muscular, wasn't nearly as sexy as Vincent's. "I can do that! I know all the best bars."

"The best drinks are served in the arena." Ria popped her head around Alex's body. His claudas on that side rose to block her view, and she growled and stepped further around him, shooting him a smirk. "I'll take you there, because Alex is too chicken to hang out at the arena. Someone might ask him to fight."

Alex's jaw tightened, a muscle ticking as he glared down at his sister. "Watch yourself, Ria. You're in just as much trouble as I am, right now. We should be sticking together."

"Good god, you two are vipers!" Valerie said with a short laugh. She shook her head and shrugged. "What the hell? Like I got anything better to do on New Year's Day than get wasted with a coupla aliens in a parallel dimension where I'm trapped for all time? Let's go see some bloodshed!"

I grabbed her arm as she moved towards the other two. "Wait, V! I don't think this is a good idea!"

She shrugged off my hold, jerking her chin towards the entry doors as one opened to reveal Vincent's towering form.

"Go spend some time with your man." Val suddenly turned and hugged me fiercely at the worried look on my face. "I'll be fine, girl. I promise. I just need to blow off some steam. Unwind a little. These kids look like they know how to party."

Vincent had joined us by the time Valerie said that last, and he clapped a hard hand on Alex's shoulder. His brother stood about half a foot shorter than Vincent and wasn't nearly as bulky with muscle. "Don't worry, Gabby. Alex and Ria will take good care of Valerie and make sure she stays safe." He narrowed his gaze on Alex. "They wouldn't dare to do otherwise."

Ria whooped as if she'd won some kind of victory and came towards us, ignoring my reflexive backwards motion as she slipped her arm through Valerie's, much to my bestie's surprise. Valerie frowned as Ria caught her close and dragged her towards the door, waving her other hand at Alex. My friend shot a look back at me, then her gaze shifted to Vincent. When she returned her focus to me, she smiled knowingly.

"Catch you later, girlie. Don't do anything I wouldn't do."

"That leaves my options wide open, V," I said, still worried though I tried to trust that Vincent's siblings wouldn't put Valerie in any danger. Given that they were responsible for her being here in the first place, it was a difficult trust to put in them. "Don't *you* do anything I wouldn't do."

Valerie snorted as Ria towed her along, Alex falling into step beside his sister after one last speaking look passed between him and Vincent. "That closes off most of *my* options."

I watched the three of them leave the medical ward, Val bending her head closer to Ria's as if Vincent's sister was telling her something fascinating. I worried my lower lip with my teeth as Vincent came to put his arm around me, dropping a kiss on my head, then nuzzled my hair.

"I promise you that they will take good care of her, Gabby. I would never have let them leave here with her otherwise."

I looked up into his eyes, feeling that odd sense of having known him forever, despite how short a time we'd spent together. "I believe you, Vince."

He cocked his head, grinning toothily. "You sure? You don't sound entirely convinced."

"I'm just a little worried about Val, is all. She's had a rough year ever since Ben cheated on her. She hasn't been herself."

His smiled faded as he slowly nodded. "I don't think her mate was very good for her, though I am sorry to hear that he has hurt her by his betrayal."

I didn't want to bring up the topic of "betrayal" again, since he had spent so long believing I had betrayed him as well. Instead, I turned to face him fully, wrapping my arms around his waist as his claudas opened for me. They tucked me in tight against his warm body as I stared up at his face.

"I'm sorry about your portal thing," I said, "and not just because it stranded Valerie here." I could tell that it distressed him to lose the Nexus.

"Our world has changed irrevocably because of this," he said sadly, lifting his hands to brush my hair away from my face. "I feel bad about that, but those negative emotions pale in comparison to the feeling of having you in my arms again. I missed you so much that sometimes, I fear this is only another dream that I will wake from."

"I'm happy to be here in your very... unusual embrace again, Vince." I wriggled against the hold of his claudas and kissed the warm skin of his naked chest. "I must admit that I'm nervous about the future, but I'm really excited to see your world for the first time. This building, while fancy with all the technology, isn't quite the same as the wonders you described."

"Then let me take you on a tour." His claws released me as he twined his fingers with mine.

We walked hand in hand through the medical ward doors, reentering the welcome center, as Vincent explained it. From there, we walked through a huge, fancy atrium, and that was when the alienness of this world first began to show in my surroundings.

Unusual flowers, trees, succulents, and shrubbery filled the garden of the atrium, and once we left the welcome center grounds, I got my first good view of New Omni.

Below us spread a city that looked chaotic and wild in its design, as if it had grown up organically, like the mind-bogglingly massive trees that rose above the city. Trees that made the California redwoods look like indoor ornamentals. Those trees were interspersed between buildings in every imaginable style of architecture, not to mention many I hadn't even imagined before, and they spread their canopies far above even the tallest buildings in the city. The canopies weren't so close that they blocked out the sun, nor the sky that now looked fairly ordinary, though I recalled my brief fall through it where I had seen the Nexus portal for just moments before I was teleported to the welcome center.

The ancilla trees shifted their colors, trees, bark, leaves, and even the occasional marble-round, tie dyed looking fruit that I spotted among their leaves. They were alien and surreal in this, as was their size as they dwarfed most of the city.

Beyond a dense cluster of buildings in the city that Vincent claimed was the main commercial center where the arena and largest and oldest marketplace were, spread a glimmering round lake, the water dark blue from this distance.

"That's where the original Omni once stood, which is why it's called Omni Lake," Vincent said, pointing out the lake. "NEX hit it with a meteor that did massive damage to the entire Fall. Only the ancilla kept this part of the Fall completely intact. My family turned the crater into a lake and built a beautiful park around it, allowing New Omni residents to decorate sections of the park to be most pleasing to them. That island in the center—it might be difficult to see from here—is a memorial built to honor those who didn't survive the meteor impact."

I could see even from here that the crater lake and surrounding lands made a beautiful parkland. Surrounding the boundaries of the parkland around the outer edge, mixed in among the trees, were massive piles of what appeared to be junk.

"The Heaps," Vincent said as if he noted the direction of my gaze and anticipated my question. "Many of the junk piles that once filled the city were toppled or buried with the meteor strike, but some remain, especially near the outermost edges of the original city limits that make up the Dead Fall, before you reach the barrens. New Omnians still scavenge from The Heaps within the ancilla forest boundaries because they're safer than leaving the city to scavenge the untamed ruins."

As my gaze swept over the city, noting all the uniquely cobbled together buildings with delight at their chaotic construction, he turned me around with his hands on my shoulders and my attention was well and truly caught as I gasped in awe.

In the center of the city stood a tree so big that it could be the World Tree of myth. It was clearly ancilla, as it shifted colors like the others, the changing tones rippling in gradients over its entire being.

Her entire being.

This was the ancilla mother tree, rising far above even her own towering people to spread her canopy the furthest of all. Surrounding her was the original grove and tucked within that grove were a cluster of multistory complexes that had made up the original New Omni.

I listened as Vincent told the history of the Dead Fall and spoke of the way this world used to be when his family founded it and began to build this marvel of a city, but I couldn't tear my gaze away from that tree.

"She's beautiful!" I said on an exhale, feeling a strange sense of peace that I hadn't expected to feel so soon after leaving my home dimension behind.

"I will take you to meet her." Vincent's voice sounded pleased as he drew me towards a path that I assumed led towards the center grove. "You're part of my family now, and the ancilla will let you close to the mother because of that. It is a rare honor not afforded to many to walk within the heart of the forest that we call the Mother's Grove, or Heart Grove—or Mother's Heart, depending on who you ask."

Eagerness sped my steps as we left the welcome center behind and made our way through the city streets towards the center grove. I noticed my surroundings only peripherally, though I would definitely want to return to all these places and take a closer look at the many different sights. So many that it would take years to truly explore them all.

For now, my main focus remained on the mother tree, which I could already tell was the most magical thing in this entire dimension, and I knew from what Vincent had told me that that was saying something.

As we entered the grove, my feeling of peace only increased, until my hand was no longer cold and clammy in Vincent's as I could breathe easily, without palpitations of anxiety or feelings of being overwhelmed swamping me.

Birds sang in the trees—or perhaps they weren't all birds. I didn't see some of the noisemakers, and their songs weren't like any I had heard on Earth. The ones I did see ranged from rather mundane avian creatures to far more interesting ones like mini winged serpents or feathered monkeys.

The extensive plant life of the city gave way to a blanket of soft loam with rare bursts of flowers beneath some of the trees. Other than that, the ground remained mostly clear, which

Vincent explained was due to this grove being tended daily, weeds being pulled and any and all unwanted debris being disposed of.

I didn't see any signs of the caretakers of the grove, but Vincent had explained that most of them were from the founding families or were trusted family friends who had been a part of New Omni for a very long time. This truly was a sacred place, and my future husband was one of this world's princes, though he probably wouldn't consider himself as such.

He came from a powerful family. The most powerful, if I read into his words correctly. Though this didn't matter in how I felt about him, it was a little intimidating to realize that my own status had dramatically altered by becoming his mate. I would not make him or his influential family regret having me as a part of it. More than ever, I wanted them to embrace me as one of their own, so that I would finally know what it was like to be a part of something greater than myself.

Then we reached the mother tree. Vincent told me she had once been an empress, and a cruel and heartless one at that. A conqueror who had wiped out entire civilizations in a never ending hunger for more power.

Now, the peace that emanated from her as we approached made that origin story almost impossible to believe.

As I moved closer to her massive trunk, a branch from the tree swept downwards to brush my cheek.

I gasped as I heard a feminine voice speaking inside my head that sounded nothing like my own.

You are welcome here, child of man. My people will bring no harm to those who come to us in peace. We guard our family well, and you are now a part of that family.

"The tree is actually talking to me!" I said with excitement, practically bouncing on my soles as I turned to look at Vincent.

He grinned at my expression as he stood with his hands in his pockets. "She does that on occasion."

"Wow!" I turned back to the mother tree. "You are so beautiful! I've always loved trees, and forests, but I never imagined any trees like you and your people." They had a weeping willow quality to them with their long, trailing branches, but also the grandness of oak trees with broad, sweeping canopies.

The thin, willowy branch brushed my cheek again, and I realized that it needed to be in contact with me to speak inside my mind, so I held still to hear the mother's words.

Destiny has brought you here, Gabriella, and we welcome your arrival. Though the change in your life might be upsetting for the moment, you will come to appreciate it. And the Dead Fall will come to appreciate you and your friend, beyond what you can know.

34

Gabby

Meeting the mother tree was one thing. Meeting Vincent's family formally was another entirely. Before he subjected me to that unnerving experience, he took me to his home, which would also be mine from now on, though a formal wedding ceremony likely wouldn't be for some time yet. As much as I wanted to plan it, I needed to feel settled first.

After spending the night in his home, blissfully locked in his embrace that was so alien and yet felt so familiar to me, I awakened to a new day.

The city was experiencing some outbreaks of rioting as the citizens realized the enormity of their loss now that the Nexus was gone, but where we were at in a funky artistic district, most of Vincent's neighbors were far too chill to bother themselves with panicking and protesting. We passed many workshops that were open to the street, allowing me to see some of the craftsmen and artists creating so many amazing things that I knew I would be walking these streets every day from now on just to get a closer look at all the wonders.

Vincent assured me that his Aunt Lauren and Uncle Asterius had everything under control as our journey to the welcome center led us past one of those pockets of citizen anger. Since the unnerving roaring and screeching and shouting eventually quieted, I had to believe he was right.

As we walked, he described everything to me, telling me stories about many of the different and unique creatures I saw. The variety of appearances was astonishing, and I did see some citizens that resembled some cryptids of legend, including a towering bigfoot-like creature that paused to regard us curiously through intelligent brown eyes as I resisted the urge to exclaim aloud in excitement after my first "eep" got his attention.

He moved on after a brief glance at Vincent, who had stiffened beside me and placed a possessive arm over my shoulder.

It didn't occur to me why until after we had gone a distance from where we'd spotted him.

"Normally," he said, playing his fingers in my hair that I'd left loose to fall around my shoulders, "I wouldn't worry about other males in this city, but now that the Nexus is gone, I'm concerned that we might have to be more guarded about our mates, like they were in the old days."

"I don't think that guy wanted to steal me from you," I said with a laugh.

When he didn't respond, I glanced up at him, surprised to see how serious his expression was. I was even more surprised to note that his claudas weren't comfortably folded on his belly but had actually loosened and extended enough that he could quickly grasp at anything—or anyone—who got too close to us.

"Vincent?"

He seemed to shake himself out of whatever dour thought he'd been having. "Perhaps not, though you shouldn't make assumptions about a male's lack of interest. I finally have you back. The last thing I want is to lose you again." He paused our walk, turning to face me. He cradled my face in his hands, his gaze intent. "I will tear this city apart to find you if someone tries to steal you away. I swear that to you, Gabby. I won't let any harm ever come to you."

I patted his hands soothingly. I expected his concern wasn't wholly imaginary, but I also felt like he was overreacting a bit, probably feeling as possessive as I did, since I'd seen one too many apparent females of various species eyeball my man's naked chest.

"I trust you, Vince."

At the welcome center, Vincent fitted me with a translator device that had every known language spoken in New Omni loaded into it. It fit neatly in my ear so I could understand even his wing-father, Veraza, as he trilled and cawed in his language.

Then it was time to meet Vincent's parents and siblings, all of whom had assembled in their housing complex recreational room.

The complex itself was surprisingly simplistic in design and architecture, but given the beautiful surroundings of the Grove, I could understand why Vincent's family didn't concern themselves with elaborate architecture.

I entered the building with the weight of Vincent's hand resting reassuringly on my shoulder, my tension building as he led me to the door to the main gathering room for the family and other residents of this complex.

Then we entered, and I braced myself, my eyes going first to the woman who stood in the middle of the crowded room—a nice, familiar-looking human face to focus on rather than all the surrounding people.

I was fascinated by this world and all the alien aspects of it, but that didn't mean I wasn't also feeling overwhelmed at taking it all in.

Then Vincent's mother, Evie, spread her hands in a welcoming gesture, walking closer to me. "Welcome, Gabby. Our last meeting wasn't ideal, and I'm afraid we've been a bit distracted lately, so we haven't—"

"Sorry we're late." Alex stumbled into the room with Val's arm wrapped around his waist, his arm supporting her as she swayed on her feet.

Her cheeks were red, and her eyes bright and glassy with inebriation. She giggled drunkenly as someone in the crowd of Vincent's family gasped, and I heard several disapproving mutters.

"Hey, what's with all the sour-blood faces?" Ria strolled in behind her brother and Val, her clothing torn and rumpled and some spatters of fluid on her clothing that may or may not have been blood. I wasn't sure I wanted to know.

Evie sighed heavily, lifting a hand to run it over her face as if she was so over it. "Alex!" she hissed as if she could keep anyone else from hearing her angry tone, even though you could drop a pin in the room, and everyone would hear it.

No one moved for a long moment, then the black-eyed man who I knew to be Vincent's older brother Sherakeren, though Vince insisted on calling him Eren, unlike the other nicknames his family used for his older brother, left his post by the horizontal pole sticking out of the wall where two winged men were perched. He approached Alex, sweeping past Vincent and me.

He caught Valerie as she stumbled when Alex guiltily released her shoulder. "I'll take her to the lounge to sober up," he said in a tight voice as Valerie laughed, flinging her arms around his neck, one of her hands toying with the end of his ponytail that was now neat and sleek.

He shot a speaking glance at Alex. "You need to do so, too. You reek of liquor."

Alex shrugged. "Be outta my system in a few." He tapped his chest. "I got good blood."

I saw Doshak, unmistakable as he leaned against one wall but still towered over everyone else, glowering at Alex, muttering something that was indistinct to me, though the way Alex gasped and straightened, then rushed out of the room on the trail of his brother and Valerie made me think Alex knew exactly what his father had said.

"How very typical of Alex," Veraza cawed, shaking his head, his two winged sons nodding from their perches.

"What am I gonna do with your brother?" Evie asked as her gaze shifted to Vincent.

I felt my mate shrug his shoulders at my back. "Send him on a barrens exploratory team?"

"That won't be necessary," the gray alien mate of Evie said, drawing my focus, though I had been unnervingly aware of him since I entered the room. "With the unrest in the city, he will have an opportunity to focus on something other than his Fayi-driven wanderlust. The bloodshed will settle him. For a time."

He was difficult to ignore, even as he appeared to be content to blend into the background of the rest of the huge family.

His words were even more disturbing than his appearance, and as I had that unflattering thought about him, his thin lips quirked in a slight smile, and I realized that he could totally read my mind, and I needed to watch what idle observations crossed it.

Evie seemed to notice my embarrassed expression as I quickly looked away from Gray, and her eyes narrowed as she glanced at her mate.

"Gray," she snapped, "you stay out of our future daughter-in-law's head!"

His slight smile widened enough to bare teeth, and he looked completely unrepentant, but shrugged. "Her thoughts are projected. It is difficult to block them."

"Yeah, Mama, I heard them too!" the youngest of the brood said, and I recognized her as Lily, the other telepathic child.

My blush burned hotter as I scooted closer to Vincent, who pulled me close to his side, his claudas spreading slightly in a gesture I realized was defensive.

Towards his family, on my behalf.

This meeting already wasn't going well!

Then Evie rushed up to me and gave me a hug with one arm while she hugged her son with the other. "I'm so happy that you're here, Gabby. Don't let some of the less polite members of my family," she shot a glare over her shoulder at her gray, "unnerve you too much. We are all happy that Vincent has you in his life again."

"Indeed." Gray nodded his pointed chin. "His misery was growing tiresome."

"Thanks, gray-father," Vincent said in a wry tone. "Glad to see you care."

Gray chuckled, winking one dark eye at Vincent.

"You're in a surprisingly good mood, all things considered," Vincent added.

"Your happiness projects even more than your mate's thoughts," Gray said serenely. "It is a welcome distraction."

Evie smiled warmly as she released us and stepped back. "We're so happy to see our little squirmie happy again! I know there were some misunderstandings between the two of you, and I'm glad you got all of that sorted out."

"I didn't betray him," I said quickly, worrying that his family hadn't gotten the whole story yet.

"They know," Vincent said before Evie could respond. "Trust me, there isn't much that goes on around here that my parents *don't* know."

I could guess that that remark was directed mostly towards Gray, who shrugged with no visible sign of concern, despite how stressful things must be for him.

"I want to help with wedding plans!" Lily suddenly hopped up and down on her little toes, her pigtails bouncing.

I hadn't had that thought so I glanced at Vincent. He was looking at his mother with an affectionate smile. "I suppose you can't wait for that, Mom?"

She lifted a hand to brush her hair away from her face, looking sheepish. I noticed how young she still appeared to be, recalling Vincent's claim that Fayi blood stopped the aging process.

"This will be the first wedding for my children." She shifted her gaze to me. "I have to admit, I'm very excited about that. It's something to look forward to, and we need that right now."

Impulsively, I broke away from Vincent and threw my arms around Evie, giving her a hug of my own. I couldn't believe I was a part of a family. A big one!

Evie hugged me back in a way my mother never had, and I felt accepted. When tears prickled against my eyelids, they came from happiness.

Things would be crazy for a while, and I imagined I would feel some homesickness for the world I'd left behind, but I was happy. Truly, genuinely, blissfully happy in a way I had never been before.

35

Gabby

Several months later...

I was happy Valerie had finally joined me and Evie as we worked on wedding decorations in the craft room of the complex. It was a huge space, but shelves upon shelves against the walls and a bunch of long worktables made it look smaller, especially since tons of craft supplies stocked every shelf.

Valerie didn't look so good, hungover from hard partying the night before with Ria and Alex and a bunch of humans from Human Town who weren't my favorite people of her new friend group.

She'd made a lot of new friends and rarely ever had time to hang out with me anymore. Despite being surrounded by my new family, who had embraced me fully and welcomed me into their homes and their lives without reservation, I still wished I saw Valerie more than I had in the last few months.

It was rare that Evie and I had time alone to do the mother-daughter bonding thing that was happening between us, but she had offered to leave me and Val to our own devices when Val had turned up at the door, offering to help make centerpieces. Valerie had brushed off the suggestion, sweeping past us with the lingering hint of alcohol clinging to her but seemingly sober at the moment.

"The more the merrier," she'd said as she made her way towards the craft room, Evie and I following in her wake.

"Doesn't Alice usually join you guys?" she asked as she plopped her oversized handbag on a chair in the craft room, turning to face us as we entered.

"Alice is spending the day with Friak and Omni," Evie said helpfully as she headed to the row of stained aprons hanging on hooks on one wall.

Fortunately, her back was briefly turned so I didn't think she saw the look that crossed Val's face. Her nose crinkled up as if she'd smelled something unpleasant.

I knew it wasn't because of an unpleasant smell. She wasn't fond of Friak.

At all.

Their first meeting hadn't gone well, as Val had been intoxicated as usual, and Friak, wrapped up in his own sense of loss, had snapped at her about sobering up. She'd accused him of trapping her here forever by being incompetent, and he'd spontaneously combusted with fury at her harsh words and disdainful tone. I had not been a witness to the encounter, but Valerie had been forthcoming about her part in their unpleasant conversation. Friak had said nothing about it, but the burned portions of the bar had spoken volumes.

Since then, every time they encountered each other, they both got uncharacteristically nasty. I think Friak was the one person in New Omni that Valerie would cross the barrens to avoid, and I think Friak felt the same way, though I didn't get to talk to him often.

He wasn't faring very well himself after all that had apparently happened to him during his time in the other dimension. A significant number of years had passed while he was in that dimension, and according to Alice, they had drastically changed his personality. It was surprising to hear that he had once been a carefree, happy-go-lucky child, rather than the brooding, angry, short-tempered, and highly flammable person he had become.

I doubted Evie was unaware of the tension that existed between them, but still, Valerie usually hid her distaste for Evie's beloved nephew better than this when she was in the company of either Alice or my mother-in-law.

Val loved Alice, on the other hand. Pretty much everyone did. Vincent's aunt was a total sweetheart, softspoken, empathetic, and always ready with a kind word for anyone who needed to hear it. I had no idea how Valerie hid her dislike for Friak so well that Alice didn't pick up on it, but she managed, and Alice was one of the few people in the older generation who never once mentioned Valerie's drinking problem. Alice was rarely critical of anyone, and I think that was one reason Valerie tended to gravitate towards her. Despite the fact that Alice, like Evie, didn't look much older than us, she had a very nurturing personality, and I suspected Val had adopted her as her surrogate mother. One far more accepting of Val's flaws than her real mother had been.

Val and Evie chatted easily as we all settled in at the worktable, supplies already laid out for today's task, making painted skull centerpieces for my upcoming wedding. Valerie might be struggling with her own problems, but her comfort and ease with socializing that I had always envied had not changed. People still loved to be around her, even if she might drink too much and get a little too loud and crude when she was intoxicated.

We had a nice visit, Val telling us both about her new place in Human Town and how well she and her roommates got along. They were both human females like Val. One had come from a primitive world where humans had not moved far beyond the hunter-gatherer stage, and the other came from a high-tech space age dimension, where galactic travel was commonplace. What they found in common, I didn't know, but Val said they made their friendship work.

Though I was happy Valerie had a new home, I knew I would see her even less now that she wasn't staying with me and Vince, as we had often hung out together in the evenings when she wasn't out partying.

Ria and Alex would occasionally join us to play games, since they claimed they got tired of the noise and chaos at the family game nights that Evie insisted on twice a month. I think they still harbored guilty feelings because even Ria would let me win and kiss up to me whenever she hung out with us.

Vincent said they were trying, though he would always shake his head with exasperation at their antics. Alex was dealing with something that had him antsy, and Evie had told me that it was because male Fayi would leave their birth nest when they reached maturity and take a long journey to find a new nest where they would gift the dominant male something valuable enough to win a place in it. She said the Fayi blood ran strong in Alex. Stronger than it did in Vincent when it came to the wanderlust and an overwhelming desire to seek a large nest.

Ria and her mother were getting along better now that Ria was feeling properly chastened after the abduction debacle. She made a greater effort to placate her family and behave in the way that they considered proper. Knowing her better now, I actually felt sorry for her. She had dreams and goals that her family wouldn't allow her to pursue because they worried about her safety. Evie had confessed that Gray had seen grave danger in almost every path Ria's future could take if left to follow her heart, so that was the real reason they restricted her so much.

Now that I understood how powerful Gray's love for his children was, I realized what a burden it must be to have insight into their fates and make the call about whether to intervene or not. It was not a burden I envied, even as the temptation would be great to guard my children from ever being harmed.

After several hours of crafting, Valerie set aside the skull she was working on and pulled out a roll of tin foil. Though I continued to paint the designs I'd sketched onto my—very real—monster skull, I regarded her curiously out of the corner of my eye.

When she finished her project, she put it on her head and turned it this way and that as she beamed at us. "What do you think? It's very stylish, right?"

"Uh...." I blinked stupidly at her, then glanced at Evie who looked just as confused. "Val?"

She patted the tin foil hat she'd created, tweaking the curlicues she'd put into the twists on the top of it. "I didn't want to do some boring old cap. I've been planning this design for days."

"Sweetie," Evie said carefully, as if she thought Valerie had lost her mind, or maybe she was inebriated. "Why are you wearing a tinfoil hat?"

Val looked surprised that she would ask. "To keep the telepaths from reading my mind, of course." She cocked her head at Evie. "Sherak says you have a whole collection of these to use when you don't want your mate or children to get inside your head."

Evie's lips twitched, and I could tell she was really struggling not to laugh, but I couldn't cut off my bark of laughter, though I put my hands to my mouth after it escaped as if I could stuff it back in.

Val looked from one of us to the other, her fancy tinfoil hat glinting in the light. "What's so funny?" Her eyes rolled upwards as if she could catch a glimpse of the hat from that angle. "Does it not look okay? I thought the twists would be cool."

"Val," Evie said in a gentle voice, "Sherak was just pulling your leg. You can't block mindreading with a tinfoil hat."

"What?" Val shot to her feet. "Are you—he—"

She snatched the hat off her head, and it was a real shame that she crushed it when she did so, because it *was* actually pretty stylish. "I am so gonna kick his—"

She cut herself off, shooting an embarrassed glance at Evie. Then she stuffed her mangled hat into her bag and threw it over her shoulder. "If you'll *excuse* me, I have a prior engagement."

She stalked towards the door, and I heard a muttered, "He is *so* dead!" before she left the room.

I couldn't help it. As soon as she was out of earshot I burst into laughter. I soon heard Evie join me, both of us clutching our guts and rolling with mirth.

After we calmed down, just a few scattered chuckles breaking past our grins, I took a long breath, shaking my head. "Sherak is *so* bad," I said, another grin splitting my face as I glanced towards the door.

Evie chuckled again. "That's my baby. I *am* glad he's feeling more playful again. I was worried after we had to destroy the Nexus. He didn't take that very well. It's good to see his mood improving."

Then her smile faded, and she regarded me with a sideways look, her expression seeming like she wanted to say something but debated whether she should. Since Evie wasn't usually circumspect, being far blunter than her sister Alice, I was surprised by her hesitation.

"Is everything okay, Mom?" I asked, calling her that because she'd asked me to, but also thrilling at the thought of having a mother figure in my life who actually seemed to care about me the way a mother should.

"I don't like to pry into my children's affairs," Evie said in a blatant lie that I didn't bother to call her on, "but I wondered if you knew if...."

I waited patiently, dipping my brush into a cup of water to rinse it.

"Is Valerie sleeping with my son?" Evie asked in a rush, as if the words were escaping past some barrier.

I laughed in disbelief as I thought about the question. "I sincerely doubt that!" I said in reassurance, recalling how Sherak and Valerie interacted.

It didn't seem to be in a romantic or even attracted way. The last time I had seen them in the same room together, she and Ria had been chucking wadded paper balls at the back of Sherak's head while he'd been trying to read in the sitting room. Though every ball was deflected by his telekinetics before making impact, and he never even turned around to look in their direction despite their best efforts to distract him, they had been giggling like two children in a classroom picking on the quiet, nerdy kid.

Pranking Sherak or messing with him in some way just like Alex and Ria did seemed to be the sum total of Valerie's interactions with him. And from the tinfoil hat she'd just spent thirty minutes creating, Sherak was giving as good as he got.

"I don't mean Sherak," Evie said, guessing that was who I was talking about. "I mean Lexie."

Well, that was a much trickier question, because I suspected the answer was yes, but Val's relationship with Alex was more of a "friends with benefits" thing than a mate for life thing. "Uh, I don't know anything about that," I said, hedging my bets, because Valerie had never come out and explicitly said they were having sex, but I knew it. Vincent knew it. And Val knew we knew it.

It was an open secret that apparently even Evie had caught on to. I was honestly surprised Gray hadn't verified it to his mate, since he had to know, but apparently, he kept some things to himself, even from Evie.

Damn.

Evie sighed and sat back in her seat, running one hand through her hair. "I hope you don't think I'm asking because I disapprove. Valerie is a lovely woman, despite her unfortunate issue," she didn't bother to elaborate, "but Lexie isn't... he's not...."

Evie sighed again. "As much as I love my boy, he's not a good choice for a woman looking for love. He's not in a good place right now for a relationship. Not the kind that I think Valerie would prefer." She leaned forward to rest her arms on the worktable. "I was hoping you could gently explain to her that Alex isn't serious about whatever they have going on. I don't want to see her get hurt like that when she finds out he's still *engaging* with other women. She's been through enough."

I nodded, amused despite Evie's concerns by the way she avoided saying her son was screwing other women besides Valerie. "If there is anything going on between them, I can comfortably say Valerie isn't serious about it either."

I didn't elaborate on that. Evie didn't know that Valerie was also *engaging* with other partners, though I was pretty sure the rest of them were more on the human side.

EPILOGUE

Vincent

The day of my wedding to Gabby finally arrived, and even though we spent every night wrapped in each other's arms after making love until she was exhausted, I still felt a sense of great anticipation. This would be it, the official union between us that would be unbreakable. That union would happen in the most sacred place, the Mother's Grove, right beneath the mother tree.

Such events were rare in that place, but my family anticipated the opportunity to have more. They were hopeful to see their other children stand in this same place, with Veraza performing the ceremony as we said our vows, the mother tree looking on with peace and joy radiating from her trunk. They were hopeful that, despite the destruction of the Nexus, there would still be moments like this, moments like the one where I took my bride's hands in mine and slid a sapphire ring on her finger that matched her earrings, bracelet, and necklace.

I still had more sapphires to give her, but I would save those for another special occasion. For now, this ring would seal my vow to her. Not just a vow, but a resolution.

One I had made before in complete seriousness, though perhaps back then, having just met her, Gabby believed I was just being playful.

Vincent's New Life Resolution #1: "I resolve to keep Gabriella happy for every day of her life, and let her know every day that she's special, just as she is."

I could tell she remembered by the way her eyes widened and then her smile beamed bright. When it came time to kiss, she caught my nape as I bent to reach her lips and lifted on her toes to close the distance as if she was impatient.

Her lips felt perfect against mine, and every time I kissed her, it felt like that first magical kiss we'd shared. No matter how many times I tasted Gabby, I would never get enough.

I should have realized that when I spent so much time in this world unable to forget her. I should not have wasted any time going back to convince her that the only place she wanted to be was with me.

She swears she loves me and that she would have chosen to be here with me anyway, even if she had not been abducted and then stranded in this dimension, yet a part of me could not stop regretting that she hadn't come here with me, to be with me forever.

Then she would remind me of her own resolution. The one where she would make sure that I knew, every day, that she was happier with me then she had ever been before.

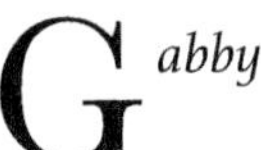*abby*

. . .

My wedding was even more perfect than I could have imagined. Forget people in costumes at my Halloween-themed wedding reception. The people surrounding me now as we made our way to the tables spread out around the main table didn't need costumes. They were as fascinating and unique and different from anything mundane as I could have ever hoped for.

And they were now my family!

I looked up at my husband, dressed in a tuxedo and cape that was *absolutely* inspired by the mythical vampires from my world, as we took our place at the central table, the trees around us glowing as the band played music so alien that I had never heard its like on my world, emanating from instruments that human hands and mouths couldn't even play.

Candles guttered, wax dripping down onto the painted skulls that decorated the centers of each table, surrounded by alien flowers with petals in dark blood red and black. None of my guests had questioned my choice of décor. None of them had raised eyebrows at my black dress. It took going to another dimension to find my home, the place where all my weirdness and oddities fit in.

I managed to break my gaze away from my gorgeous husband to glance out over the crowd of guests. Vincent's parents and siblings were all in attendance, the youngest, Lily, being the only one who had insisted on coming in costume—an adorable little dragon suit Aunt Alice had made for her that looked a lot like one of Omni's shifted forms.

They made quite a crowd on their own. A wild, boisterous crowd that I had come to love in a way I had never felt for the mother who had borne me and spent my entire life resenting me for that. In addition to that was Alice's mates and children, and Friak and Valerie had made a temporary truce—likely just for this one night—that allowed them to be in the same vicinity without making their enmity clear to their loving family—because Valerie had been adopted into this family too, and since she had always been like a sister to me, I was thrilled to see how well she fit in.

In fact, she was doing a little better now, drinking less, partying less. I hoped she would continue to improve, but it was enough to have her there with me, serving as my maid of honor in a gorgeous blood red dress that she rocked with her curvy body.

Aunt Lauren and Uncle Asterius were also in attendance, along with their sons, both of whom watched Valerie with some interest, clearly crushing on her, though Asterion was too young to even be considering dating yet. At least, according to Aunt Lauren, who was somehow both a badass and an easy-going woman at the same time. Her charismatic mate was also chill, and I enjoyed talking to them both. It was an honor to have the governor of New Omni at my wedding, not that there was any doubt they would attend.

I loved this world, and these people. And most of all, I loved Vincent. I turned to gaze into the eyes of my mate, still wanting to pinch myself to prove that all of this was real, but too afraid that I would wake up to discover it was all a dream.

"I think we need a new holiday for New Omni," I said just loud enough for him to hear me over the music and loud conversation.

He grinned down at me, flashing his sexy fangs, his golden eyes dancing with his happiness. "We already have a holiday similar to Halloween. It's the shedding of the leaves." He gestured to the surrounding ancilla. "It's a very somber affair focused on death and the spirit world. You'll love it!"

I beamed at how he totally got me. "I meant a holiday like New Year's Day. Your mother gave me the list of holidays, and I didn't see a single one for the turning of the year, the time of new beginnings."

He considered that thoughtfully. "We should bring that up to Aunt Alice. She loves coming up with new holiday traditions." He leaned towards me, and I moved in closer to him, breathing in deeply of his heady scent. "Perhaps, we could make it a holiday where everyone who is unmated goes on a blind date. That worked out very well for me." He pecked a kiss on my lips, but his words distracted me momentarily, despite the way that the touch of his lips always made my body buzz.

"You know, Aunt Alice *did* say we should do something to encourage matchmaking now that the Nexus is gone," I said thoughtfully, looking out at our guests, all laughing and talking and enjoying each other's company and the celebration itself. "We need more happy days like this!"

There was a whole generation of people in New Omni who faced growing up without the Nexus on hand to seek their destinies. But maybe they didn't have to travel so far from home to find them.

"Just don't suggest a dating show," Vincent said with a crooked grin. "Aunt Alice would love to try that again, but such activity has been banned for all time, according to gray-father."

I cocked my head in curiosity, wondering about the story behind that. Before I could ask, I heard a commotion to my side and turned to see Valerie falling backwards as her chair slid out from under her when she went to sit down.

She tumbled onto the loam, her skirt flying up and her legs kicking wildly. One heel flew off her foot towards the next table, hitting Friak's hand just as he raised a mug to his lips. His drink splashed over his face, dripping down to the collar of his formal shirt as he scowled while all the younger guests burst into laughter.

I helped Valerie right herself and get back to her feet, the mermaid style dress making it difficult, hearing a peal of laughter coming from Ria and Alex's direction.

"*Damn* you, Sherak!" Valerie screamed, her hair coming

undone from her updo and her face flushed red as she shot an infuriated glare at the culprit.

My mother-in-law groaned and put her hand over her face in exasperation and embarrassment. All three of her mates burst into laughter, even Gray chuckling loudly.

Friak shifted his glare from Valerie to Sherak, who sat quietly at Evie's table pretending to be wholly invested in examining the remains of his roasted redbird. At least, until Valerie stormed up to him, snatching a mug of stone-mold ferment out of Omni's hand as he lifted it to his mouth on her way to Evie's table.

"Hey!" Omni stared from his suddenly empty hand to Valerie's back as she stalked past him.

"Valerie, wait! Don't!" Sherak hopped up with a panicked look on his face, holding up both hands as she tossed the contents of the mug at him. His telekinesis couldn't stop every drop of the alcoholic beverage and more than enough made it through to splatter all over his face.

Vincent burst into laughter as Sherak sputtered, lifting a hand to swipe his face while Valerie dropped the mug to the loam like a mike-drop and then turned on one bare foot and stalked back to her seat, her head held high like a queen dismissing her servant.

"You asked for that, brother." Vincent's sexy, deep voice boomed out over the laughter at Sherak's expense.

My focus returned to my mate, and I couldn't get over how handsome he was as he laughed aloud, fangs flashing, golden eyes twinkling. Then he turned to me, and his smile grew more serious, his look more intent, and the rest of the world fell away.

He lowered his head and claimed my lips in a long, hungry kiss. As he lifted his head, he whispered against my lips, just loud enough for me to hear. "You said at least five children, right?"

I smiled against his mouth. "At least."

"It will be chaos, just like this," he murmured softly.

It would be. I could tell.

I couldn't wait.

"I know."

"We should probably get to work on making that happen then." I felt the stretch of his anticipatory grin brushing my lips.

AUTHOR'S NOTE

Thank you all for reading Vincent's Resolution, my addition to the loose collaboration of Blind Date with an Alien New Year's Eve holiday romances. Be sure to check out the other books in the collaboration. Each author did their own take on the theme, setting their stories in their own universes with their own characters:

Blind Date with an Alien New Year's theme collaboration books:

It All Started With A Kizss by Jeanette Lynn release date 12-14-21

New Year, New Planet by Marina Simcoe, releasee date 12-16-21

Vincent's Resolution (This Book!)

Her Alien Farmhand by Honey Philips, release date 12-23-21

Tattle Tail by Nancey Cummings, release date 12-26-21

I hope you are as excited about returning to the Dead Fall as I am, and I hope the first book in the series didn't disappoint.

When I was invited to write a book for a loose "New Year's Eve blind date with an alien" collaboration, it sounded like a lot of fun, and I immediately sat down to play with some ideas, trying to decide which series I would write the book in and what characters would be involved. I quickly came to my decision. I've been itching to return to the Dead Fall for some time now, as it is one of my favorite worlds to write in, and it allows me to bring in elements from other series because of the Nexus portal, so it gives me the best of all worlds. I have many plans for the Dead Fall, New Omni, and as you will discover in future books, the underground settlements and even beyond the barrens, but first, I wanted to revisit much-loved characters from the original series to see how they're getting along and reconnect with their children now that they are becoming adults.

It was so fun to write about the Hibbett sisters and their mates and families again, and it makes me want to write a few short stories about their lives and what they're up to, just for fun, for myself and fans of the series. I may be doing that at some point, depending on how much time I get to play with these passion projects.

Until then, I am getting a little more involved with the stories of the children, as this first book was about Vincent, one of the Evie's first set of "squirmies," who has set out to meet his match. (For those unfamiliar with the original series, Vincent started his life as a giant grub worm :D) He and Gabby are a permanent MF couple like Lauren and Asterius. There won't be any RH in their future. Although, this series *will* feature RH groupings as well as more MF pairings, and at least one MFM mating in future installments. I have the next three books completely outlined (they will feature the same heroine and three different heroes, each book building off the last while focusing around the relationship between the heroine and a specific hero and deepening the relationships developed in previous books), two are finished in first draft form, and the third is in the works, five other books with different heroines are in the conception stage that will likely be passion projects to work on between other books I plan for 2022 and 2023. (Like I mentioned, I am *really* excited to return to the Dead Fall, and have had ideas percolating since Veraza's Choice wrapped up!)

My current plan is to release the second book for the series, tentatively titled "Sherakeren's First Date," in February 2022 and then go from there as I work around the release schedule for other upcoming projects. I know that extending one heroine's story out to three books isn't necessarily the most popular way to do things, but in this case, this was the way I felt the story would be at its best. It has been an absolute pleasure to work on these books, because I have the time in each one to really build and develop the romance with a specific hero, without feeling any rush to keep the book a reasonable length that causes me to drop scenes I might have wanted to add. I hope my readers will agree that this is the best way the heroine's story could be told and will end up loving it as much as I do, even if they have their initial doubts about the format. Rest assured, I won't be rehashing the same scenes over and over. Each story will show scenes that weren't shown in previous books, or will show new perspectives if there happens to be any overlap.

I know that there might be some readers who will be disappointed that the series will veer into RH territory after this first book is MF. Trust me when I say I don't make these decisions lightly or without a lot of consideration and forethought. The characters in the upcoming RH were already set up for sharing a mate based on their unique backgrounds, and the way things come about truly does fit how I envisioned their character arcs. I will not gratuitously add heroes to a harem just to spice things up. Every pairing has meaning for all the characters involved. I hope my readers will give the series a chance and decide the journey was worth the step outside their comfort zones.

I also hope my readers will forgive some of my characters

their flaws and understand that part of their journey is in facing those flaws and the consequences they bring, and overcoming them to become their best possible selves. These arcs are important to me, and again, I don't bring things into a story without thought or simply to add conflict or interest to a story. My characters' struggles are real, and how they ultimately end up dealing with them might not be the same as a reader's experience, but I write from my own perspectives and experience and can say I try to give their journeys and struggles the gravity they deserve.

And if anyone is asking "But what about NEX?" all I have to say is... you'll see. ;) (You don't think I'd just *delete* NEX, do you?)

Vincent's Resolution was a joy for me to write, and felt very fulfilling, especially to my muse. That being said, I am not certain how it will be received by the audience. I think fans of the "Into the Dead Fall" series will enjoy this return to that world, and I hope newcomers to the Dead Fall will be excited to see more, and may even decide to check out the original series to learn about the parents and their own stories and about how they became legends in New Omni.

As for the other projects I have planned, I have three currently in development. Sentinel's Journey will be a return to the Children of the Ajda series, with Kevos, my handsome but grumpy lizardman, heading out into the human world to meet his mate—though he doesn't know it yet. Uriale's Redemption will return to the Shadows in Sanctuary world to catch up with the big, bad villain now that his wings have been clipped to see if he can find his way back into the light. And the third book I have planned for 2022 is The Director's Mate, (working title that may change) which is a return to my Iriduan Test Subjects series where a heartless Lu'sian and his crew find themselves in possession of an alien-obsessed human female named Ava who is so fascinated by them that they discover their bodies—and their minds—changing for her. Though this will be book 9 in the series, it will span the timeline of the earlier books to (finally!) tell Ava and Roz's story, as well that of their misfit crew.

I'm really excited about my 2022 lineup, and I hope my fans are too! I want to bring a little bit more of each of my most popular series to my fans next year, and we'll see if any new story ideas shake up my muse along the way too.

I really want to send out a big heaping helping of thanks to Pam and Kimmie for taking the time to beta read this book and give me their feedback. You two have really helped me refine and polish my latest book baby, and I can't thank you enough. I really appreciate it! Y'all are awesome. Huge hugs from me!

Finally, I want to thank each and every one of you readers and fans out there who continue to support me by buying my books or reading them on Kindle Unlimited, by spreading the word about them, by leaving ratings and reviews on them, and by simply giving them a chance and hopefully discovering some new worlds and characters to love. You have no idea how much it means to me to have so many amazing people embrace the worlds I've created and choose to spend time in them. Your kind words and encouraging feedback keep me coming back to the keyboard with my enthusiasm sky high to create more words! A thousand times thank you for making it possible for me to do what I love!

Be sure to subscribe to my newsletter for updates and announcements. I have added a section to my newsletter where I feature exclusive content for my subscribers, such as sneak peeks, excerpts from unpublished or pre-published works, character art and interviews, and anything else I think my fans will enjoy. I only send out newsletters when I have something to announce, so you won't be spammed. You can sign up at this link:

Susan Trombley Newsletter

Other Links to keep updated on news:

Blog: https://susantrombleyblog.wordpress.com/

Facebook Page: https://www.facebook.com/The-Princesss-Dragon-343739932858

Instagram: susan_trombley_author

Email: susantrombley06@gmail.com

Bookbub: https://www.bookbub.com/authors/susan-trombley

Goodreads: https://www.goodreads.com/author/show/3407490.Susan_Trombley

Amazon author page: https://www.amazon.com/Susan-Trombley/e/B003A0FBYM

Book Links:

Iriduan Test Subjects series

The Iriduans are up to no good, determined to rule the galaxy by creating unstoppable warriors using monstrous creatures found on their colony worlds. Can the courageous heroines captured by the Iriduans to be breeders to these monsters end up taming them and turning the tables on the Iriduans themselves? This is an action-packed science fiction series where each book features a new couple, and there is an overarching storyline in addition to each individual happily-ever-after.

The Scorpion's Mate

The Kraken's Mate

The Serpent's Mate

The Warrior's Mate

The Hunter's Mate

The Fractured Mate

The Iriduan's Mate

The Clone's Mate

Into the Dead Fall series

Ordinary human women are abducted by an enigmatic force that pulls them into a parallel universe. They end up on a world that is in the aftermath of a devastating apocalypse and is now just a vast, inter-dimensional junkyard. There they will encounter alien beings from many different dimensions and discover the kind of love they never imagined, forming a life for themselves out of the ashes of a lost civilization. This series is an exciting reverse-harem, post-apocalyptic alien romance that introduces beings from many different worlds and includes a mystery that spans the entire series, though each book ends on a happy note.

Into the Dead Fall
- Key to the Dead Fall
- Minotaur's Curse
- Chimera's Gift
- Veraza's Choice

Children of the Dead Fall series (Spin-off of Into the Dead Fall series)

Twenty years after Evie and her family defeated NEX and Jagganata and Gray took control of the Nexus interdimensional portal, things are peaceful in New Omni, a growing city reclaiming the post-apocalyptic ruins of the Dead Fall. Now, as their children become adults, they are eager to begin their own adventures—and find their own mates—by traveling to other dimensions in search of love. But sometimes, adventure comes looking for them, and brings a whole host of problems with it. This series will feature both MF and RH romances, though every book will end on a happy note.

Vincent's Resolution (MF romance)

Shadows in Sanctuary series

The humans of Dome City have been raised to view the horned and winged umbrose as demons, but when their separate worlds collide, these brave heroines must face the truth that nothing is ever what it seems. Can love alone bridge the divide between human and umbrose and put a stop to the tyranny of the adurians, who are the enemies of both? This futuristic science fiction romance series features a different take on the demon/angel paradigm on a world where humans have forgotten their origin, but still cling to their humanity. Each book features a new couple and can be read as a standalone with an HEA, but there is an overarching story throughout the series. (This series has some domineering heroes and darker elements that may not be for all readers.)

Lilith's Fall
Balfor's Salvation
Jessabelle's Beast
Executioner's Grace

Children of the Ajda series

An ancient reptilian species has shared a secret underground boundary with Earth for many millennia after humans chased them from our world. Human governments know about their existence but hide the truth from the populations of the world to avoid panic. When the yan-kanat people, children of the mighty dragons they call the Ajda, encounter humans who stray into their territory, they usually deal with them swiftly and permanently. Unless they discover that those humans are their fated mates. Then chaos ensues and love finds a way to turn mortal enemies into lovers and bridge the chasm between humanity and the yan-kanat.

Guardian of the Dark Paths

Fantasy series—Breath of the Divine

When a princess is cursed and transforms into a dragon, she falls in love with a dragon god and sparks a series of events that plunge the world of Altraya into grave danger. Myth and magic collide with the cold ambitions of mankind as those who seek power will do anything to get it. The dragon gods work to stop the coming danger, but it might be the love of a human woman that holds the key to the salvation of the world. This fantasy series features a different couple in each book and a satisfying ending to each story, but there is also an overarching story throughout the series.

The Princess Dragon
The Child of the Dragon Gods
Light of the Dragon

Standalones or Collaborations

The well-known story of Rapunzel gets a science-fiction twist in this fairytale retelling featuring an artificial intelligence and a plucky princess determined to prove herself to be much more than a pretty face. This is a futuristic science fiction romance that introduces a new universe where humans live on colony worlds after being forced to flee a deadly AI on Earth centuries prior to the story.

Rampion